A N G E L

K I L L E R

BOURBON
STREET
BOOKS

An Imprint of HarperCollins*Publishers*
www.harpercollins.com

ANGEL KILLER

A JESSICA BLACKWOOD NOVEL

ANDREW

MAYNE

Originally published in a slightly different form
in the United States in 2012.

HarperCollins books may be purchased for educational,
business, or sales promotional use. For information please
e-mail the Special Markets Department at
SPsales@harpercollins.com.

FIRST BOURBON STREET BOOKS EDITION PUBLISHED 2014.

Designed by Fritz Metsch

Library of Congress Cataloging-in-Publication Data
has been applied for.

ISBN 978-0-06-234887-6

14 15 16 17 18   OV/RRD   10 9 8 7 6 5 4 3 2 1

To my parents, James and Patricia.

My professional life has been a constant record of disillusion, and many things that seem wonderful to most men are the everyday commonplaces of my business.

—HARRY HOUDINI

ANGEL KILLER

WARLOCK

You're going to die." I tell her this not to be cruel, but out of compassion. It's the uncertainty of things that tears our souls apart. She still thinks this is a dream, but her eyes are focused now. My words are working their way through her broken mind.

She was a pathetic sight in the rain. Standing by the Dumpster in back of the diner with her torn jeans and smeared makeup, hoping for enough money to get a fix from one of these backwoods dealers and their crude concoctions.

When she got into my truck she had to know that in at least one reality something like this would play out. Well, not quite like this . . .

The glow from the dashboard casts an orange pallor on her cheeks. She resembles a jack-o'-lantern made from the last pumpkin in the patch. Puffy, bruised, sad and, most of all, unwanted.

I've given her purpose. I've given her a role to play. What happens next will be a secret for only me to know. But her part will echo through eternity.

The gnawing at the soul by those tiny cat teeth of doubt will be soothed. This experiment will tell me things I assume, but need to be certain of. Physical things. Things of this nature. This world.

What does she see when she looks at me? A man. But it's not the man that scares her. It's the purpose of the man. A purpose can be larger than a man. Even if the man dies, the purpose can become a cause. If it holds on long enough, it will grow into a belief and then a religion.

This is how gods are made.

It starts with a purpose that others don't understand.

A purpose that frightens.

I reach over and unbuckle her seat belt. Her limbs are paralyzed, so she can only track me with her eyes. There's a shudder as I touch her.

She thinks I'm going to violate her. I'm going to set her free.

I push the door open and the wind rushes inside. Her hair flies about like wildfire. She doesn't look outside. She knows what's out there.

I give her a push.

Her small body falls out.

Her shoulder hits the wing. Her mouth opens, but no words come out. She vanishes into the darkness.

I'm left with the hum of the propeller and the wind.

I envy her.

Her journey.

Her certainty.

Someday I will know it too. But not now.

I have purpose.

• The Eternicon*

---

* Case 093478-89 from a .txt file found on a forensic examination of a server used to coordinate a DDoS attack on the Justice Department servers.

MURDER IS A WORLD away from me in the children's hospital as I watch Elsie's pink fist close around the red sponge ball and squeeze. The scars on her hand turn red from the exertion, but she's not paying attention to the pain. When she opens her hand again, two large red balls appear and almost roll off her palm. Her eyes light up and she breaks into a smile. It's a million megawatts of energy in a face half covered in waxy skin still healing from the skin grafts.

My grandfather taught me this trick. It was the first one he ever showed me. We were backstage watching my father entertain a half-full theater in some forgotten town in the Midwest. I remember the glow of Grandfather's cigar in the dark wings as he muttered and shook his head. Tall, with a '40s leading man mustache grayed by age and hair slicked to the side, he was always immaculately dressed in a suit and ascot, even when it was his son standing before the crowd.

"Fool doesn't know his hands from his own ass." He looked down at me, then took the red sponge balls from his jacket pocket. "Even you could do it better than that jackass."

I watched and learned. I was five.

Grandfather gave me a pat on the head when the two red

balls appeared in my other hand. I gave him a toothy grin. I'd
been practicing sleight of hand with balls of cotton after bed-
time in the dark.

I got one of his rare genuine smiles. "You're clever. Too bad
audiences would never take to a girl magician."

It was an offhand comment not meant for me. He leaned
back against a road case and puffed away at his cigar, swearing
every time my father messed up a trick in his eyes.

To the audience, the show was going fine. But to Grandfather, every little missed subtlety, every less-than-perfect sleight
of hand was a disaster. Watching his son, his legacy, fumble
through his art was like watching someone burn down the
home he spent his entire life building, room by room.

He had a penchant for the overly dramatic, but it wasn't just
his legacy either. Great-Grandfather, a rival of Houdini, really
made the name for the family. And in Grandfather's mind, it
was all coming to a crashing end.

Elsie makes the sponge balls vanish and reappear again. Her
eyes wait for my approval.

"Wonderful," I tell her.

I've had to learn how to smile and hold in the tears every time I
see her face. She's still too self-conscious to play around the other
children at the clinic. This Saturday afternoon we have the playroom to ourselves. Our audience is a nurse doing some paperwork in the corner and a wall full of cheery Disney princesses
accepting kisses from frogs and cavorting with cute animals.

Elsie had us sit in the pirate section of the playroom. A mural
behind her depicts a valiant battle between lost boys and a hag-
gard crew of buccaneers. The first time she sat me down here,
I thought it was so she could look at the princess murals. After

several magic lessons, I realized she's an adventurer at heart and likes being close to the action.

So much potential, ruined by the burns . . . I have to stop myself. I'm already prejudging the rest of her life. I'm deciding what she can and cannot do, which is what everyone did to me. That's what Grandfather did. That's what Father did. Even Mother, God rest her soul, even she did that.

"Can I learn how to do the next part?" Small teeth bite the edge of her lip expectantly. A lock of dirty blond hair falls in front of her eyes and I have to resist an inborn motherly urge to brush it aside. The skin is still healing and sensitive. I can smell the balm the nurse rubbed on it before my visit.

"Of course, Elsie." I show her the move I used. She watches every minute detail.

I think more and more lately about what it would be like to have my own child. Apparently that happens when you're closer to thirty than twenty. I'd sworn it off when I was younger. I didn't want to put anyone else through the fractured childhood I had. I was loved, to be certain, but loved by people who didn't know how to love themselves.

I feel guilty when I see Elsie sitting there on the colored carpet, struggling with the magic trick. My dysfunctional family has nothing on hers. The scars I have are only the ones I hold on to. She has to go through life with hers visible to the world.

A little while later she's able to do the trick. Crudely, but she has the idea. She's eight but has the patience of a much older girl. She's got the drive of nobody I've ever met. I wish I could have known Elsie before her mother threw the pot of boiling water in her face. Was she this strong before that?

I was introduced to Elsie two months ago when I showed up at the children's hospital and volunteered to teach magic tricks as a form of therapy. It's something I've done since college and continued all the way through my career in law enforcement. It's probably the only part of me I haven't tried to reinvent in some way.

I try not to think about how she ended up in the burn ward as I help her practice the magic trick. The first two lessons I'd given her had to end early so I could go cry in the bathroom. I'd felt guilty. My pity wasn't helping her.

I don't know if doing this is any more helpful than the physical therapy she's getting. What I do know, because I've seen it before, is that magic gives kids something they didn't have before, a kind of confidence. Pricked and prodded a dozen times a day, always being talked down to in an infantile voice; sick kids begin to regress and feel helpless. A magic trick, even one as simple as making a red ball vanish in one hand and reappear in another, gives them the upper hand in a small way when they interact with adults.

For a girl like Elsie, who is too afraid to look in the mirror, much less let other children look at her, magic gives her a special ability the other children don't have. Scarred, unloved, she's still magical.

"Remember to keep it a secret," I remind her. I avoid giving her the long speech my grandfather would give. He didn't ask you to keep it a secret, he commanded it. Even the smallest trick, the kind you might find on the back of a cereal box, he'd admonish you to protect, lest you met an untimely end like a handful of others who dared to reveal how our world worked.

He called it "the Secret Library."

Elsie nods her head. I'd already explained to her the

importance of the secret. The real power of a trick is its mystery. If you reveal all your mysteries, perhaps because you think it will make people like you, the power is gone and you're back to being just as normal as them. It's a power trip for sure. But I think Elsie can use whatever power trips she can get.

Her hands make the balls vanish and reappear again. "I can't wait to show Mommy."

The words are a kick to the stomach. That urge to forgive is so strong in Elsie, making the act even more evil.

I'm not supposed to know the details of how Elsie ended up here, but I can't stop thinking like a cop whether I wear a uniform, a suit or yoga pants. When I see a hurt little girl, all kinds of instincts rise up.

Her mother is a piece of trash that moved from one drug-dealing boyfriend to another. She'd had a number of minor arrests for possession and an acquittal. She has never been convicted of dealing, although that's what she obviously does. The court system looks at her like a troubled addict and will probably reunite Elsie with her sooner or later. Her daughter's disfigurement will be remembered as an unfortunate "accident." No one wants to believe a mother could really do that. They'll all embrace the fiction and send Elsie back.

God help the poor girl.

What will Elsie's mother see every time she looks at that face? Will it reflect her own guilt? Will it make her want to be a better person and stay clean? I already know the answer.

Elsie whispers, "I've got a secret."

"What's that?" I ask in a hushed voice.

She leans in and whispers, "Dr. Peter was asking about you. I think he likes you."

Dr. Peter? "He's a very nice man, Elsie. I think he likes

everyone." He was one of Elsie's pediatricians and I'd spoken to him once or twice. He's the rare kind of doctor who can talk to kids without talking down to them.

Elsie reaches out and grabs a lock of my black hair and squeezes the strands between her fingers. "I want to be like you when I grow up."

"An FBI agent?"

Elsie lets go of my hair and shakes her head. "A magician," she replies. My real job is of little interest to her. The dark-haired woman who can do miracles is more fascinating to her than the lady FBI agent. Sometimes she looks at one of the Disney princesses on the wall and then back at me.

My visits are magic for her. For a little girl so badly treated by reality, I can't blame her for wanting to believe magic is real.

I take her hand. "You can be anything you want when you grow up."

Her eyes light up and the tooth bites the lip. "Anything?"

"Of course," I tell her.

Her eyes widen like she's about to see another magic trick. "Can I be beautiful like you?"

My heart stops.

The nurse in the corner looks up at me. I notice for the first time that she's been crying as she watches us. From her angle, all she can see is Elsie's scarred side. Unconsciously, I've positioned myself by the unharmed part of her face.

My phone rings. It stops Elsie from seeing the look in my eye. I've promised myself that I will never let her see me cry.

I pull the phone out and check the number. The office is calling on a Saturday. A voice on the other end asks if I can make it there in thirty minutes.

I don't want to leave Elsie right now, but I have to. Not for work's sake, but for hers. I put my mind into practical matters away from my emotions. If I can't even see past that scar, how will the rest of the world?

Getting to the office will be tight. No time to go home. I'm dressed in my casuals; sneakers, jeans, a T-shirt and a hoodie. My backpack contains my yoga clothes and some deodorant. I don't look FBI proper, but I get the feeling that this is an exceptional situation.

I can't imagine what, though. I've been spending the last four months away from the D.C. headquarters and in a cubicle in Quantico, doing forensic accounting and answering to a supervisor with all the charisma of a library card.

I tell the dispatcher I'll be there. He gives me the name and building to report to. I ask him to repeat the name, just to be sure.

Dr. Ailes.

As in Jeffrey Ailes, the Witchfinder.

He's not even an FBI agent. He's a DOJ computer scientist working with a team of geeks in a remote corner of Quantico.

This can't be good.

The last time I heard his name, it was rumored that he had been using the FBI's own profiling system to look for leaks within the agency. Invasive questionnaires had been passed around, and we all felt as if we were being insulted by some pencil pusher who'd never carried a gun.

I'd heard Ailes was an African-American professor of mathematics turned businessman who got rich designing black box computers for Wall Street before one day deciding what he really should be doing is telling us how to do our jobs. Being rich and having political connections helped him make that a reality.

God knows what he wants with me. I can only assume his

computers flagged me for something. I haven't done anything wrong.

Not technically . . .

This doesn't help my anxiety. I've got things I'd rather not have brought up. Ailes is the kind of guy who would find them if he connected the dots.

I look over at Elsie and give her hand a squeeze. I'm tempted to tell the dispatcher I need another half hour. But to be honest, I don't think I can make it another thirty seconds.

I give Elsie the sponge balls to keep. She acts as if I just asked her to take possession of the Ark of the Covenant. Before I go, she throws her arms around me to give me a hug. I look over at the nurse. Elsie has never done this before. The nurse raises an eyebrow over red eyes, then smiles.

I lean over and let her put her arms around my neck, being careful not to touch the sensitive skin.

Her tiny mouth whispers into my ear a little too loud. "I think you're my favorite person."

I know being a favorite is a fleeting thing with children, but it lifts me enough to face the Witchfinder. I can leave there with a happy smile. I'll avoid crying until I get into my car.

I don't care what Ailes's computers and his geeks think about me. I've just been told by the purest soul I've ever met that I'm the best in the world.

 THINK I'VE SEEN Ailes a few times on campus. He has a stare that goes right through you. Like you're a spreadsheet with a red flag pointing out something you're trying to hide. The Witchfinder. He could fit into a movie where a medieval bishop points out the person guilty of evil deeds against the church and sends them out to the courtyard to be stood atop a pile of logs and set on fire. There's an intensity and certainty about him that's intimidating.

My Uncle Darius has that kind of look. Purely analytical, like he's counting verbs as you talk and noticing how many times you blink.

Out of sight, but not out of mind to those of us wondering what he does there, Dr. Ailes's unit is in a nearly abandoned facility at the west end of a sprawling compound of government-gray structures. The whole building feels like a secret court hidden away in the bowels of the Vatican. Only we're in Quantico, Virginia, and the building is a relic of a bygone age in law enforcement. Brown plastic signs on doors for divisions that no longer exist line the forgotten corridors.

Decades ago, several of its floors were filled with refrigerator-sized computers compiling data on license plates, hair dyes and carpet fibers entered by hand from physical files. Now it's a ghost town of hallways with burned-out fluorescent lights and missing ceiling tiles. The custodian has more computing power in his pocket than this whole building once held.

The Ailes group is tucked away on a floor that used to hold thousands of binders indexing things like tennis shoe prints with year of manufacture, how many were sold in each size and in what regions. The FBI has always thrived on this kind of data. A 1983 Puma running shoe can help you narrow a list of thousands down to just one or two people.

Almost all this information is now digitized. The section of indexed tire prints once took up an entire floor. Today you can fit it into an e-mail attachment. In the academy, our professors would regale us with stories about spending weeks hunting through catalogs of fibers to find out the make and model of the trunk where a victim had been stashed. It was a different kind of detective work, one where you could still touch all the evidence.

When I enter, I notice the linoleum floor still has deep gouges from where the massive walls of cabinets once stood holding all those physical bits of information. Half-repaired light fixtures dangle from the tennis court–sized room. At the far end sit six desks pushed up against one another, bullpen-style. Three heads lean over computer screens. Two young men and a woman. All of them are dressed in proper FBI ties or polo shirts. None of them look like the barefooted hippies I'd been led to imagine or the red-robed cardinals I'd feared.

This isn't as sinister as I was expecting. This looks like a bunch of college kids trying to get out a school newspaper.

A young woman, maybe a year or two younger than me, looks up from her computer screen. With short auburn hair and big cheekbones, she has that Nebraska farmer look but an athletic build. She clicks a window closed before I can get a proper glance. What I see looks like a profile of an agent.

"I'm looking for Dr. Ailes?"

She points to the conference room. "He's over there right now." She turns back to her computer before I have a chance to reply.

I thank her anyway and walk over to the door. I'd been expecting an office, but I realize his desk was probably at one of the terminals back in the bullpen, alongside his geeks.

Ailes's voice calls out from the cracked door. "Have a seat, Agent Blackwood, and close the door behind you."

I'VE BEEN SITTING here for several minutes at a table filled with file folders, watching my inquisitor finish something on his computer. This is either a test of my patience or he's genuinely overwhelmed.

Ailes holds up a finger, telling me he'll be another moment. Even seated, I can tell he's tall. Although graying at the temples, he doesn't look like an academic. I remember something about him serving in the Navy before getting his PhD. He still has a lot of that bearing. Okay, maybe he doesn't look like a bishop. He could be a Moorish knight.

My eyes drift around the files on the table. They all have numbers for identifiers. I can see the edge of a magazine poking out of one. Something looks familiar . . .

I know the magazine instantly from just a few centimeters of the cover.

I feel my heart sink.

"Why did you go over Agent Miller's head on the Hashimi case?"

"Pardon me?" I pull my attention away from the magazine.

Ailes looks up from his screen and sets his reading glasses down. "Miller. Why'd you go over his head?" He gives me the intimidating stare I'd seen across the Quantico campus.

I'd feared repercussions on this. We were trying to pin down a ring of credit card thieves. Three of them worked in the same restaurant chain. I had been tasked with going through miles of credit card receipts to look for other possible accomplices by cross-referencing other fraud cases. The kind of humdrum police work you'll never see on television.

I reply in a flat tone, "I found fourteen suspicious charges and flagged them. Miller ignored them."

"So you went over his head?" Ailes raises an eyebrow.

I've never been very good at being political. "I think of it as around him. We were on a time crunch."

"But he's your supervisor. The FBI put him in charge of the case so he could decide what was important and what was not. Do you think you're smarter than him?" Ailes emphasizes the word "smarter."

I shake my head. "He's got a dozen open cases to supervise. I think if he'd had time to read my memo and look at the data, he would have reached the same conclusion. Nothing more."

"Why did you suspect Hashimi was the Greenville Killer?"

I don't know what to say. When I went through a list of flagged charges, I noticed some odd purchases. Rope, bleach and a few other items that would seem innocuous in other situations but not on a credit card fraud case. I got curious and placed them in locations where the Greenville Killer had murdered three people. Part of the reason I went over Miller's head was it was only a suspicion. I never told anyone. It was a total potential wild-goose hunt. If I'd told my boss I thought one of these low-level credit card thieves was also a potential FBI most-wanted killer, I would have been laughed out of his office and maybe a job.

Hashimi just smelled wrong. Sometimes you can't put that on paper. We'd never have gotten a search warrant based on the Greenville case. There was plenty of cause with the credit card fraud case. The problem was the bureau could take a year before knocking in his door and following that lead.

I had to nudge things a little . . .

It was simple enough. Miller was sending a group of cases to his supervisor to be expedited. Hashimi wasn't on that list. All it took was a hastily written note that looked a lot like Miller's handwriting, but no actual signature (so I couldn't be accused of outright forgery), taped to the file. How it ended up on a desk in the supervisor's locked office is beside the point. The supervisor's secretary only saw Miller go in and out . . .

When they got the search warrant on Hashimi's house they found IDs and documents tying him to the murders. Miller got the credit for the catch. I was just happy they got him.

No one has ever asked me this before. Ailes is the first one to realize I suspected Hashimi of being the killer in the Greenville case. When they busted him, I kept my mouth shut and congratulated Miller when he got his commendation.

Ailes is waiting for me to respond. I say nothing.

"I see . . ." he replies.

What does he see? That I went around my supervisor? Miller never told anyone I'd gone around him. He never mentioned it to me either. He knows that file came from somewhere. He suspects who, but doesn't want to admit it.

Ailes drops the matter. "Why do you think you are here, Agent Blackwood?"

I don't understand the question. "The dispatcher asked me to meet you here."

He looks at my hoodie and jeans. "Didn't expect to get called in on a Saturday?"

"No, sir. I did not," I reply.

"Any idea why you're here?"

I think about the magazine. The only obvious physical piece of evidence in the entire building. It's embarrassing, but it's not the kind of thing to cause this much fuss. Is it? Maybe the Miller thing blew up. "I'm not sure I know."

His eyes squint for a moment, then he remembers his glasses. The glasses seem like a prop he uses to stretch moments of time and make me keep talking. He can tell I'm not giving anything up. "What have you heard about what goes on here?"

"Just the rumors. That you and your number crunchers are mining through personnel files to find leaks."

Ailes nods his head. "That's a minor thing. More of an assist we're doing for internal affairs." He points toward the bullpen visible through the window. "Most of what we do here is quite boring. Even more so than the kind of forensic accounting you've been doing. Jennifer out there is finding ways to reduce the number of boxes on an expense report by half. Terribly dull. But exciting at the same time. If she can find a way to save twenty percent of the time each agent spends filling out forms, then that's the equivalent of adding eight hundred agents into the field by freeing up their time from bureaucratic bullshit."

Ailes sets his glasses down and rubs his eyes. "We did a study that showed if you calculated the amount of time some supervisors spend going over incidentals like phone calls and fuel expenses, it'd be cheaper to keep all the cars running non-stop and never hang up a long-distance call. Inefficiency is the creeping death of bureaucracy and accountability. It's what brought the Roman Empire down. While they were filing reports, the barbarians were storming the gates. You can bet at least one senator demanded a census of the number of invaders before he decided whether or not to support repelling them."

I say nothing. It's a topic we're all familiar with. When you join the FBI, you think your days are going to be spent going after bad guys. The reality is that you find more and more of your time being eaten up by paperwork and procedures and hierarchy, and it only gets worse. It's how the Greenville Killer could have slipped away from us. If I hadn't subverted the chain of command in my own way, he'd still be out there murdering people.

The bureaucracy keeps getting thicker. Every few months another form comes along because some manager somewhere decided that if we all just spend an extra ten minutes filling it out, everything will be better, ignoring the hundred other geniuses who had the same thought about some other form.

Ailes waves his hands in the air. "My goal here is efficiency. Helping you do your job faster. One of the ways we can do that is by making sure the right person is in the right job. Decide who belongs where. You don't seem to care much for lines of authority. Are you better than the FBI?"

"No." The word blurts out of my mouth.

"Yet you went around Miller. You could have told him your suspicions."

"He . . . he wouldn't have believed me."

"How do you know? Did you try?"

I shake my head. Miller is a well-intentioned accountant. He has no street experience. He wouldn't believe a serial killer was hiding in a spreadsheet for a credit card case.

I only saw because I grew up learning how to do suspicious things while looking innocent. I know how to create deceptions in front of people prepared not to be fooled. It's in my blood. Hashimi was using a stolen credit card to purchase things that he didn't want to appear on his own credit card statement. If you're a professional thief like him, you'll buy iPads, TVs, pre-paid gas cards; things that have a high resale value. Not rope, bleach and cutting tools. Hashimi was hiding these purchases on the stolen cards because he was more afraid of someone suspecting he was a serial killer than a credit card thief.

"Did you try?" repeats Ailes.

"No. I didn't." I was new in the division. Miller had little patience for me.

"Don't you like it here? Are you sure you're really FBI material?"

So this is what it comes down to. I'm being asked if I'm happy in the FBI.

I've asked myself that question a lot lately.

It's the kind of routine I always longed for after growing up in the back of a tour bus, sleeping in airports; the FBI has a kind of stability I always craved. I wanted to help people. I just didn't know it would be so hard.

People have been waiting for me to slip up, for my past to catch up with me. "We're show people," Grandfather used to say. Show people, with our own values, our own way of doing things. Gypsies who work in the open. People like us don't belong in places like this. We belong to the fringe. Some of us, even people close to me, belong on the other side—in those file we search through . . .

My eyes drift toward the magazine. I get the feeling I'm about to be set up for a fall. I pull the folder out of the stack and flip it open to show the magazine cover.

"Am I here because of this?"

3

AILES NODS AT THE MAGAZINE. It's me on the cover at nineteen. I'm wearing a red sequined tuxedo jacket with my cleavage on display and what could debatably be called a thong, although I was wearing flesh-colored tights under the fishnets.

Magician Magazine. At the time I was proud to be the youngest female magician to ever grace the cover of a major magic magazine. Even if the cover suggested the kind of thing that comes to your mailbox in a brown wrapper.

After Grandfather taught me that first trick, I pushed to learn more and be in the show more. Neither he nor Father would let me onstage until I could perform flawlessly. Better than them.

I produced playing cards from my hands until the skin cracked and bled. I didn't go on dates. I didn't have friends. I had magic.

I needed to prove that I could be just as good as them. When I was fifteen I booked myself as a featured act at the national magic convention. I won that audience over. Grandfather still took time.

"You're just a novelty," he'd tell me.

"Magic is a novelty act," I'd remind him.

He would puff away at his cigar and just stop arguing. I

wasn't going to be a pushover like his sons. I was in awe of my grandfather, but I knew he was just a man. My father didn't have his technical skills and mind, and my uncle lacked his charisma, but people told me I had both. People except for my grandfather.

The year I got the cover of the magazine, the International Magic Alliance also named me magician of the year. Younger than my father or grandfather. They treated it like a joke. They didn't want to admit that I'd done it mostly on my own.

My famous last name helped. It's probably why my father got it a decade earlier. But it didn't help me keep practicing on the concrete loading dock in freezing rain while I waited for them to finish their after-show drinks at the bar across the street. It didn't help me get up at 4 a.m. to practice so I could have enough time to catch the city bus to Venice Beach Middle School—where I'd had to register myself.

My family's name opened doors. Practice is what kept them open. I learned the game. I was a girl in a man's world. I knew my looks were an asset. I played that card.

The sexy vamp on that cover is nothing like me as a person then or now, but it was a role I had to embrace. "Come for the tits, stay for the skills." I heard Grandfather say that once when he didn't think I was listening. Or maybe he was speaking loudly enough so I would hear. With him, it was hard to tell.

In the world of show business, the magazine cover is a point of pride, not a scandal. In the puritanical world of the FBI, where you're expected to spend six days serving J. Edgar Hoover and the seventh in a church pew, it would look not much better than a sex tape. You become "that kind of a girl." The wink, the pout; I stole the pose from a men's magazine. I knew as much about sex then as I did the far side of the moon.

I lift the magazine and show the cover to Ailes. "Do you mean, should I be doing this, instead of working in the FBI? I disclosed everything when I signed up. The agency knows my background."

"An interesting family history," says Ailes. "Not something you need to be ashamed of."

Shame. There's the word. Is that how I feel? I don't know. I really don't know. I tried to hide it. But only because I wanted to fit in. Maybe that's the definition of shame? I toss the magazine down on the table. "Then why is this here? Why am I here?"

Ailes looks at me for a moment, then a light goes on behind his eyes. "I see. You have my apology, Agent Blackwood. Let me start over."

I'm confused. There's almost a kindly look on his face. He turns the magazine facedown, telling me the photo is not the point of the conversation. Then what is?

He points to his laptop. "We go through those question-naires that you fill out and we look at other data points. Your name came up and I was curious as to why. I did some digging in our archives and found the magazine and made the connec-tion. I forget sometimes the holier-than-thou bent of some of your peers. I'm not here to embarrass you."

I flip the magazine over so my younger self is visible. "I'm not embarrassed." My eyes look at the sequins and skin. "Not that embarrassed. It's my past. Just my past. Cheerleaders dress like that now."

"But you weren't a cheerleader."

"I wasn't much of a team player." The words flow before I realize what I just said.

Ailes ignores it. "I don't care about photos, Blackwood. I was interested in what I read. You were a magician. A professional magician. And from what I've found out, not just a pretty face who used the family name long enough to pay her way through college working cruise ships and casinos. You performed and you invented magic. In all the FBI, do you know how many agents have that level of experience?"

I shake my head. I've seen some guys playing with decks of cards. There's even a small magic club at the D.C. office, but that's it.

"None. Zero. I did some research. In the entire history of the FBI, we've never had an agent with that kind of knowledge. And now you're sitting there asking yourself, 'So what?' I'll tell you. My job here is efficiency. And that means putting the right man or woman on the job so it gets done quickly. I flagged your name so when the right opportunity came along, I could test this theory."

"Is the director having a birthday party?"

It takes Ailes a moment to realize I'm making a joke. My humor, my real sense of humor, has that effect. Grandfather used to say, "The little witch is drier than the Sahara."

Ailes shakes his head. "The director is having nightmares. We all are. We're faced with something big. It doesn't fit the paradigm. I think it's time we try something different." He reaches into a bag by his chair and pulls out a folder, then sets it in front of me. There's only one word written on it, "Warlock."

I heard the name a few days ago. Someone had managed to take our website offline and redirect the URL to another website. Not the same as actually hacking our internal computer system, but still a serious security lapse. The page that came up was a series of numbers and the name "Warlock."

The hack was pretty big news and caused all kinds of panic and embarrassment. Other than that, I didn't realize it was this much of an area of concern. For all I know, someone just used a bad password and it wasn't some large-scale brute force hack. "I don't understand. This is a computer crimes case. That's not my area."

Ailes nods his head. "It was a computer crime until two hours ago, when we unlocked the code." There's a pause. This code isn't a joke. I can already tell from the tone that there is something more sinister in play.

"The numbers were encrypted GPS coordinates. We sent local police to the point on the map. We were expecting some kind of hacker stunt. None of us expected this. Hackers don't do this kind of thing. But the code led us to a body. Now it's a murder investigation."

"I'm in forensic accounting. What does this have to do with me?"

"I could go into the complexity of the code and why the FBI should be throwing more resources into this, but that's not your concern. I brought you here because of the body."

"The body?"

"It's an impossibility. A puzzle. A mystery we can't solve," he replies. "The kind of thing you'd need a magician to understand."

I shake my head. I'm still not sure I get it.

Ailes continues, "The problem is, the person we've identified as the victim is supposed to have died almost two years ago. But the body is only hours old. You get my drift? A magical mystery at the moment. Complicated by the suspect's intentions. He calls himself a warlock. Another word for a necromancer. Someone who can raise the dead. In twenty-four hours, the news is going to get ahold of this. Short of having him in custody, we need to figure out how he did it. We're already dealing with the blowback of the hacking. To the public, he defeated the security of the most advanced law enforcement agency in the world. Granted, that was just a public Web server. But it doesn't matter. He left us a code that told us where to find the victim before she was killed. He knew almost to the minute how long it would take us to break the code."

"But she was already dead?"

"We don't know what to think. It's unprecedented. And I'm sure this is only the start."

I still don't know what I can do. I shake my head. "This sounds like a forensic matter."

"Can you pull a card from behind my ear or make all the aces come to the top of the deck of cards?"

It's an odd question. "Yes. Of course."

"If I sent that deck of cards to the forensic lab, what would they tell me?"

I understand what he's saying. Maybe they'd find a few fingerprints and creases, but that's not enough. The real answers are in the mind of the magician. In other hands, those cards are just thick pieces of paper.

He slides the magazine toward his end of the table and flips it open to a page with a yellow Post-it note. "You said in the interview that you like to be fooled by something firsthand, rather than have someone describe it to you?"

"Yes, that way you might think of possibilities nobody else thought about before." Magic works by misleading expectations. You assume the hand is empty or the box doesn't have a false bottom. Magicians can be just as easily fooled. We assume the awkward hand at the performer's side is hiding something or the thick table has a trap door.

Ailes nods. "Well, let's test your theory. I won't spoil you with what we know. If you're game?"

"Game for what?"

"I want to spring you from the paper jungle and let you work on this. I want to send you out into the field with the team. But I want your raw experience. I don't need another FBI agent. I need a magician. The Warlock is trying to convince us that he's the genuine article. He wants us to believe he's created a miracle."

I look down at the folder. I've never worked a homicide. "I'm not sure this is my area."

"Maybe not. We just want your eyes and brains. Agents, we have plenty. Magicians, I have only one."

He's been working me all along. He knows I've been trying to put all of that behind me. The magic, the family drama, all of those other connections I've been trying to sever.

This would mean revisiting that. It means bringing a part of my past I want to forget about in front of my peers. They'll know about the magazine and everything that goes with it. They'll think they know me.

Pride wants me to refuse. The scared girl that had to learn how to shut down overbearing males wants me to tell him to drop dead.

But I didn't become a cop because of ego. I did it for a lot of reasons. The most important one is that when I see something wrong, I need to do something to make it right, no matter the personal sacrifice. No matter the ridicule. No matter what the people who are supposed to love you say.

"Sure," I reply. Part of me wonders if it's my sense of justice that said yes or my ego refusing to accept that I can be fooled.

"Excellent. We have a plane leaving in twenty minutes from the airfield. There's a seat on it for you. We're sending some of our forensic people out there to assist the Michigan office."

"Excuse me? Plane? Michigan? Twenty minutes?"

"Sorry. I couldn't get them to hold the plane any longer. They want to get there before nightfall. We have only a few hours before they begin the excavation. Everyone is onboard waiting for you."

"Excavation?"

Ailes puts a finger to his lips. "Let's not spoil anything. I think you'll do your best if you form your own thoughts. Just remember, as per the assistant director's suggestion, you're only there as an adviser. Still up for it?"

I agree, but feel like it was a setup all along to get me to say yes.

4

TWENTY MINUTES AGO I was in Ailes's office. Now I'm sitting in the last row of an FBI jet flying toward Michigan. Six other agents, specialists in forensics, are in front of me making small talk about baseball games and what colleges their kids are applying to. I don't know any of them or have anything to offer the conversation. I was given polite smiles as I boarded the jet, but that was the extent of things. They look like a closed group. I get the impression they weren't too thrilled about being kept on the tarmac for me. Explaining it wasn't my fault is pointless.

After the seat belt sign is off, I take a trip to the rear lavatory to try to freshen myself up. At least that's what I pretend to myself I'm doing. The rear section of seats has been ripped out to make way for several large containers of equipment. I want to get a look at them to at least get an idea of what we're heading into. I know I could just ask someone, but I don't want my cluelessness to get back to Ailes, much less show the others here how out of the loop I really am. Nobody needs to know how out of place I am. They'll figure that out for themselves soon enough.

MY GRANDFATHER, my father and my uncle would perform mentalism as part of their acts—pretending to read someone's mind. If you wanted an example of their different personalities, watching them try to do the same thing was illuminating.

During an interview, Grandfather would excuse himself to use the restroom and flirt with the coat check girl so he could rifle through a reporter's jacket for ticket stubs, receipts, sometimes even a lover's note. Father liked gimmicks. They were safe. He'd slip a credit card carbon under a notepad and have you write down a word, then crumple the paper. He'd take the notepad back and look for the impression when nobody was watching. Uncle Darius took a different approach. Purely analytical. He'd look at your shoes, your wedding band. He'd watch what you ate, then he'd make a deduction. It'd be phrased like a question if it was a miss. His technique was similar to those of psychics. He could tell in a glance if your dog nipped at your shoes or if your five-year-old spilled ketchup on your tie.

Grandfather would have the most stunning revelations. Father would have the most practical. Uncle Darius was the only one who really seemed to see right into people.

He tried to teach me how to see too. Sometimes I think he taught me too well. But it was this skill that made me think I had a chance as a cop. I couldn't go around making tigers appear to stop bank robbers. But seeing what was in front of me, drawing conclusions that others were oblivious to, that was a useful skill. I guess that's what made Hashimi stand out as the Greenville Killer.

I move past the containers and look at the labels. Only one is visible. It's a ground penetrating radar system I'd read about in some briefing. Not the old kind they have at field offices, but the new experimental one that can resolve high-resolution images through concrete. This is military-grade.

Interesting.

It was a pipe dream until 9/11. After that, nobody thought it would be silly to spend a hundred million dollars developing machines to look through several tons of rubble for bodies. I can assume the other cases probably contain field versions of equipment we have back at the labs or more experimental gear.

I splash some water on my face and try not to look at myself in the mirror. It doesn't matter how many people tell you that you look great without makeup, you still notice. Seeing my face from a decade ago on that magazine didn't help either. I'm still fit from jogging and yoga and get hit on by college guys, but I know youth is a diminishing asset. I'm afraid there's going to be a point when I start counting the compliments and the looks that I now ignore and feel bad when they come up shorter than before.

After I broke up with my last boyfriend I caught myself looking on his online profile to see if his new girlfriend was younger than me. She wasn't. It shouldn't matter, but it does.

As I find my way back to my seat, I think about what I've seen on the plane and what I know so far. Body. Ground radar. Not much. The bureau is taking this very seriously. The stunt with the website must have rattled them. It's not often you get someone capable of doing something like that as well as pulling off a murder. Semi-smart computer types try to hire outside help. They think it's something you order like an Uber. That's why they get caught.

Most killers have a below-average IQ. Even serial killers. Movies like to make them out to be cunning masterminds, but most of them would fail a fifth-grade math test. They fit into the category of disorganized killers. They don't set out to kill their victims, they just end up murdering them out of some violent impulse. It could be motivated by shame in the middle of a sexual act. A feeling of insecurity. Violence is a way for them to try to assert control. It's usually messy and unplanned.

The rarer kind, the organized killers, are the ones who tend to be smarter than the average person. The Unabomber is a textbook example of that. His targets were chosen well in advance and his method, a bomb, was designed to allow him to murder from far away. Bombers tend to be the highest-IQ killers you come across. It takes intense planning and discipline. Of course that could be self-selecting. The dumb bombers usually only end up killing themselves.

Less premeditated, but intelligent and opportunist, are killers like John Wayne Gacy and Ted Bundy, who were almost in plain sight. They knew enough to stay ahead of suspicion. And when it fell on them, they were so much cleverer than the average killer, the usual rules didn't apply to catching them.

Understanding the difference between criminal minds is at the core of FBI behavioral analysis. But being able to describe someone isn't the same as being able to catch them or really understand them.

A criminology professor once shared with us a disturbing statistic. He plotted out the average IQ scores of various professions. He drew a circle around law enforcement: 104. Above average, but not by much. He then explained the amount of deviation from this number was very small and the chances of someone with an IQ in the 150 or genius range working in this field are almost infinitesimal.

If you throw five hundred law enforcement officers after one highly organized killer, statistically speaking not one of them is going to be as smart as him. When you're dealing with someone like the Unabomber, not one in ten thousand.

The key, he reminded us, wasn't being smarter. It's being

persistent. It was logic. Smarter isn't always an advantage. You could beat a Doberman in a battle of wits on *Jeopardy!*, but not if you're locked in a room with one.

Generally, you catch the less intelligent, disorganized killers because they screw up and get caught with a body in the trunk or their intended victim manages to escape. They leave lots of forensic evidence that makes it easy to connect them to their crime.

Organized killers take much longer to find. You have to decipher their patterns and you can often spend years narrowing down suspects. Sniffing them out like a dog in a hunt. Ted Bundy's name cropped up lots of times as a potential suspect, along with hundreds of other names. There's no way to know which one is the real bad guy until you get a lucky break. With the Unabomber, it came because he wanted the world to hear his manifesto. It was his estranged brother who saw the connection. The physical evidence didn't lead us to him, his ego did. The manifesto was his scent.

At first glance, the Warlock is all ego. The attention we're giving to this asshole is starting to make a little more sense to me. Only one presumed victim, but he's shown himself equally adept at two areas of crime that take high IQs. He hacked one of the most well-protected networks in the world, and he committed what looks like a highly organized murder.

I flip through the folder Ailes gave me. Just a few sheets of paper summarizing the website hack. The GPS coordinate was encrypted with a key that took the FBI's code-cruncher computer a week to crack.

A note from Ailes points out that the Warlock knew how long it would take because the body was only hours old in the spot when they found it. He's underlined the words "extremely organized."

Not "highly."

Extremely.

This sends a chill down my spine. Ailes is suggesting what my professor had talked about, that this man could be smarter than any of us.

I remind myself that anybody with a subscription to *Wired* magazine could make a guess at how long it would take to tie up the computer, and the defacement wasn't anything that hasn't been seen before, but this in a way makes it more disconcerting. This may not have been done by a computer expert at all, but by someone who is smart enough to pick up the skills on the side to make a point.

Computer hacking is beyond me, so I focus on the facts I've been told. There's the fresh body of a young woman who's supposed to have been dead for two years. Some sicko calling himself the Warlock hacked a website and the forensic team has brought along a ground radar system that costs as much as this jet.

Maybe I do know something.

I unbuckle my seat belt and stand up. I call out to a redheaded woman in an FBI parka who's standing in the aisle, drinking a cup of coffee and talking to another woman, "How far away is the cemetery from the airport?"

She replies in a polite Southern accent. "About a half hour, darling."

So we're headed to a cemetery. There's no point in high-fiving myself for something everybody else already knew. I guess it should have been obvious. If you're going to raise the dead, you might as well go to the source.

5

Two SUVS ARE WAITING for us at the airfield. Danielle, the sweet redhead, finds an FBI jacket in an overhead bin and hands it to me as I exit the plane. On the ride to the cemetery I answer a few of her polite questions. Nobody is talking about where we're going. The driver, a special agent out of the field office named Shannon, tells us we're going to get a briefing at the location.

He looks to be in his late thirties. He's got a muscular build and a shaved head. His eyes occasionally flicker back at me from the rearview mirror. He's asked me twice who assigned me here. I explain that I've been sent as an adviser, but decline to explain why. I already feel out of place.

The sun has gone down and the sky is filled with dark, slate-colored clouds. Drab houses with lawns of yellow weeds give way to concrete and corrugated-metal buildings set back in cracked black asphalt and gravel yards. There's a light rain that makes the roads slick. We pass through a bend in the road, and the red and blue lights of the emergency vehicles parked on either side come into view. Two television news trucks are across the street with their microwave masts pointed to their towers back near the city.

The cemetery is in an industrial area. There are a few open fields and lots of neglected warehouses. A sheriff's deputy in a yellow raincoat uses his flashlight to direct us to a parking spot. We get out and I help Danielle and the rest of the team with their cases. Shannon does the same and we carry them to the iron gates at the entrance.

Reporters and onlookers are standing behind the ropes trying to get a glance as we pull up. Cameras flash when they see our jackets. The FBI is here.

Wet and gloomy, the air has a cold nip to it. Perfect cemetery weather. I'm grateful for the jacket Danielle found me. Besides being warm, with "FBI" written across the back in bold yellow letters, it'll let me fit in a little more than I would in just my hoodie and jeans.

At the gate, a detective named Gimbal wearing a drenched suit and tie introduces himself to Shannon. He fumbles with his umbrella to shake hands. "These your D.C. folks?"

Shannon nods. "Pretty much."

I'm not sure if that was directed at me or not. I just keep to the back and focus on helping. When Grandfather was in a rage, or Father in a manic mood, I just did what Uncle Darius did, move a piece of equipment or clean something.

The detective glances at our faces, then nods. A thick black mustache almost covers his mouth. He looks like a charter boat captain. "All right. Hurry up. Gladys can't wait to get the girl on the table."

As we enter the cemetery, he explains that Gladys is the county medical examiner, well respected and often brought in for outside opinions. He walks us past the stone markers toward what looks like a large catering tent. It's actually a wall of white fabric to block the crime scene from the front road and the press.

"We've cleared the area, but please don't pick anything up or touch anything you don't have to." He knows he's talking to professionals, but he has to say it. "When we got the GPS coordinates we had someone call the caretaker. He was the first one on the scene this morning and didn't let anyone else in the cemetery."

I look around at the grave markers. Most of them are small. There's none of the really fancy sculpture or stonework you'll see in big city cemeteries. Like the houses we passed on the way in, this feels working class. Clean, utilitarian, but nothing more. The dates are all over the place. Some are recent. Some are a half-century old. The recent ones tell me it's the kind of place that could get visitors on a Saturday morning.

Shannon turns around and gives us the field report. "We called in local police to verify, then I came out here. County did a preliminary forensic examination on-site and drew blood samples before we contacted the parents of the girl and showed them a photograph. They confirmed her as their daughter. And there begins one of several mysteries." Shannon looks at the grass and realizes he's resting his foot on a grave marker. He pulls it away. "Chloe McDonald was declared dead almost two years ago. Her body was found in the bay three miles from here. She'd died from multiple stab wounds. Killer still unknown. An autopsy had been performed. There was no doubt about her identity, cause of death and, well, the fact that she was dead."

I notice the way Special Agent Shannon says the last words. There's a moment of hesitation there. He meant them to sound forceful, but they weren't. He has a sense of doubt about everything. This can't be the same girl, but it's gnawing away at him.

Obviously this is just some sick game the killer is playing. However, I get the feeling that something about it unsettles

Shannon more than usual. Guys like Shannon tend to like straight-up, predictable crimes. Bank robberies, kidnapping for money, a murder of passion. It's the kind where the motives are the most alien that give them stress.

I suspect because it's easier to think about things when you can imagine yourself doing them. We can all fantasize about the perfect caper, like how we'd pull off the perfect bank robbery. But to try to understand the motivations of someone who is just plain disturbed is much more difficult and stressful. There's no predictability there. We don't want to see any part of ourselves in people capable of that.

We want to hunt monsters, not be them.

Danielle speaks up. "What kind of forensic evidence do we have that it's the same girl?"

Shannon walks us over to the edge of the white screen. "Blood tests. We're trying to do a hair sample too. As I mentioned, the parents confirmed it was her. There are even scars in the same spots where Chloe was stabbed. They had no doubt."

"What about fingerprints?" asks Danielle.

"Well, that's a little complicated. You'll see in a second." He nods to a deputy who waves us through a gap. "When we found her, the first thing the examiner did was take a core temperature and measure elasticity and other signs of necrosis. This girl died less than twenty-four hours ago."

A field technician is taking photographs of the scene. I blink from the light of the flash. As my pupils dilate, the body of Chloe McDonald comes into focus.

Danielle gasps. I'm sure I do as well. It's not the dead body that unsettles us, it's the look on her face. Mouth open, eyes wide. It's a look of sheer terror frozen in time.

This is the gut reaction Ailes wanted me to have. I think of him as a sadist for not warning me. He had to have known. I'm sure on his desk or on his computer screen was a photograph of the crime scene. But he didn't show it to me. He didn't prepare me for this.

He wanted me to see what the Warlock wanted us to see. This wasn't watching from the wings, this was sitting in the front row. The reaction is visceral.

6

CHLOE MCDONALD'S FACE is filled with horror. It's an expression of agonizing fear because her body is still half buried in the ground from which she appears to have emerged. Her fingernails are a bloody mess, and deep furrows in the grass where it looks like she tried to claw her way free of the earth are still visible. Her burial dress is in dirty tatters, torn to expose her left breast and a red scar presumably from where she had been knifed two years prior. Her skin still has the pink sheen of the living.

This is no two-year-old corpse. This body is recently dead. She was probably alive this morning while I went jogging.

I was sipping coffee and going through e-mails while she was being murdered.

The grave marker behind her is her own, showing her name, dates of her birth and her death. Yet in defiance of that, her apparently recently living body is thrust out of the earth, as if she climbed out of her own grave.

A heavyset young man with a ponytail kneels down beside her. He's wearing thick rubber gloves up to his elbows. His ID says he's a county forensic technician. "We did a gas chromatography examination of the soil immediately around the body. Its oxygen levels indicate it hasn't been disturbed in over a year." He points to the grass. "We haven't found any evidence that the roots have been cut either. It would appear as it seems."

That last sentence is a peculiar way to phrase things. It's like an honest magician. "The box appears empty." He doesn't want to describe to the apparent truth that a dead girl came back to life and crawled out of her grave.

Words are scary. Spells and prayers are words we use to ask for magic. The technician, by all accounts an intelligent young man, is afraid to say what we all see, lest he make it real with an invocation. He can only affirm that we all see the same thing.

Danielle gives the girl a sad look and shakes her head. She's not worried about the trick. She just sees the girl. I like Danielle for this. The emotion is gone from her face and she's all business. She has purpose. "All right, then. Let's take a look at what's down there." She and the other members of the team open their cases and begin taking out equipment.

I stand back and hand them cords and boxes when asked. Out of the corner of my eye I feel like I'm being watched. I turn around.

A few yards away a middle-aged woman with her arms folded is observing us with a cross expression from under a canopy. Her dark hair, streaked with silver, is pulled up into a bun. She looks like a professor in her lab coat. I'd bet anything she's Gladys, the medical examiner.

I can tell she's not thrilled with us near the body, even though we're careful and trying to be mindful of jurisdiction and the chain of evidence. I keep my distance because I don't even want to get into the reason for my presence. Her eyes still drift toward me as she notices that I'm not really helping set up the equipment. I get the feeling I'm about to be grilled by one of my professors. Smart and analytical, she's trying to decide why I'm here.

I realize part of the look on her face is probably due to the fact that she did the original autopsy report on Chloe. I don't think she buys the idea that the girl crawled her way out of her grave almost two years later. But the presence of this body in such a state suggests that she made a mistake somewhere. I don't see how that could be. Yet the evidence is right in front of us.

To this woman, it's a professional insult to her made worse by a group of FBI techs flying in from D.C. to go over the scene. It's not personal, but it always feels that way.

The most basic thing a medical examiner should be able to do is spot death. When you hear stories about infants coming back to life or grandmothers waking up at their own funerals, they always happen in other countries—places where stethoscopes are considered high tech and your average medical professional has less education than a high school teacher.

A woman like Gladys doesn't make those kinds of mistakes. They're impossible on a body you've autopsied. In one of my college classes we watched a human dissection. The examiner made the offhand comment after he sawed into the chest that if the subject isn't dead at the start, there's no doubt by the end.

One of Danielle's team members places a disk-shaped object a few feet away from the girl. A black cable leads from it to a laptop set up on a foldout table. I walk over to have a look at the display behind everyone else.

The screen shows an overhead green grid. I assume the disk is in the center. Danielle presses a button, and a low humming sound comes from everywhere, like the woofer on a stereo. Circles radiate from the center of the grid, indicating the sound waves. I don't know if they are the actual sound waves or a simulation the programmer put in there so people would know the thing was working. It reminds me of a submarine's radar.

She presses another series of buttons and the disk makes the weird sound again. The circles radiate away and a rectangular outline becomes visible on the screen.

The image resolves and I can see we're looking at the coffin below our feet. I've seen hazy ground radar before. This is nothing like that. This image is clear, like a monochrome picture. I imagine what it would be like to use that on the other side of a wall in a hostage situation. Along with armor-piercing rounds, you could take out the bad guys without ever setting foot in the door. I get why this is military grade.

One of the other agents calls out a number from the screen. "Two-and-a-half meters depth."

Danielle nods and hits a key.

Two-and-a-half meters. Eight feet under. Most coffins aren't buried this deep. In some places you can bury them under just eighteen inches. This cemetery is old. They probably do so out of habit. Occasionally you bury them deep because you have animals that like to dig. Sometimes those animals walk on two feet.

The screen pulses again and another image begins to form. We all lean in to get a better view, consciously ignoring the gruesome body just a few yards away. The screen is reassuring. The numbers are precise and scientific. The body is unearthly.

Gimbal whispers something to Shannon about them already doing this with the local field office radar.

Danielle overhears him. "Can your system do this?" She touches the trackpad and the coffin spins in 3-D space. It's not just a 2-D image system. The computer has built a 3-D map of everything underneath us.

We're watching a real-time image of the entire area below our feet. Gimbal grumbles something, then shuts up.

As the coffin rotates, the resolution begins to improve. The hinges and engravings stand out. Danielle spins it to one side, then to the other and stops.

We all see what she's looking at.

The lid is partially open.

The edge is raised only a few inches, but as she switches to a closer view, we can see the gap.

It looks like Chloe pried the coffin open and climbed through eight feet of dirt. This isn't just a planted body. This is a complete illusion.

"Holy shit," mutters Gimbal.

I quietly second that reaction.

"I can also check the moisture and the soil density." Danielle glances up as a tech hands her a memory card. While we were staring at the display, he'd used another disk attached to a handheld computer to take readings from other grave sites to create a baseline of the surrounding soil. She plugs the memory card into her computer and a row of numbers fills the screen. "This dirt is just as old as everything else here. Ain't nobody been digging here for some time—down at least."

"Impressive," Gimbal remarks. It's obvious he's talking about the machine and still hasn't processed what that means.

Danielle clicks back to the 3-D image. "You ain't seen nothing." Danielle types in a sequence and there's another wave of humming coming from the disk. "Y'all want to take a look inside the coffin?"

7

THE EXTERIOR IMAGE of the coffin begins to dissolve away and reveal the interior.

Empty.

Chloe's coffin is empty.

I catch myself looking back at the body of Chloe. Her glassy eyes, still moist, gaze out in terror. In my mind I can see her crawling out of her grave.

I know that's not what happened. It can't be.

I'd say it was impossible, but I know better.

The sight of the coffin gives me a chill different from what everyone else is feeling. I've had my own close encounter with death in one. It was the breaking point for me with my family. But I came out on the living side. Not Chloe.

I walk away from the display while it renders and start searching the ground. I know why Ailes wanted me here, or at least part of the reason. It didn't hit me until I saw the empty coffin.

It's a magic trick.

The whole thing is one giant magic trick.

Ailes must have known about my own history with that coffin. What happened in Mexico . . .

Coffins and magic have gone together for hundreds of years. It's the ultimate symbol of death, and the greatest miracle a magician can perform is cheating death. It's what made Houdini famous. People didn't watch to see him escape from shackles and chains, they came to see him punch the Grim Reaper in the jaw. A defiant little man with an attitude to challenge fate.

Ironically, Houdini never performed the buried-alive stunt. Tanks filled with water, ice-covered rivers, barrels full of beer—he tried them all. His next illusion, before he died, was going to be an escape buried beneath the Egyptian desert. Others have done the trick. It's simple enough; a magician gets sealed inside a coffin and covered with dirt, only to miraculously emerge. It's more than a hundred years old. The most famous version started a religion you may have heard about.

Before Mexico, before I had enough of the life of performer, I did the buried-alive stunt on Japanese television when I was seventeen. Wearing a diamond bustier and short miniskirt, chained and shackled, I was placed into a clear plastic coffin and buried in a corner of the Tokyo Dome. It was a dumb trick, really. My father and my uncle had created a secret passage the night before. But on television it looked great. I'd done more dangerous things. Stuff that almost got me killed. But none of that ever involved me literally crawling out of the grave. It's probably physiologically impossible. The weight of the dirt is too heavy and you'll run out of air.

Alive or dead, Chloe couldn't have crawled out of her grave. Not without a trapdoor or a secret passage.

I pace the ground looking for some evidence of tampering. Some proof of a method. A telltale flap of grass like the one that hid my secret passage. I don't see any. I kneel down and pull at the turf, just to see if it comes free. It doesn't.

I wipe my hands off and stand up when I notice the medical examiner is watching me. I ignore her gaze and look down at the grave markers.

What if this isn't Chloe's grave?

For a moment I wonder if it's a kind of puzzle. Did the man who did this just move the markers? That would be the easiest way.

I count twelve in this row and move on to the next.

Agent Shannon walks over to me. "Counting plots?"

"Yes," I reply. My eyes stop on a marker for a woman who died the same week astronauts landed on the moon.

Shannon gives a reverential nod to the markers. His voice is hushed like we're in a church. "We did that earlier. Pulled the records on the graves. No dice."

"I didn't think there would be any. But it's worth a check." I'm glad they already thought of it.

"Ever see anything like it?" Shannon asks.

"Besides in a magic trick? No. But that's what this is." I don't mention that the last time I saw something like this I was on the inside of the coffin, or that I almost died. I don't want to sound hysterical or try to make it about me. I don't think my particular experience is relevant, just my general knowledge.

He folds his arms and looks back at Chloe's body. "Hell of a trick."

He's trying to understand what's going on here. I'm sure he's imagining her crawling out of the ground, while the medical examiner is wondering how she possibly could have screwed up and declared a living girl dead. Danielle and her team are trying to figure out the soil chemistry and look for clues there.

I think of Ailes's example with the deck of cards. We're looking at the pieces of cardboard, but not seeing what really happened.

We're all distracted. Each one of us thinking along our own biases. Shannon, the physical solution. The medical examiner, the procedural error. Danielle, the scientific explanation.

I walk back over to the table with the ground radar. The tech who had the handheld scanner, Agent Davis, is offering his theory. He waves his hand toward Chloe and shakes his head as he dismisses the whole thing. "We get this in the South all the time. The soil gets real damp, cracks open a coffin, and a body floats to the top in the mud. We even have tombs where the coffins get rearranged because of the flooding. People think it's ghosts." He seems confident in his theory, but I notice he doesn't look over at Chloe when he says "ghost."

Words have power.

He seems happy with his explanation and looks at the other members of the team, waiting for their approval.

The medical examiner speaks up behind us. "Do your bodies manage to change their cause of death? Miraculously heal from their wounds, only to die two years later from asphyxiation? Spontaneously dry the mud in hours?" Gladys's words are bitter.

Detective Gimbal tries to calm her down. "Gladys, your judgment is the last thing anyone here is going to question."

She gives him a sharp look. "I'm not worried about that. I just want to get her out of the ground and onto my table so I can do a proper exam. The sooner you finish with the technology demo, the better."

"You got your blood samples," replies Shannon. "And I think we're going to need to evaluate where we do the autopsy . . ."

Gladys's eyebrow shoots up. "I see." Her tone is chilling. "If I'm no longer needed here, then I guess I should be going home. Give my regards to her family. Again." The last word punctures the air like a knife.

Gimbal chases after her to try to calm her down. It's obvious she feels like she's on trial here. I reach her first. I can see the hurt in her eyes.

She turns to me. "Who are you?" The question is cold and clinical. I feel like I'm on her autopsy table, about to be dissected.

"Special Agent Jessica Blackwood. But that's not important." I try to find the right words. "We need your help. There are two murders here and a killer to catch."

Shannon is just over my shoulder. "We haven't established that it's a murder investigation yet."

I wheel around to him. "Of course it is. You have two murders. The one two years ago and the one of this girl. The real question, besides who did this, is which girl was the real Chloe McDonald."

I'm speaking my gut. It's the only logical conclusion. Someone has to say it.

Shannon is about to say something, then stops. The words are soaking in.

Gladys's expression softens a millimeter when she realizes I'm not attacking her.

To be perfectly honest, I spoke without thinking. I'm missing something. We're watching a magic trick, but only seeing part of it. There's something more. The Warlock wanted us here to see this. He probably stood right where I'm standing, just a few hours ago. Everything is planned. From the code on the FBI computer, the two killings two years apart, to this moment.

We're his intended audience. The show is only getting started.

I turn around as two county techs are preparing to pull Chloe's body out of the ground.

Something is wrong.

I scream, "Stop!"

8

ALL EYES ARE on me. A deputy reflexively puts his hand on the butt of his gun. I sound like I'm insane. My voice is shrill and panicked.

I ignore the looks and run back to Chloe's body.

"Just step back," I tell the techs in a calmer voice.

They set down their plastic shovels and move away from the body, not sure if I'm making a threat. One of them looks for a supervisor to tell them how to handle the crazy woman yelling at them.

"What the hell, Blackwood?" Agent Shannon's face is red with fury as he runs over to us.

"The body." I point to her as I try to find the words to explain. "There are only two possibilities. It's either Chloe McDonald or another girl. Either way, we know this girl only died a few hours ago. But we're supposed to think that this is the same girl who died two years ago, yet miraculously came back to life and crawled out of her grave. Which we know is bullshit. We know it's not Chloe."

Shannon shakes his head. "How?"

I point to her bloody fingers. "Because her fingerprints would show us that. That's why he made it look like she shredded them climbing out of the ground. So there wouldn't be any. It's misdirection. It's the weakest part of the illusion, so he eliminated it."

Something is still nagging at me. It's the easiest way to explain why they shouldn't touch the body. I still haven't wrapped my mind around what's really going on here. It's bigger. So much bigger . . .

"The blood matched." The ponytail tech's voice is almost condescending.

I spin around. "So what? How much blood did you find in Chloe when you pulled her out of the bay? What do you want to bet we'll find an IV somewhere on her body if we look closely enough. Maybe even inside a body cavity. Whoever killed Chloe took blood from her so he could put it in this girl's veins."

It's just a theory, maybe one of many, but I have to stall them.

Gladys is shaking her head. "But we'd figure this out during an autopsy."

I bite my lip as I stare down at Chloe's, or whoever's, face. It's still screaming silently. "I know. He knows that. That's why he doesn't want it to happen. If it does, it destroys the illusion." I step back and point to the body. "If it were me, I'd do something to the body. Rig it so that when you moved it, after you got the effect, it would somehow destroy the evidence. If it's not her body, he doesn't want us to find that out."

Gimbal doesn't even hesitate. Put in simple terms of bombs and booby traps, he gets the point. "Everyone step back." He raises his radio to his mouth. "Get the bomb squad here stat!" He looks back at me.

I nod. "It might not be a bomb. Something." I turn to Gladys. "What would you do?"

She's about to speak but stops at the sound of rushing air. The fake Chloe's mouth emits a rumbling sound and orange sparks begin to shoot out. Her cheeks glow bright red and thick smoke pours from her lips and nostrils. Instantly, her whole body is engulfed in flames and turns into an inferno. We all leap back as it blazes into a fireball.

I shield my head with my arms and try to avoid the heat. I take Gladys's hand and pull her away. She's too stunned to move. The fire spits up into the gray sky, raging twenty feet into the air. A pillar of smoke climbs even higher.

I throw my jacket on the body, only to watch it melt in seconds. Shannon pulls me back as a fire crew rushes from the street with extinguishers and starts spraying.

Gladys snaps out of her shock. "Use the chemical extinguishers and watch for acid burns!"

A fireman nods and runs off to get more equipment. They fight it for several minutes. Despite the foam, the body continues to burn. Her face is a black cinder. A ghastly angel spewing dark smoke and fire. The dried flesh turns to ash and begins to disintegrate in the wind.

The plume is a hellish spire reaching into the sky. Cameramen across the street climb on top of their news vans to film the conflagration.

I look at Gladys and can tell what she's thinking. There will be some forensic evidence left. Maybe enough to prove there could have been another girl, but not enough to prove this wasn't Chloe's body. Even her parents were fooled.

And that's the point of this cruel illusion.

Uncertainty.

To plant doubt in people's minds.

The magician never wants you to look into his pocket or up his sleeve. Great illusionists would take axes to their old equipment before they'd give a rival a chance to dig through the trash pile in the alley in back of the theater and steal those secrets for their own.

The Warlock needed to make his deception perfect. If we had absolute proof the girl wasn't Chloe, he'd just be another charlatan. He wanted us to watch as he destroyed the illusion before our eyes. Even still, something is missing . . .

Grandfather used to call it the long burn. It's a setup within a setup. It's how you fool the smartest ones in your audience. It's the kind of thing you do to destroy just one person. It was how he bested his rivals.

I'm letting myself get too distracted and forgetting the present. I need to focus on the here and now. We're still in the middle of the Warlock's show.

Shannon turns from the fire and squints at the buildings around the cemetery. We're all having the same thought. Someone is watching us. The fire could have been live-triggered.

At the back of the cemetery there's an ivy-covered fence. Just beyond is a row of warehouses. I'm sure the police cleared the area, but there's something too convenient about the location. Shannon notices me looking in that direction.

I almost miss the figure at first. Hard to see against the night sky, there's an outline of someone lying flat on the roof of a building.

I'm about to suggest that we quietly call it in to the local police when Shannon shouts, "You on the roof, freeze!"

I don't wait to see if they follow orders. I know he's about to bolt. I take off running to try to reach him before he has a chance to climb down and get away.

Shannon and Gimbal are behind me, far behind me, by the time I make it to the fence.

I thank God for yoga as I slip my body over the top rail and land in a crouch without hurting myself. I should wait for them to catch up, but time is everything.

I slip my Glock from my holster and run to the other side of the building. Footsteps echo from the alley. I can't tell if they're running away or running toward me.

9

THE WATCHER WHO was on the roof can only be a few hundred feet away. On the other side of the building I reach a narrow alley between the warehouse and a chain-link fence topped with razor wire. Wild grass and torn-up garbage bags litter the empty lot on the other side.

The sun has set and the alley is lit only by stray streetlights and the dark silver sky, hiding the moon. My knee bangs into a broken crate that slams into a metal Dumpster. I have to keep my eyes on the ground to avoid tripping on the abandoned machinery.

I can't see anyone moving, but I decide to shout anyway. "Freeze! FBI!"

I'm answered by the sound of wind whipping at tattered newspapers. I step forward, keeping my gun trained on the darkest corners. I know I saw someone on the roof, I just don't know who. It could be our perp or some kid who wanted to get a better look and was scared off by Shannon's shout. I proceed carefully, more afraid of shooting an innocent person than for my own safety.

My eyes adjust a little to the shadows. I can't see where

anyone could be hiding. The rusty door on the loading dock looks as if it hasn't been opened this century. I continue along and hear the sound of Shannon climbing over the fence. The metal makes a rattling sound, followed by a groan as he lands.

He catches his breath and shouts to me, "Anything?"

I keep my eyes trained ahead. "Negative."

I reach the end of the alley without seeing a thing. At the back end of the warehouse is a fire escape leading to the roof. Gimbal approaches from the other side with his gun leveled at the ground.

The street in front is empty. Rain-filled puddles are still rippling from the drizzle. Across from us are a few more buildings like this one and a trailer park several blocks over that we passed on the way in.

The wail of squad cars grows louder as they try to cordon off the area. I think we're too late. I holster my gun and look up at the ladder. The rungs are rusty. It's doubtful they'll get a print off of it. But I decide not to climb up. I don't want to chance it. Besides, they might get something from the metal sidings on the top.

Gimbal holsters his gun too. "You sure you saw someone?" he asks us.

Shannon nods.

"I know, I'm positive," I reply. "I saw the shape and watched it move."

Gimbal scratches his chin. "Could it have been a bird?"

Shannon and I ignore the question. His eyes scan the ground and come to a stop. Almost invisible in the darkness, it's little more than a triangle.

Shannon squats, takes a pair of tweezers from his pocket and holds the object up to the street light. Blue cardboard, torn at the edge. He gives me a look. We both recognize it. I use the same brand.

"What?" asks a confused Gimbal.

"Memory card packaging," I explain. "Everything was being recorded."

Gimbal finally understands. "Reporter?"

I shake my head. "I don't know. Maybe our perp. Maybe a gawker."

Shannon stands up and takes another suspicious glance across the street. "We need to check with all the drugstores around here. If they needed to get a card, it means they probably filled up the other one."

A cold wind blows down the street as a police car races by. The rain has soaked through my sweatshirt. My FBI jacket is somewhere in the cemetery, a pile of ashes on a corpse.

Shannon makes a gesture to give me his jacket. I wave him off. I've dealt with worse. Cold doesn't bother me. It's only a sense. When Grandfather and Father first refused to teach me how to perform escapes, telling me that I was too young and that it wasn't appropriate for a girl, they found me later that night in a motel bathtub, half frozen from all the ice cubes I'd packed in there to practice an endurance stunt.

"We either teach her, or we have to come up with a convenient explanation for her suicide," Grandfather had remarked after they dragged me out of the tub.

I look back at the roof and think about the fact that we were being watched the whole time. Our reactions, everything. Somebody was studying us.

I hope there's enough evidence in the body to tell us if it was a timed fire or something remotely activated. If it was done by remote, then I'd bet everything on our voyeur being the Warlock.

The problem is that he would be cutting things very close. He's seemed smart so far, why would he risk being this near to us? One of the first things investigators do is scan the scene for potential suspects.

Maybe it's the thrill.

Or maybe it's part of a bigger deception. He might just want us to think he's that predictable. I'm overthinking things, but I can't get the idea of the long burn out of my head.

Gimbal calls into his radio for someone to come bag the piece of cardboard. Shannon and I walk back to the fence, still the shortest path to the cemetery. He asks if I need a hand over the fence, but I'm already on the other side before the words leave his mouth.

A moment later he lands next to me, trying to hide the fact that he's out of breath.

"Yoga" is all I can say.

Fire crews have managed to put the blaze out or it burned itself out. Gladys is still standing there, trying to make sense of it. As I get closer I can see her eyes are scrutinizing every detail. The fire marshal says something to her and she nods her head.

There's an acrid tang in the air. "Potassium permanganate?" I ask.

She nods. "You study chemistry?"

"No. Only the kind that makes pretty flames." Our garage was filled with many wonders for a child. Magic cabinets, costumes, props from a dozen different shows. My favorite part had been the workbench where my father has tinkered away on projects. Next to the tools and cans of paint was a rack of chemical compounds used to make puffs of smoke and magic flashes. Through trial, lots of error, and dog-eared science textbooks that belonged to Grandfather when he was a boy, I learned the basics of chemistry.

Her face has a pained expression. "I think he probably filled the poor girl's stomach with the stuff and the body with glycerol." She shakes her head at what's left of the body. "Wants to make it look like spontaneous human combustion or something equally ridiculous." She waves her hand at the body. "Of course, it'll just be our word against theirs."

"Theirs? Who do you mean?" I ask.

She points to the masts of the television trucks. "The people who want to believe this sort of thing. The ones that think you can talk to the dead or that ghosts are real. My niece even watches that garbage. We'll try to explain what we think happened, but they won't listen. I'm sure some of them will even accuse us of trying to destroy the body to hide the truth they think we're hiding." She gives me a frustrated look.

I don't know what to say. In my mind it's clear, or at least mostly clear, what we saw. But I think I understand. The Warlock only needs to create enough doubt. Tomorrow's headlines are going to be filled with news about a dead girl crawling out of her grave and then erupting into flames in front of an army of helpless FBI agents. It's a story too sensational to ignore.

The discussion is going to be about what happened. Not why. A girl was murdered just hours ago but the story is going to be on whether or not we've witnessed a miracle.

It's a dirty, evil, vile trick.

The Warlock turned one girl's death into a publicity stunt, killing another.

I search the rooftops again for any sign of someone watching. I know he's long gone, but part of me still has that feeling that I'm being watched. This dark show has only started.

10

Our jet leaves Michigan a little past 4 a.m. When I check my phone there's a message from my ex-boyfriend. He's in from New York and wants to know if I want to grab a late dinner.

I send him an e-mail explaining why I couldn't return his call and tell him maybe next time. Secretly, I'm thankful I didn't have to turn him down over the phone. Our breakup was long and awkward. A campaign fund-raiser for a New York senator, he seemed like my workaholic match until I caught him reading the CNN closed captioning in the middle of sex. I may not be the most imaginative girl in the bedroom, but I have to draw a line somewhere.

By the time we land, there's already a meeting scheduled for later that day to fill in the rest of the bureau on what happened. I make it home long enough to get a shower and take a three-hour nap. While I change into something more suitable for the office, I watch the news for the media reaction from yesterday.

What should be a quiet Sunday morning is filled with high-def video of the flames from the body over the iron gates of the cemetery. The fire looks like a stretched-out tornado as it twists into the sky and ends in a dark plume of smoke.

Photos are already popping up online. Some people saying

they can see ghastly images and spectral eyes looking down on them. A commentator flicking through different images calls attention to the most striking ones. I have to admit that some of the freeze frames are ominous-looking. No matter what I know about statistics and psychology—you're bound to get some photos that can be anthropomorphized into faces—it doesn't change my emotional reaction when I see a dark skeletal image leering at the camera.

I send a quick e-mail to Ailes while I put on my makeup, something I never learned properly until a college roommate showed me how. All I knew up until then was show makeup, designed for bright lights and big theaters. I used to either look like a drag queen or wore none at all. Now I go for a simple not-made-up-unless-you-look-closely style. It takes just as long as anything else.

We're so image-obsessed, if the Warlock really wanted to mess with us, it would be simple for him to Photoshop an image or digitally manipulate some video and then post it somewhere online. It would be the twenty-first-century way to leave a calling card.

Watching the news replay the video and play up the mystery is frustrating. I keep hearing the phrase "a case that has the FBI baffled" over and over again.

For Christ sake, we've only been on the case for less than twenty-four hours. Give us some time . . .

But there may not be time, I realize. The Warlock may be playing a game with us, but it's not one we're meant to win.

A young paramedic, one I think I remember from the scene, is talking to a reporter. His face is wide open with surprise. Not shock. It's awe.

"I can't explain it. It's like nothing I've ever seen. One

moment the girl is just there and then BOOM! She's erupted into flames reaching the sky." He looks up, expecting to still see the fire.

"Do the authorities have any idea what caused this?" asks the reporter.

The paramedic shakes his head. "No. Nothing. They don't have a clue. Look to your Bible, that's all I'm saying."

I turn the television off, disgusted. I don't think it's time to give up on rationality and reason just yet. I hope he's just one excitable young man, but I can't help think that his reaction is similar to that of many other people watching this around the world.

Somewhere the Warlock is also watching this. Laughing to himself.

I finish getting dressed and head back to Quantico for a conference with Danielle's forensic unit, the assistant director, the head of behavioral sciences, in addition to a man from behavioral analysis and a few other people I don't recognize. It's a large room with about thirty seats around the table. Another thirty people are sitting and standing around us. When Ailes sees me, he pulls me from a chair by the wall and sits me next to him at the table.

I'm sitting still, trying not to call attention to myself. I don't belong here. Everyone else has piles of folders in front of them, like they're showing off their homework. I just have a folder with the notes I wrote on the plane, which I already typed up and e-mailed to the newly appointed supervisor of the investigation, a squat bald man named Joseph Knoll. He has a face like a prizefighter, the calculating kind that knows where to hit.

After getting a nod from the assistant director, Knoll calls the meeting to a start and begins with a PowerPoint presentation of what happened between the hacking and yesterday. He plays a video of the body in flames, taken by a sheriff's deputy. This is a much closer view than the one on the news taken from atop a news truck.

"One week ago, the FBI's public information website was hacked into and a number was placed there and an invitation for us to decode it. Almost seven days to the hour later, our cryptanalysts using our best number cruncher found the hidden code. It was the GPS coordinates of a cemetery in Michigan. That's where we found the body of a girl that resembles, in every detail we could check, a murder victim from almost two years prior. However, a preliminary investigation showed that she had died just hours before. Apparently from asphyxiation and exhaustion from trying to crawl out of her own grave.

"When we proceeded to move the body from the grave, it erupted into flames caused by some chemical reaction we're still trying to determine. It's been suggested this was done as a means to conceal the true identity of the girl. Despite what the Warlock wants us to believe, the dead do not come back to life." He ends the recap by freezing on the face of the girl we're still calling Chloe, fire erupting out of her mouth.

It's a hellish sight, much higher resolution than anything on the news. She looks like a demon screaming fire in a medieval painting, almost biblical.

Knoll points to Danielle. "Our forensic team brought back what we could to look at in our labs. We'll probably know within a few hours if we can get a tissue match between this and the preserved samples from the first murder victim nineteen months ago. As you can imagine, it's a bit of a challenge. We still haven't identified the particular incendiary device used to cause the combustion. Field tests show high levels of potassium, indicating that it was some kind of autocatalytic re-action. This still leaves two questions: who and how. Danielle?"

A tech pulls up the 3-D image of the coffin in the ground as Danielle walks over to the screen. Her voice is clipped. I can tell she hasn't slept since she got back. I feel guilty for my nap. "Density tests and soil oxidization levels indicate this casket has been in this position for at least six months, likely much longer, which implies that this was planned at least that far back. The real Chloe, or original victim, was probably removed at that time. The whereabouts of her body are still unknown. It would seem evident that the original Chloe was murdered by the same individual who staged this. He drew her blood, saved it and injects it into the second victim to confuse a preliminary forensic examination. Or at least that's the prevailing theory."

As she says this I begin to have doubts. I don't know why. Something is out of place. The long burn . . .

A blond woman with glasses stops taking notes and raises her pen. "Would a more thorough examination have revealed the transfusion?"

"I think so. Given the extreme circumstances, we would have done skin scraping as well and compared them with sam-ples from the original autopsy. If it was just a regional medi-cal examination, then possibly, but I'd like to think they would have caught it too."

"Are we sure there are two girls?" asks the woman.

Danielle thinks the question over carefully. We all know it can't be just one girl, but she's rational enough to know we can't always go by what we "know." "The first girl's body would likely have much more advanced necrosis. It's possible the body could have been preserved. But a cellular analysis would confirm this. Because we stand a good chance of getting a skin sample from the portion of the body that was still in the ground and didn't undergo complete combustion, I'm reasonably confident we will be able to know in a few hours." She looks in my direction. "Thanks to Agent Blackwood, we can be thankful we have that much. If the techs had pulled the body all the way out of the ground, we might have a different story and be looking only at a pile of ash."

I feel awkward about the praise. If I'd said something sooner last night, if I hadn't been distracted, we might have had more to go on. Like everyone else, I was still too dazzled by the show to see where it was going. Danielle may be trying to pay me a compliment, but it's just a reminder to me that I failed.

Knoll thanks Danielle and takes over the podium. "We have several areas we need to investigate. We need to identify who the second victim is. How was she chosen? Does she fit a type the Warlock has? Was she just a lucky find for him? Did he find her after murdering Chloe McDonald? The scars on her chest matched the original stab wounds. The question we have now, without the full body, is whether those were genuine or makeup effects? If they were genuine scars that healed over, that suggests a whole different level of premeditation. Based upon the evidence on hand, the assistant director has suggested we proceed to treat this as a serial killer investigation. To help us with that, we've brought in an expert to assist the analysis unit in giving us a profile."

I turn to look at the head of behavioral sciences, but he's looking at me. Everyone is facing my direction. All the FBI chiefs in the room are waiting.

Ailes leans in and whispers to me, "You're on."

Me?

11

MY FIRST STEP onstage was by accident. I was three years old and my grandfather was performing a series of shows in London's West End. My mother had run off a year before, leaving me in the care of my unprepared father and my equally unskilled grandfather—his solution was to use dancers in the troupe as nannies. I had more "aunts" and "uncles" than I can remember. I was watching from the wings as usual. I used to sit in the lap of the dancers before they would go on, and this time my designated sitter was filling in for a girl getting ready on the other side of the stage, so I was left unattended.

Grandfather was performing the Mischief Rabbit, a trick invented by his father. He'd pretend to attempt to make a rabbit appear out of a silk top hat, only to fail. Each time he turned to the audience with an exasperated look, the rabbit would poke his head out of the top of the hat.

The trick was accomplished by a pneumatic lift built into the table. Each time Grandfather stepped away, a stagehand would push a button and raise the rabbit on its little rabbit elevator, bringing him into view.

I loved the trick. The rabbit delighted me. I used to feed him carrots and look after him and his six brothers like they were my own pets. When Grandfather performed the trick, I paid no mind to the machinery and thought it was really the rabbit poking his head out of the hat, giving Grandfather a hard time.

On this occasion, with no one there to mind me, I ran onto the stage and pulled the rabbit from the hat when my grandfather looked away. The audience screamed in delight. When Grandfather turned around, the rabbit was gone and so was I. He didn't realize I'd stolen the rabbit and continued on with the routine, baffled as to why he didn't get the laughs in the right places.

At the end of the effect, when it was time to produce the rabbit, he reached into the hat and his face turned red. The rabbit was gone. Suddenly he knew why everything was off. Then he saw me in the wings cuddling his finale.

I'd seen his enough of his temper to be frightened. Rather than run away, I joined him onstage, handed him the rabbit, and said in my high-pitched voice, "Don't be angry, Grandpa! You can pet him too!"

The audience roared. Grandfather's scowl melted. He knew a good bit when he saw it. I was in the act from then on.

Until he taught me the trick with the red sponge balls two years later, he'd never thought of teaching me to be more than a prop. I was used onstage but never as a magician until I took the initiative.

Since then, I've been on national television and performed for tens of thousands of people in outdoor arenas in Asia. But none of that has prepared me for this. I look at Ailes, not sure what I'm supposed to do. He taps his pen to my folder with its single page of notes.

I decide to just start talking and let my brain catch up. Just stick to what I know and not go into some bullshit theory about how I think the Warlock sees things—a mistake I've seen a lot of green analysts make.

I take a breath. "What we saw was a trick. I mean that in the strictest sense of the word. This is a magic trick designed to fool us and keep us fooled."

Ailes and Knoll are waiting for me to continue. "A trick assumes a trickster—a magician. There are two kinds of magicians: the type that acknowledges to the audience that what he's doing is a trick, and the kind that uses deception to pretend he's the real thing—like a psychic or a spoon bender. The first one just wants your attention. The second type wants to continue to deceive you. He wants you to believe in him."

Knoll raises a pen. "Why?"

I shrug. "I don't know. Dr. Chisholm or behavioral analysis would have to answer that. I can only tell you about the kind of magicians I'm aware of." I point to the screen and the girl's hellish scream. "This man is the second type. He doesn't want us to know how he did his trick. He wants us to believe in him. He wants us to believe he's real. He's not just trying to prove how clever he is. He doesn't just want our attention. He wants us to think this is a miracle. Maybe he knows that a room full of people like us won't be fooled into believing that a man can raise the dead, but he knows some of the public will be. A dead girl crawling out of the ground who spontaneously erupts in flames? That's a powerful idea." I think of what Gladys told me. "No matter how much science and logic we have on our side, if there's any room for doubt because we can't figure it out, he'll consider a win. It's about the spectacle."

The blond woman raises her hand. "How do you think he wanted the illusion to play out?"

Illusion. I guess that's the right word for this. Usually an illusion is much more benign. It only looks deadly . . .

I think for a moment. "If it was me and I wanted to convince you I was some kind of necromancer, I mean a real magician, I'd try to destroy the evidence that could contradict that, just like he did. Maybe I'd rig the body to combust when it was pulled out of the ground. Or perhaps I'd plant some kind of pressure sensor so it would burst into flames once it was in a confined space like a morgue truck. Maybe I'd try to make the combustion even more significant by having it burst into flames when the sun came up."

The last observation gets several raised eyebrows. I realize I'm overstepping. "I'm just speculating. He's obviously obsessed with the occult. It's a theme for him."

Knoll interrupts me with a question. "Do you think this person is a trained magician?"

I've been thinking about that a lot since last night. I don't have a specific answer. "I don't know. I'd say not. Magic techniques are available to just about anyone who wants to find them. Most magicians aren't creators. And to be honest, magical thinkers, I mean people who invent tricks, are extremely rare. They usually find work elsewhere, in Hollywood, designing games and other stuff." I leave out joining the FBI. "His method here is nothing like what would be used for a traditional buried-alive illusion. Superficially similar, but it ends there. He's just very, very clever."

I pause for any further questions. None. I breathe a sigh of relief. Everyone turns their attention back to Knoll.

The long burn is in the back of my mind. "There's one other thing."

Knoll sits back down and raises his eyebrows. I'm afraid I'm pushing, but it has to be said.

"If he's thought this through, he doesn't want us to solve it. That means he'll do things to lead us down blind alleys. He'll distract us. He'll make us reach for the wrong conclusion."

"How do you mean?" asks Knoll.

I remember an illusion I used to do for reporters and reach out to the conference table to pick up a set of keys from Knoll. I pass them from one hand to the other with my fists closed. "Which hand are they in?"

Knoll points to my right. I open the hand and show that it's empty.

"I think this is more than sleight of hand tricks, Agent," sneers the blonde.

"You're right," I reply. I open my left hand. I'm holding Knoll's BlackBerry. There's silence followed by a few stifled laughs.

"Well shit," shrieks Danielle. "That girl just burned a room full of us FBI folks." She gives me an approving look.

"My point is that smart people are smart because we are generally very good at knowing where to focus. Which means we're sometimes the easiest ones to fool." I look around the room. "Me too."

Ailes speaks up. "Jessica, do you think this is the last we've seen of the Warlock?"

I glance at Dr. Chisholm. "I think your division and the people at behavioral analysis would have a better answer than me."

Chisholm gives me a smile. "We have our thoughts. But I'd like to hear yours."

I'm still in the spotlight. The room is looking at me, expecting me to pull off another stunt. I'm not an expert on behavior and hate to be put on the spot for something outside my expertise. I go with my gut. "No. This isn't the last. He's just getting started. This is how a magician gets your attention. The website defacement was the poster calling us to the show. The Chloe murder is his opening effect, something quick, to the point, which tells us to take him seriously. Now he's going to follow through with something else. Something bigger. You saw the news today. This is only the start."

Chisholm nods his head. He knows this too. "Why do you say that, Agent Blackwood?"

"Because he's that second kind of magician. The dark kind. He doesn't want us to show that he's a fake. He's the kind of magician that thinks he's special, that despite the trickery there's something about him that is magical. Jim Jones used to do mentalism and hypnosis. That's how he got nine hundred people to follow him down to the middle of nowhere. Their kind only get stopped one of two ways. They either get exposed or they die."

"Either way is fine by us," replies Knoll.

I shake my head. "I don't think you understand. The ones that die without being exposed have religions built around them. I can name a handful of religions that really took off when their founder died. In a sense, they became immortal by dying. That's what the Warlock wants, what every dark magician is after, to be thought of as a god. And gods don't care how many people they kill." I shut up and sit back in my chair.

Chisholm follows up my comments with some analysis about the Warlock being obsessed with the occult and the suggestion that Chloe and her double were meant as a kind of sacrifice to demonstrate his powers. People keep glancing my way, expecting me to say something or add on to what he's saying.

I focus on Chisholm as he recommends looking for possible connections between the victims and the Warlock through occult online groups and related subcultures.

As the meeting is about to wrap up, a young agent barges through the door and whispers something into Knoll's ear and hands him a note.

Knoll tells us to stay in our seats. "They exhumed the coffin and found something else." He checks the note again. "Sand. From initial inspection it doesn't appear to be from the Michigan area. Apparently it's still damp and smells like salt water."

The blond agent raises her pen. "Wet sand in a coffin that was supposed to have been buried for two years? How is that possible?"

Everyone turns to me.

How the hell would I know?

12

Two days later, the assistant director of the FBI waits for me to perform a literal miracle in his office.

After that meeting I returned to my job in the cubicle hunting down fugitive decimal points. But I'd been active in the online working group for the Warlock case, following its development. The forensic lab sent samples of the sand over to the Navy and the Woods Hole Oceanographic Institution for analysis and I was asked again to offer my explanation as to how fresh sand got into the coffin.

I tried describing to Ailes that there could be any number of ways. Without more evidence, I wouldn't be able to say exactly how.

He'd shake his head, "Agent Blackwood, we're not asking how exactly he did it. We just want to know that it could be done. Could you do it?"

"Of course," I replied. It seemed to me like the backwards version of the buried-alive stunt. Instead of getting a living person out of the ground, you were putting something in the grave after the fact.

"Could you do a demonstration?"

He must have seen my face go white at the thought of being buried alive in some field at Quantico. He clarified, "I mean, can you just show them you can get something inside a sealed box under difficult conditions? I just want them to keep their minds open."

"A small demonstration?"

"Yes. Just a proof of concept."

"Okay." I told him my idea. He gave me a grin and asked if I'd do a demonstration for the assistant director as well as Knoll and Chisholm. I resisted the idea, but he was relentless.

"You need to show these people, Jessica."

"I think they'll get the idea if I just tell them."

He shook his head. "I mean, you need to show them what you're capable of."

"It's just a trick," I insisted.

"So is the Warlock's stunt. We need to be reminded of that."

I gave in. I knew he wouldn't stop. I don't want to be the performing magic girl. I just want to be a good cop.

THE WOODEN CHEST I asked Ailes to bring to Assistant Director Breyer's office the day before is sitting in the middle of his desk. Breyer pokes a finger at it and gives me a smile. "I had them lock this in a safe overnight. So what gives?"

I check my watch. "You're an Orioles fan, right? What's the score?"

He clicks open a screen on his computer to check. "They just finished. Ouch . . . Sox beat them by two."

"You have the envelope I asked Dr. Ailes to give you?" I'm standing while everyone else sits, looking at me like it's a god-damn magic show. I guess it is.

Breyer pulls the envelope from his desk and hands it to me. I check the seal and open it up. There's a key inside. I put the key into the lock on the chest and give it a turn. It makes a click. I step back and motion for Breyer to open the chest.

He gives everyone a look, then lifts the lid and peers inside. He takes out the envelope inside the chest and holds it up. "Am I supposed to open this?"

"Please."

Breyer takes a letter opener from his desk and slits the top open. There's a smirk on his face.

His smug expression vanishes when he looks inside. "Holy crap!" He pulls out his business card. Written on the back is the final score for the game. Breyer presses his intercom button, still holding the card. "Jill, did anyone get into the safe?"

"I hope not . . ." she replies from the next room.

Breyer shakes his head at me. "All right, witch. Explain."

It's an old method. Nobody uses it anymore. Not that I would feel any guilt explaining it to a room filled with FBI agents trying to solve a murder.

"Look at your business card."

Breyer gives the back a closer inspection. "It looks like it was rolled up."

I point to the key on his desk. He picks it up to examine more closely. Breyer shakes his head and hands the key to Chisholm when he sees the hollow end. He lifts the chest and looks through the keyhole. "The prediction was inside the key? You slipped that in there while we were all watching you?" He nods his head and gives me a smile of approval. "Clever, Agent. So the sand?"

"It's only a theory," I reply. "At first I thought he might have tried to drill a hole from above into the casket. Then I realized he didn't need to. When he took out Chloe's body out he probably installed a piece of PVC pipe going straight into the open lid and hid the other end under a few inches of dirt. When he planted the second body, he just poured the sand and water in through the tube, then pulled the tube out of the ground. If Danielle's team still has the density data, they'll probably find something odd in the direction the sand was pooled in the coffin. Maybe."

Breyer nods and gives Ailes a grin. "All right."

Ailes replies, "Maybe we can reassign Agent Blackwood to work on this full-time with Dr. Chisholm and give behavioral analysis an assist too? I think she's being wasted in the paper jungle."

I hadn't expected him to ask that, much less in front of me. He just put Breyer on the spot. I didn't want him to. I'd love to be able to work on this full-time, but I'd never dreamed about asking myself.

Breyer's eyes go to the floor in contemplation as he sits on the edge of his desk and taps his fingers. "I think Agent Blackwood is very clever. I don't doubt that." He waves a hand toward the chest. "But I think we got this mystery under control now." He looks at me and raises an eyebrow. "And we need clever people in the paper jungle as well."

A polite rejection. "I'm happy to do my part wherever I can." My words are half true, yet I feel like I've been rebuked for wanting something I didn't ask for.

He thanks me for the demonstration. Ailes and I head for the door.

Dr. Chisholm calls out after me. "Just a second, you didn't tell us how you got the prediction into the key locked in his desk."

I turn around. Ailes catches my arm and calls back, "I

thought you had the mystery under control?" He gives me a wink.

Breyer has his arms crossed. "Noted."

In the hallway I turn to Ailes, barely able to control my anger. "What was that all about?"

"I'm sorry. They're a little resistant to a change in the status quo."

"I didn't ask to be reassigned full-time. I'm happy to still contribute to the online working group." I feel like I just made a fool of myself in front of the assistant director. My little magic show was turned into a plea for a better position. It looked desperate and pathetic. They're probably laughing at me now.

Ailes can see the hurt in my eyes. "Agent Blackwood, when you give up one thing to be taken seriously in another, you can't expect it to come easy. It's going to be hard. Just look at me. Do you know how many other black men got their PhD in computational mathematics the year I did?"

"Not many."

"They didn't know if they should treat me like a prodigy or a special case. All I wanted to be was a mathematician. They don't know what to make of you. But you're not going to conceal it by hiding what makes you special. Even if sometimes that means being a little pushy."

"I don't know if those men will ever take me seriously again."

"They will. Trust me. Things are converging. It's hard to explain. I don't even understand it. But trust me," he reassures me. "They're about to realize how badly they need you."

I give him a skeptical look.

"It's in the numbers," he replies.

13

BEFORE MY APARTMENT was broken into as I slept, I was dreaming about being forced onstage to perform a trick that went horribly wrong.

I look on in shock as Elsie is burned alive in one of my magic illusions. It's an older Elsie who looks like Chloe. But the scars and the smile are the same. Fire and sparks spew from her mouth as she stares at me helplessly. Only I can't do anything to help. I'm eight years old and made up to look like one of those poor girls in a Texas beauty pageant. I'm doing one of my first shows in a theater full of magicians at a magic convention. My dad is giving me stern directions from backstage while my grandfather, drunk, is sitting in the front row shaking his head in disapproval.

Elsie is in flames and nobody will help me.

The dream hurts because parts of it are true. I know my family has always loved me. I've never doubted that. But sometimes having three generations of ambition forced on you is too much.

I was persistent with my family, pushing them to let me become a magician. Once they saw the potential, at least the novelty of it, I became the center of attention. Father was relieved to have someone else fall under Grandfather's hyper-critical eye. Grandfather, having given up hope on his son, began to increasingly look to me to continue his legacy.

After the incident in Mexico, my contact with them has been minimal at best. I didn't invite any of them to my graduation from college or the FBI academy. It was a selfish thing. I try to pretend they wouldn't have cared. But I know that's not true.

Ailes asking me to put on a show for Breyer and Chisholm scratches a little too deep. I can remember being a teenager, not quite fifteen, and noticing the way some men looked at me. The glances were different from when I was a little girl. It made me self-conscious about my magic and so I practiced more. I made sure my show was better. I created illusions, I took it seriously. I didn't want them to see me that way. I wanted them to respect me for my skills. Some did, but most others continued to look at me like a piece of ass in a tight costume. Then there were the men like Breyer and Chisholm, who just saw me as a little girl putting on a show because she couldn't get enough attention.

As I lie in bed trying to put the dream out of my mind, I realize the television is on in the other room. Half asleep, for a moment I think it's Terrence, but we broke up months ago.

I know who it is.

It's Damian.

Of course it would be him.

At one of the worst moments in my life, of course he would drop in like thunder from a rain cloud.

I reach over to my nightstand and take my pistol from the drawer, then get out of bed. I move toward my door and slowly turn the handle.

The news is on in the living room. I can feel cold air coming from under my door. He must have slipped in through the veranda and left the sliding glass door open.

I keep the gun pointed to the ground with my right hand and open the door with my left. I swing it open.

He's sitting there on my couch dressed in khakis and a blue polo shirt, with his feet on the coffee table like he owns the place. Today his hair is a light brown. It's cut close and he has a tan and a lean build like a tennis pro. With Damian, I never can tell how he'll appear next.

He looks up at me and gives me a broad smile.

"That. Is. Hot." He emphasizes each of the words. "The gun especially." His eyes linger over me. I'm still wearing the T-shirt I slept in and a pair of pink boy shorts.

"I've already called the police," I lie.

He shakes his head and points to a cordless phone on the coffee table. "No. You did not. But I did." He checks his watch. "I've got about six minutes until they get here."

Knowing him, he did.

Damian Knight, the world's only known instance of serial personality disorder—a clinical designation a friend of mine studying psychology made up when I explained his case to her.

I FIRST MET him at a magic convention when I was seventeen. He was polite and charming and said none of the creepy or suggestive things the creepy men who go to magic conventions like to say to the few women who stray into their domain. We spent a few hours sitting in the hotel lobby. He showed me a few sleights with card tricks I'd never seen before or since then. Mostly he asked why I wanted to do magic, where I thought I was going with it and about my philosophy of life.

I was a teenager trying to impress someone older and did my

best to sound as intelligent as I could. At the end of the conversation he said good-bye, and I didn't see him again until I was twenty-one and majoring in criminal justice at the University of Miami. He was working on a graduate degree in biology, or at least that's what he told me when he sat next to me in the library. He looked almost the same as when we met at that magic convention four years prior. In fact, the conversation started where we left off as he leaned over and asked me if my philosophy on life had changed.

We ended up dating for several months. He was funny, charming and always knew how to say the right thing. He was the first man I had sex with that I more than just liked. He was perfect. Because that's what he does, he tries to be perfect at anything he tries. He's the type of man that surprises you by speaking Thai at a Thai restaurant or sits down at a piano when nobody is looking and plays something as beautiful as anything you would hear in a concert hall. He could remind you of your friend's birthdays and would pick out a flower arrangement you couldn't imagine doing. Perfection was a kind of game for him. Or the illusion of perfection. The relationship ended when I found out that he wasn't enrolled in the university and his entire story was a fabrication. I confronted him about the lie and he just nodded his head and walked out of the restaurant.

I thought that was the end of things. I was heartbroken. I hated myself for being a fool. I hated myself for ending it.

Three years later I was at a bookstore and met a man with dark hair, a bit of an unkempt hipster beard and a Radiohead T-shirt. He invited me to coffee and we had a fascinating conversation. He asked me for my phone number. As he leaned in to watch me write it down, I noticed a mannerism that seemed familiar. You can change your voice, your hair, even your face.

But it's the little things we overlook. His habit of scooting back while straightening his back, like someone sitting down to the piano. You pick up a lot of things when you love someone.

Deep down I knew something was wrong. I looked up at him and couldn't understand for a moment. He was thirty pounds lighter, looked taller, and his eyes and hair were a different color. But it was him. Damian. Again.

I couldn't feel myself breathe.

He didn't say anything. He just gave me a smile and left.

I sat there stunned for a half hour trying to understand what had just happened.

Since then, Damian has kept showing up in my life. Each time with an almost unrecognizable look. It's uncanny. I've tried to run his fingerprints, but he discovered a trick a long time ago of putting super glue over his fingertips and manually etching them with the tip of a pin.

After the encounter at the bookstore, I got a friend in the police department to run his prints from the coffee cup I swiped from the table. When the results came back, she asked if I got William Shatner's autograph too when I met him. It was one of Damian's little tricks. God knows how long it took him to etch that. He knew I had studied criminal justice and probably thought it would be fun to see how far I'd push my professional life into my personal.

He's crazy. Certifiably insane.

I once ran an old photograph I have of him from college through a facial recognition database. It came back with a newspaper article from the 1980s of a teenager who was arrested for posing as a train conductor and taking a train cross-country to Seattle. A hundred-car-long train. Technically speaking, it was the biggest theft of an object in history.

His name was left out because he was a minor and the records were sealed. The grin was unmistakably his. When I asked him about it, he just replied that he's had lots of different careers.

That's what Damian does when he's not pursuing me. He pretends to be other people. The role he wants more than anything is to be my lover again.

But that's never going to happen. He's dangerous.

"Why are you here?" My knuckles are white on the grip of my gun.

Damian points to the television. "I just want to make sure you have sunscreen. I'd hate for something to happen to that beautiful skin when you go there."

14

I'M TOO DISTRACTED by Damian sitting on my couch to realize what he's talking about.

He takes a sip from a beer he stole from my fridge. "When I saw that Michigan trick, I figured you'd show up eventually. I could have sworn I saw you in the news footage in the background. I'm glad you're living up to at least part of your potential."

"Get out." I don't point the gun at him, but I give it a flick with my wrist.

He looks away from the television and stares at me. His eyes are almost ice blue. That's the reason he often uses contacts to color them. His one unforgettable trait. His gaze drifts down to the gun and smiles. "Jessica, if I could die right now from your bullet, looking at you like that, I can't think of a better way to go."

The scary part is I think he's telling the truth. He knows I won't kill him. But I think he likes to toy with me in that way. He's never harmed me other than with his lies and his total ignorance of personal space.

It's hard to call him possessive. I think "fixated" is the better word.

I've been in criminal justice long enough to know a harmless fixation can change into something deadly. That's why I'm holding my gun.

He might die for me, but I also strongly suspect he may have killed for me. He's never admitted it, but he's hinted at it before.

Before I joined the FBI I spent two years as a street cop in south Florida after graduating college. Eleven months into the job, I answered a domestic disturbance call about a man beating his girlfriend. He was a known drug dealer and a pimp. As soon as he saw a lady cop at the door, he kicked me down a flight of stairs and broke my nose. It happened so fast I didn't have a chance to react.

His girlfriend later testified that I'd entered the premises without knocking and threatened to kill him, so he was acting in self-defense. It's hard for me to hate her, knowing what her life was like. He had two other witnesses, who probably worked for him. The judge dropped the assault case and the asshole walked.

It was a raw deal. Two days later his attorney filed a lawsuit against me to sue for damages.

It's stuff like that people forget cops have to deal with. I'm not even a cop for a year and I get a broken nose and sued by a drug dealer who drives a car more expensive than the house I was renting. It's why our suicide rate is so high.

I was at rock bottom after that happened. I don't complain about being a woman in a man's field, but I felt like everyone around me was just waiting for me to snap. They have no idea how close I came.

Three days after the process server presented me with the lawsuit, the drug dealer was found facedown in a Dumpster with a piece of wire wrapped around his neck. He'd been strangled to death. There weren't any leads or an overwhelming desire to put too much effort into solving the case. It was written off as a robbery.

The jack of spades they found in his pocket didn't seem important to anyone other than me.

The jack of spades was the first card I picked when I met Damian at the magic conference and he showed me a trick. It's his favorite card.

I think about the murder every time I see him. I can never let myself forget what he's capable of doing. No matter how charming. No matter the smile. I'm pretty sure he has the capacity to be a cold-blooded killer.

"I've got three minutes, Jessica," he says.

The television is playing a news report about an airplane that landed on the beach. It looks like Fort Lauderdale.

Damian turns up the volume. "Navy officials are trying to confirm if it is indeed one of the original Avenger bombers last seen in 1945 that some claim were lost in the Bermuda Triangle . . . Authorities have sealed the sandbar off and aren't allowing news crews close enough to take photographs of the body inside . . ."

I forget about the gun in my hand.

The World War II plane is sitting on a sandbar with Coast Guard boats on either side. Thick fuselage and stubby wings, like a huge engine with a plane built around it. A tarp is over the long cockpit section. The bomber looks as if it's been sitting on the bottom of the ocean for a hundred years. Maybe it has.

Damian points to the television. "I bet you anything the pilot is going to be a dead ringer for one of the missing airmen from 1945. Your bad boy loves duplicates. Doesn't he?"

Damian flashes me a smile. He has an almost gleeful look on

his face. The Warlock connection doesn't hit me at first. The screen flashes a close-up look at the bomber, then a graphic of the Bermuda Triangle like you see on those paranormal shows, and some archival photos of the bombers.

I knew on some level the Warlock was going to try something bigger and even more impressive, but this is just beyond the pale.

The plane looks exactly like the photograph of one that went missing more than fifty years ago. Now it's come back with a corpse inside.

A reporter on the beach says the Pentagon is trying to track down the serial numbers. They haven't made any comment about the body. But I bet Damian is right.

"One minute." Damian stands up.

I'm still looking at the television.

"A word of warning, darling. What's the one thing magicians hate more than anything else in the world?" He steps out onto my balcony and leans over the railing.

I turn away from the television. "A skeptic."

"Clever girl." He blows me a kiss, then climbs over.

"Damian!" I call out to him.

By the time I get to the ledge, he's gone.

I live on the nineteenth floor.

My phone rings at the same time the police knock on my door.

I try to explain to the cops that it's a false alarm. They look a little suspicious and want to stay longer and ask me questions. I think it has to do with how I'm dressed. Meanwhile, Ailes is on the phone telling me to get to the airfield in forty minutes. Assistant Director Breyer had a change of heart.

They need me in Fort Lauderdale as soon as possible.

15

BARELY MAKE IT to the airfield in time. Fortunately, I'm not the last one on the FBI jet. It's a full plane. All forty seats are taken up by forensic specialists and some naval officials teaching at the FBI academy who requested to come aboard. Our last passenger is an older man, a retired pilot who teaches history at the U.S. Naval Academy at Annapolis. Although we've all been looking up the same Wikipedia page on our laptops and phones, he gives us the overview of the mystery on the trip down.

The Avengers were torpedo bombers launched after Pearl Harbor and used to turn the tide of naval warfare in World War II. Flight 19 was a routine training mission out of the military airbase in Fort Lauderdale, Florida, now the site of the city's airport. On December 5, 1945, months after the end of the war, five Avenger bombers with a total crew of fourteen took off in the afternoon under clear skies. At some point they appeared to become disoriented, reporting erratic compass readings. They were under the impression that they were hundreds of miles away from their radio position. Contact was lost and a rescue mission was launched. A Mariner seaplane with a crew of thirteen exploded in midair during the search and all hands were lost.

The wreckage of Flight 19 was never found. Dozens of Avenger bombers had been ditched in that part of the Atlantic during similar missions and never recovered. The pilot in charge of Flight 19 had bailed out of similar planes twice in the past. What made Flight 19 notorious were the erratic radio and compass readings, the loss of all the crew, the complete lack of wreckage and the loss of the rescue plane, all in clear weather.

The historian explains that statistically, this kind of event was to be expected, given the number of flights flown out of that base during World War II. In all, ninety-three men lost their lives on similar missions.

But the numbers haven't detracted from the mystery. Conspiracy theorists love to hold up Flight 19 as one of the big unsolved unusual events of the twentieth century. The fact that the ocean is vast and it's hard to find things there doesn't do much to dispel the idea that something paranormal has taken place.

Before we land, we receive confirmation that the body of the man dressed in a pilot uniform found in the plane resembles one of the missing airmen physically. By the time we get to the scene, the bomb squad from the Miami field office is going over the plane inch by inch looking for a trap.

A1A, the highway that runs along the beach, has been blocked off, but that hasn't stopped several hundred people gathering to see the missing plane. Our van passes at least six news trucks before we get to the police line.

This is chaos. The sun is barely up and the streets are filled. Although I shouldn't be surprised in a town that specializes in bars that open before most places stop selling breakfast.

After the cemetery incident, people are primed for another so-called miracle. When the news broke about the plane, they all came. Nobody has said it aloud yet, but I get the sense people believe these things are connected. This is the age of dark mysteries.

On the trip down I surfed the Web and found hundreds of articles and discussions making religious connections to Chloe's graveyard spectacle. Everyone has an opinion. From the secular to the religious. The Warlock started more than one fire. Nothing sparks a discussion of religion like bringing back the dead.

I follow our team over the barrier that blocks the sand from blowing into the streets of Fort Lauderdale. The crowd, pushed back to the sidewalk, is filled with a mixture of locals and tourists. I notice more than a few holding crucifixes and watching with what looks like worry on their faces. I spot a man carrying a picket sign with "Leviticus 24:16" written on it. I make a note to look it up.

Clear as can be, several hundred yards offshore, there's the plane. We all stop to look. Several people pull out their phones to snap photos. I glance behind us at the rows of hotels and restaurants and see onlookers crowding every balcony and roof with access. I spot several long-range lenses, the kind professionals use.

I can't deny the spectacle. The scene reminds me of something out of the opening of *Close Encounters of the Third Kind*, where the missing fleet of planes shows up in the desert. I guess that was the idea—if this is staged by the Warlock. But I already know it is. I get the feeling the crowd is waiting for something else to happen, like an alien stepping out of the Avenger.

There's only a handful of law enforcement officers on the sandbar. FBI agents dressed like armored beetles probe the aircraft for a bomb. The bureau's hazardous devices unit is trained to dismantle everything from letter bombs to suitcase nukes.

This situation is made even more complicated by the shifting ground. To fight the afternoon tide, Broward sheriff's deputies and the Fort Lauderdale police have improvised a barricade of sandbags around the plane. They've also beached several boats on the sandbar to serve as work platforms.

After we introduce ourselves, an FBI field agent hands Knoll a radio. Knoll tells the head of the bomb squad that our biggest concern is the body. He turns to me and raises an eyebrow, asking if I think that's correct.

I can't remember ever being put on the spot like this with people's lives at stake. I can see the men we're talking about. I shake my head. "We shouldn't take the chance. If the plane is a fake, he'll want to cover his tracks on that too." I turn to one of our naval experts who took the flight down with us. "Are there any serial numbers or markings that wouldn't be known publicly?"

He folds his cap over in his hands. He's got that close-cropped hair and boyish look a lot of military men still hold on to, like overgrown Boy Scouts. "There are four standard markers. One in the cockpit. Two in the engines and one on the tail. Parts are switched around a lot, but those would remain constant."

I'm sure the Warlock knows this. "Yes, but if all four match, would you say that was the plane? Definitively?"

He thinks for a moment, then shakes his head. "No. We'd then look for serial numbers on the engines and other parts. Those can be switched out, so they're not as definitive, but they'd tell us something." I can tell he's as nervous as I am. We don't want to see the men on the sandbar blown apart by our mistaken assumptions.

One bomb tech is on a ladder looking into the cockpit, while another is examining the engine behind the propeller shaft with a mirror. With that metal casing, the whole plane looks like a bomb to me.

I don't know what to say to Knoll. I decide on just being honest. "I'm not sure. If the Warlock thinks he could be exposed, he's going to destroy the evidence. And if that's not one of the missing planes, then I think we're in a bad situation."

All of us are thinking about the duplicate Chloe bursting into flames. We're afraid that this could end even more spectacularly. Besides the fuselage and wings, he could have buried something in the sandbar. The bomb squad is sweeping the area with handheld metal detectors and chemical sensors.

Knoll leans into me and half whispers. I can tell he's embarrassed to ask the question. "Could it be the real thing?"

I've been wondering too. Unlike a girl coming back to life, it's theoretically possible someone found the long-lost plane. But still. "Maybe. Maybe."

The naval officer disagrees. "That can't be one of the planes. Maybe something else pulled off the floor of the ocean, but it's a million to one it's from Flight 19."

Knoll takes the cautionary approach and radios over to the head of the bomb squad. "I think we should pull back for now. There's a chance the whole thing could be set to explode in our faces." He pauses, then adds, "Again."

16

THERE ARE MORE than a thousand people observing us from the highway along the beach. The wide sidewalks are packed with locals and tourists. Everyone is here to witness the miracle they saw on television, waiting to find out if it's a hoax. Crowds have filled the area between the water and the streets on both sides of the barrier. News helicopters are flying around in a circle, covering the scene from all angles.

It's a sunny day. That water is sparkling and a nice breeze fights back the heat of the sun. If you ignore the airplane on the sandbar, news crews and law enforcement, it could be the crowd that shows up for a Fourth of July display or air show. A great day to pull off something like this. I look at the faces observing us. The Warlock has to be among them somewhere. He's enjoying every minute of the show. He watched us pull back the bomb squad and congratulated himself on making us overthink everything.

Him. I keep thinking of the Warlock in the singular. I look back at the plane sitting on the sandbar. Could one man pull that off?

"Lieutenant, how much does one of those planes weigh?"

The naval officer answers without hesitation. "Unloaded, ten thousand pounds."

"Could one man get that out there by himself?" Local police had been checking for witnesses, but so far none have shown up.

"I don't know. I've been wondering that myself."

I rephrase the question from the abstract. It's always been a good trick to get people to think of the possible. "If you had to do it, how would you?"

The lieutenant crosses his arms and squints at the plane. "I'd use flotation rings. Basically make a raft around it. You could use salvage balloons to do that. That's how they move concrete blocks around under water for construction. They take forever to inflate."

"But he doesn't have to inflate them while people are watching. He just has to tow the plane from wherever and park it over the sandbar at high tide and let it drop." I pull out my phone to look up tides on the Internet.

"Three-fifty a.m.," he replies from memory. "That's high tide."

Knoll has been listening while he waits for the head of the bomb squad to report back with an alternate plan. "We'll start looking in on that. Meanwhile, they're going to try to rig a robot against salt water and get it out there to do the inspection. Anyplace we should look first?"

The lieutenant thinks this over carefully. "We already got the first four serials. Can it take a look inside the engine compartment? The serial number there is actually etched into the engine block."

"I think so. We can cut it open. The robot has a diamond saw." Knoll radios instructions to the head of the bomb squad.

I feel a wave of relief that we're going to continue the

inspection with everyone at a safe distance. Although I get the feeling the Warlock isn't going to repeat the first stunt.

All of this inspecting and prodding reminds me of the setup for one of my grandfather's illusions. For the premiere show, the police chief of whatever town we were in would be invited onstage to inspect the locks and the packing case. Local warehouse workers would manhandle the chains. Grandfather would make a big show of proving everything was real. The subtext was showing how much smarter he was than all the idiots onstage.

That was part of why Houdini was so popular. He cheated death and defied authority. Now the Warlock is teasing the ultimate law enforcement authority in the world. We're all amped about the plane exploding because there's just no way it could be the real missing Avenger and pilot. But maybe that's his trick . . .

A half hour later, the bomb squad is bringing the plastic-wrapped robot over to the plane on a boat. A technician in a truck on shore will control it while the supervisors watch the robot's camera feed in handheld monitors. Knoll holds up his screen so we can see.

Bomb robot work is a slow process. Because of the dangerous nature, the tech doesn't want to make any mistakes, like overcompensating on the controls. It's like trying to fix your car with baseball gloves on both hands.

An armored tech places the robot on the inside of the sandbag barrier. Thick treads push it across the sand to the plane. The robot comes to a stop near the front and starts to extend an arm on a telescoping base. At full extension, it comes halfway to the engine compartment.

To help the robot operator, a mechanic familiar with the

make of the plane is on the radio explaining where to cut. He sounds so specific that first I think he's reading from a manual. Then I overhear he's actually on the phone from an air museum outside Orlando, describing the plane they have on display as he takes it apart.

On Knoll's screen, the diamond-tipped blade starts spinning. The tech moves the edge a few centimeters and it begins cutting into the casing over the engine. The rusted metal sprays out a cloud of brown dust as the saw carves a hole the size of a book. The grinding sound carries across the water. Once the smoke clears, the robot uses an arm to pull the piece away and sticks a camera into the engine compartment.

The technician takes several minutes to get the camera over the location of the engine serial number. When the numbers finally come into view, he calls them out over the radio.

A new voice, someone who sounds like he's indoors somewhere, calls the numbers back out for confirmation. He's probably in a dark basement library under the Pentagon poring through a repair log that hasn't seen light in half a century.

I look at the two dozen other officials watching the monitor Knoll is holding up for us. I know what they're thinking. It's what the Warlock desires. He wants us to hope the numbers match.

Forgetting the dead man in the pilot's seat, probably another innocent victim, we all want this to be true. We want this to be one of the missing planes . . .

We want the mystery to be bigger than us. We want novelty of the unexpected.

We want to be entertained.

There's a disconnect around me between the horrible acts and the spectacle.

That sickens me. I can understand the power fantasies men

sometimes have about serial killers. It's something else when we're waiting for confirmation that would give proof to this asshole's illusion.

We have this strange desire for symmetry. Humans are pattern seekers. We're designed by nature to get a little buzz every time something connects in a novel way. It's why we play Sudoku, enjoy simple video games, and watch TV shows with different characters but the same plots.

We love patterns.

Even dark patterns.

The tech continues calling numbers.

We wait for the man in the basement to respond. No one is breathing, for fear of missing the moment.

I look at everyone around me. I know it's not real. Somehow we're all about to be deceived, or it's going to fall apart. Regardless of what the man in the Pentagon basement says, it's a trick.

But I know it won't fall apart here.

Damn him.

I know the answer before the man in the basement says the words. I get that goose-bump feeling.

I feel guilty for wanting it to happen.

The serial number etched into the engine block is a perfect match.

17

KNOLL LOWERS THE MONITOR. "Now what?" His voice is low and grave. He knows what the match really means. "There are a dozen other serial numbers we can look for. Do we just keep at it and take the whole plane apart out there?"

There's got to be a better way. Serial numbers can be faked.

It's not a Flight 19 plane we should be matching.

The pilot. He's the key.

I remember the girl in the cemetery. Her hands had been stripped raw of flesh so we couldn't fingerprint her.

On the monitor, the pilot's hands look intact.

I get an idea and turn to the naval officer we spoke with earlier. "Lieutenant Droves, does the Navy still have the fingerprint files of the pilots?"

"We had them digitized a few hours ago and e-mailed to the FBI prints division," he replies.

I turn to Knoll. "We need a print off the pilot. If it doesn't match, then we know the Warlock is going to want to cover his tracks. Maybe have the body rigged so that when we remove it the whole thing will explode."

Knoll shakes his head. "Blackwood, the robot can't take a print. And if we use it to pull the body out, we're still going to have to deal with things possibly exploding." He looks at all the bystanders. "This is not a contained environment."

I've already thought this through. I don't know how else to say it, so I just lay it out there. "We just need the robot to cut off a thumb."

Everyone standing around Knoll gives me a strange look. The thing about being an attractive female is that if you say something morbid, people get this look like they've finally figured you out. A little bulb in their head lights up and they go, "Of course, she's crazy."

Knoll doesn't look at me like I'm crazy, surprising me. He gets it. He turns to the lieutenant, as if he needs to ask permission from the Navy.

The lieutenant nods his head. "I think we're better off cutting a thumb off a dead man than putting everyone in harm's way."

"All right. Let me clear it with upstairs." Knoll makes a call on his phone. While he's waiting for a reply he asks the lieutenant another question. "How would the Navy handle this?"

"The easy way. We'd blow it up ourselves and go look at the pieces the seagulls didn't get. Of course, we usually have the advantage of knowing who the bad guys are."

Knoll puts away his phone and picks up the radio. "Hey, robot boy, let me ask you a question. Are you the squeamish type?"

TWENTY MINUTES LATER the robot drives to the edge of the sandbar, away from viewers on the beach, and drops something into a bag held by a bomb tech waiting on a boat. He places it into an evidence bag, then into a toolbox, and brings it back from the sandbar. The thumb is rushed to a mobile forensic lab before the media have any idea of what a grisly thing we've just done.

Dr. Chisholm steps over a small sand dune and approaches me. I hadn't realized that he wasn't around while we were watching the bomb robot cut open the plane.

"Your idea?"

I can tell he means the thumb. "It seemed . . . pragmatic."

"Probably the safest thing to do at this point." He looks over his shoulder at the crowd behind the barrier.

"Anything interesting?" I ask.

Chisholm turns his attention to the plane and speaks in a low voice. "We've got plainclothes out there taking photos of everyone and photographing all the license plates we can find. Hotel records too. Of course in a crowd this size . . ." He glances back over his shoulder. "At least three thousand people now. We can expect at least sixty clinical sociopaths. Maybe more because it's a workday and these people don't seem to have anything else to do. At least several hundred convicted felons and God knows what else are out there."

"You must be a blast at a football game."

"Forty." He throws the number out there for a moment. "That's how many people in an average football stadium have murdered someone in the last ten years."

"And that's just when the team shows up to practice," I reply.

Chisholm lets out a laugh. Not too loud, but genuine. "You have a dark sense of humor, Blackwood."

"You should meet my family."

"I have. Your grandfather signed an autograph for me when I was a boy. I was a little magician myself. Just a magic set. Nothing serious. Nowhere near your level. Never had much coordination. I loved seeing how adults could be fooled. That's what got me into psychology. When I realized that some people thought magically all the time, thought angels or dogs were talking to them, whispering for them to kill, I didn't need trick decks anymore."

"Me neither, I guess." I didn't know he'd met my grandfather. I wonder what he makes of me and my career choice.

"So, as a former magician, what's your reaction going to be if the thumbprint comes back as a match?"

"You mean am I going to believe that a man vanished in the middle of last century, only to reappear just as young as the day he died?"

"What else is there?"

"Somebody switched the paper card in the basement of the Pentagon with the fingerprints on it."

"Really?" replies Chisholm. Is he skeptical?

"I could do it with fifty bucks and a sheet of fake letterhead from a university." I'm thinking of a stunt my father pulled on the *New York Times* by planting something in its archives when they were still physical. I'm sure doing the same at the Pentagon is an order of magnitude more difficult, but they all have the same weaknesses: people. Records like that aren't national secrets.

"Occam's razor. Fair enough. Assuming the uniform and badges is war surplus. What about the plane? What if it holds up when we put all those serial numbers under our electron microscopes and start looking for aging in the abrasions on the metal inside the grooves of the etching?"

"The plane could be real and it's still a trick. Maybe the Navy records for the plane were tampered with too," I reply.

"So it's always a trick?" he asks.

I've known enough highly educated men to realize that almost all of them want to believe that there's some magical part of life we can't explain. Psychologists especially. "If it's packaged like a trick, there's probably a reason why."

"Does the idea of being fooled bother you?"

"No." I've had to deal with this question all my life. "Not if we catch this guy. I mean, that's why we're here? That's why I'm here?"

"Yep." He sticks a hand into his pocket and pulls out a photograph of the pilot. "We just processed a bunch of stills the techs took. Nobody else has seen a good close-up of the face. What do you see?"

He looks like he stepped out of a *Life* magazine from the 1940s. Unlike Chloe's double, his face is almost peaceful, as if he died in his sleep. On a closer examination I can see abrasions on his face. The kind my grandfather and uncle had from years of alcoholism. "Burst blood vessels."

Chisholm takes the photograph back from me and points out the discoloration in the cheeks and around the eyes. "I won't know until forensics gets a closer look, but it looks like he died in a vacuum. Some might say it's as if he and the plane were transported into the middle of space."

"So why does he look recently dead while the plane is like something Columbus flew over on?" The Warlock is giving us too much proof.

I see his eyes twitch at my metaphor. "Maybe because this void or wherever he's been makes things age differently."

I don't think Chisholm believes. He's testing the limits of my belief. "Maybe because if the plane showed up looking brand-new, nobody would believe it was the original artifact. If he had an old corpse in there, people might just assume it washed up from below. It's an inconsistency. Like a tell in poker. It's like in a card trick how I might flip a card over in a way that doesn't make any logical sense if you think about the action. But taken as a whole, it makes sense."

Chisholm nods his head. "Keep reminding us how it could be done. Maybe we can figure out who did this."

He hands the photograph to me again. I try to imagine the mind that would go as far as killing a man in a vacuum chamber to create an illusion.

I'm glad that Chisholm and his group are the ones who have to get inside the Warlock's head. I only have to take apart his handiwork.

I just hope he's not as clever as I'm afraid he might be. I'm still having nagging thoughts about the cemetery murder. We reached a convenient explanation. Too convenient for a man capable of making the world think he just ripped a hole through space and time to produce a long-lost mystery.

I get the feeling something else is about to hit us there. We've been leaking to the media the inferno didn't leave enough of the body to confirm that it was Chloe. It's a small public relations victory, but one that's about to fall out from underneath us as the long burn plays out.

18

A FEW HOURS LATER we're gathered in a hotel conference room down the strip from the airplane. It's a hastily arranged operations center put together on the fly.

Knoll's making a pained face as he holds the phone. He's listening to the forensic lab report the results on the thumb.

The print is a perfect match for the original pilot of the missing Avenger.

Chisholm and behavioral analysis have been compiling a profile and looking for a historical precedent while others comb the beachfront hotels for suspects. From the look of things as they huddle around their laptops, they're not having much success.

The Warlock appears to be a black swan. A thing so rare, there's nothing to compare it to. On the far wall overhead projectors flash images of the cemetery crime scene and the Avenger bomber. The forensic team is talking about doing radiocarbon and chlorine-36 testing on the pilot to prove he was born after World War II, and possibly isotopic testing to determine where he was born.

I was reminded by one of the techs of the fun fact that because the U.S. and Soviet governments freely tested nuclear weapons in the 1950s, different isotopes made it into the food chain and effectively gave us all internal timestamps based on bomb blasts.

We can measure the rate of decay of certain radioactive elements given off in an atomic blast and find them in your teeth and bones from when you consumed said elements at some point.

This approach is made more complicated, however, because of what happened when the bomb squad decided to test the plane for radioactivity in case it was some kind of dirty bomb Trojan horse. That's how paranoid we are now. The plane had negligible radioactivity, but the pilot was red-hot.

It could be proof that he was tampered with to hide his actual date of birth, or evidence that his body experienced some kind of cosmic trauma from teleporting through time and space.

The Warlock is playing all the angles.

Chisholm motions me over to a table where he's talking to the head of the Miami field office, Robert Jensen, who we met briefly on the beach. Jensen has neatly combed gray hair and the look of a principal who's decided he hates children. He gives me a moment's glance, then turns back to the conversation. Absentmindedly, he pulls a chair out between him and Chisholm for me to sit. I keep my mouth shut until Chisholm asks me a question.

"How'd he do it, Blackwood?"

Again, I'm being put on the spot, frustrating me. "I don't know."

Jensen rolls his eyes. "Heck of an expert you got. I don't have to guess why she's really here."

I speak calmly. "Maybe I should come back later." I step away from the table.

"Please have a seat, Blackwood. Jensen is just a bit rattled because he doesn't like not knowing," replies Chisholm diplomatically.

I sit back down on the other side of the table, across from them. Chisholm asks me to elaborate.

I can only lay out my inner monologue. "I guess my point is that all I have is a theory. I don't presume to know how he did it. I just have Occam's razor. That tells me he didn't pull the thing through time and space and drop it on our doorstep. He's covered his tracks enough with the pilot to confuse things. A DNA test won't help because we have no tissue from the original pilot. Even next of kin might be doubtful if there's no match. Failure to show a match between the body in the plane and a family member only means they didn't share any genes. Somebody could have been fooling around and nobody knew." I point to a group of forensic techs. "According to them, we can't even use dental records because looking at tooth fillings would help, but his are all gone and the teeth have been washed with an abrasive that would take away any tool marks inside cavities. No matter how much we insist the Warlock tampered with the body, we can't prove he wasn't born in the 1920s. That's what people will remember. Either way, the real trick here is the sense of wonder. The plane. It's an artifact out of time. Where did it come from?"

"How did he do that?" asks Jensen.

I can tell he's not expecting much of an answer but I surprise him. "I have an idea. You're not going to like it." It makes the most sense out of everything.

I'd been thinking about it before they called me over to the table. "It's the real thing," I explain.

"What?" Jensen almost spits out his coffee.

There's a trace of a smile on Chisholm's face. I think he can read me more than I care to be read. I ignore him and turn to Jensen. "If I wanted to really impress you, there are two advantages that I can use to make that happen. The first is planning. When a magician steps onstage, he has years of practice going into the things you're only going to have a few seconds to ponder. The Warlock has been planning these stunts for a very long time. So much so, like a good magician, he's tried to think of every contingency. That's why the Chloe's double caught on fire when we wanted a closer look. That's why our fake pilot is setting off Geiger counters."

Jensen shakes his head. "How do you arrange for the appearance of an airplane that went missing in the Bermuda Triangle over fifty years ago?"

"You don't. It's the second thing you hope to have happen as a magician. Opportunity. I think he tipped his hand more than he wanted to with this plane stunt. But it was too good of a chance to pass up. If you know it's a trick, but the plane is real, then answer is obvious."

Jensen's face is a mask. Chisholm had asked me over to the table to show the local field director that we weren't as clueless as we seemed.

I raise up my hand and show it's empty. I snap my fingers and a silver pen appears. "Opportunity."

Jensen is dismissive. "Neat trick. But I don't see your point."

I toss the pen onto his notepad. "Look familiar?"

His nostrils flare as he realizes that I took his pen. He picks it up and tucks it into his jacket pocket. "Okay. So you're a kleptomaniac." He gives Chisholm another eye roll. "My grandson could pull that off."

Chisholm holds up a finger. "Would your grandson see a hard-ass skeptic a mile away and find an opportunity beforehand to make a point? I think Agent Blackwood is telling us that the Warlock has been waiting for something like this."

I continue my demonstration, even though I can see it's not getting through to Jensen. "The Warlock probably cast a pretty wide net searching for something to exploit. Who knows what else he was looking for or hoping to find. Amelia Earhart? Who knows. My point is Flight 19 has been a pervasive mystery, partly because nobody has ever spent the resources using modern technology to find the planes. The Navy stopped looking half a century ago. What would it cost? Time more than anything else. Maybe a little luck, but not as much as it seems. This tells us a lot about him. It also suggests he has other things planned." I reach into my purse and toss Jensen's watch on the table in front of him.

His jaw hangs open. I keep talking without missing a beat. "Planning and opportunity." I look over at Chisholm. "For what it's worth, the Warlock might have a background in drug running. Maybe he's not a smuggler himself. Possibly a chemist. But someone who could have had the opportunity to find the plane and a reason not to tell anyone. He could be one of those treasure hunters too. This state is filled with people searching the ocean for lost Spanish galleons and gold. Boats and planes are the connection I'd make."

Jensen snatches the watch from the table and shakes his head.

Chisholm gives me a smile. "That's what we think. Anything else?"

"Well, he could also be a guy that really wanted to find Flight 19 and spent a lot to do that. I wouldn't rule that out. Either way, if this is like the last stunt, he's left us a clue in there somewhere. The website told us where to look for Chloe. The sand in Chloe's coffin came from here. If it hasn't already been matched to this beach yet, I'm sure it will be. There's got to be another clue to direct us to his next performance."

I leave out telling him what he already knows; that the next victim could still be alive.

19

JENSEN GRUMBLES SOMETHING that sounds like a compliment and walks over to a table of his agents who are going through a database of images of the crowd on the beach. They're looking for anyone who stands out in the files of the Miami field office.

Chisholm thanks me for the demonstration I gave Jensen. I'm clearly part of a little power game between D.C. and the local bureau that I can only guess at. I get the feeling I was just shown off as a pet freak. If that's what it takes to stay on the case, then I guess I'm okay with that.

On the far wall, a video feed from the beach shows a crane getting ready to move the Avenger to a flatbed truck. A forensic team is doing a last-minute pass on the plane before they wrap it in plastic for transportation.

I count all the different law enforcement personnel in the hotel conference hall. There are more than fifty people working on this case while it's hot, not counting the ones back at D.C., Quantico and the field office in Michigan. Most of these people will be back to their normal workload in a day or so, but that's still a lot of human resource hours being spent on this.

Chisholm goes over to a side of the conference hall where

his people are reviewing the profile they're creating of the Warlock. He's one of the most important people in the FBI, and yet he's in the field trying to scrape together something to give us a lead. I respect his dedication.

I think it's the black swan factor that has drawn him in. The Warlock is just so atypical. Since leaving the behavioral analysis unit for sciences, Chisholm spends more of his time teaching and on research. Back out here he's in the presence of something real. Something immediate.

My phone rings. It's Ailes. I walk over to a quiet corner of the hall.

"Anything exciting to report, Agent Blackwood?"

"You're the mathematician. What are the odds that someone would find a missing Avenger bomber in the middle of the Atlantic?"

"Higher than you might think. Jennifer looked into this and noticed all the previous documented searches fell into the classical search pattern mistakes."

"What are those?" I ask.

"Giving too much weight to one data point and ignoring the fact that at least some of your data points are going to be manufactured."

"You mean somebody lying?"

"No. Not exactly. Go to a high school science fair where kids are measuring the height of daisies or size of diatoms in ocean water and you'll notice a strange effect. Scientists do it too. If someone measures something that's exactly one centimeter, or some other number that sounds too perfect, they change it to .9 or 1.1. The same thing happens with coordinates. We ran a test on some naval log books and found that you almost never get an exact coordinate like ten degrees mark ten degrees. Nobody wants to look lazy. I've got a bet with Gerald that I can predict something about the signatures on the logbooks when those kinds of numbers do come up, the round ones."

"What's that?"

Ailes lowers his voice. He must be calling from the bullpen and not want Gerald to hear. "There will be two signatures with the nice round numbers. If two people witnesses it, then they're not as worried about appearing dishonest by using what they imagine is an overly convenient number. The positions for Flight 19 smell of very scared people trying to cover their own asses and not be asked why their numbers are too round. I bet a search that takes this into account might be more fruitful."

"You think the Warlock knows this?"

"Maybe. If we can figure it out in a few hours, a man as smart as him, who seems intent on showing how clever he is, might come to the same conclusion. Or maybe he got lucky. Maybe both. What's it like down there?"

I describe the scene in the conference room. He's getting the live feeds at Quantico too. "I see a lot of clever people trying to pick up the pieces after the fact." It reminds me of an observation my uncle shared. "You know the difference between a comedian and a magician?"

"What's that?" he asks.

"A comedian waits for the laughter and applause to die down before moving on to his next bit. A magician uses it as a distraction to start his next one. I think we're very distracted."

"What do you think we should be doing?"

"I'm not in charge. I'm out of my element here." The room feels busy. But that's not the point.

"So are the rest of us. Indulge me," replies Ailes.

He knows something is bugging me. I let it out. "I guess what it comes down to is the victims. The deceptions are incidental. If we found their bodies in a forest, no dramatic staging, we'd focus mainly on trying to find out who they are."

"Their faces have popped up on every television so far. We're getting hundreds of calls, but no missing persons."

"I know. I know," I reply. "But doesn't that strike you as odd? I mean, these people didn't come from Mars. The other Chloe and the man in the plane don't look like drifters. I didn't see any signs of heavy drug addiction. As harsh as it sounds, they look like people who would be missed."

"What are you getting at?"

I'm trying to put my finger on it. "This is the real deception. Or at least the one nobody in this room wants to pay attention to just yet. We've got two victims nobody says are missing. The Warlock has given us impossible explanations for their deaths. If we don't figure who they really are, the mystery is going to remain and we'll even have failed them in giving them some sense of peace. They'll remain a Jane and John Doe as long as we buy into the illusion."

"A good point. You mention this to Chisholm or the field supervisor there?"

"No. Knoll seems like a sharp guy, but I don't think Jensen was impressed with my demonstration."

"You need to be mindful, Jessica. You have two strikes going against you when you walk into a room."

Two? I can only think of one. "I'm a woman."

"The worst kind. You're attractive, which wouldn't be an issue if you didn't have the burden of usually being the smartest person in the room. They know you're smarter than they are. It's in your eyes."

"I don't feel so smart."

"Trust me. I spend all day around people smarter than me." He holds the phone aside. "Except you, Gerald. I keep you around to feel smarter than someone."

It's comforting to hear him kid around with his subordinates like that. I get the feeling that all they want to do is impress him and be impressed by each other.

Ailes adopts a sympathetic tone. "Well, unless you want to dig around down there, you're welcome to come back to the brain trust up here and bounce ideas around. Maybe we can figure out the next one before it happens."

I look over at the chaotic room and realize that there's really no place for me. Everyone has their task. Maybe if I'm with Ailes and his geeks we can make some headway.

"Sounds good. Let me talk to Knoll."

"Hold on . . . You seeing this?" ask Ailes.

I look over at the overhead screens. An image appears from inside the engine duct. The metal is dark green and rusty. But the thing we're supposed to see stands out clear as day.

The Warlock's clue.

A feather.

A solitary white feather.

20

THE INSTANT THE feather appears on the screen, a group of forensic techs are on the phone with local zoos and universities tracking down an expert on plumage.

Since I don't know much about birds, other than how to hide them in a sequined tuxedo, I clear things with Knoll so I can head back to Quantico.

Knoll's standing over the shoulder of an agent who is flipping through online images of birds. "What can you tell us about birds, Blackwood?"

"I got bit by my grandfather's macaw when I was ten." I still have the scar on my arm. A nasty bird, he clamped onto my arm when I was changing the newspapers in his cage.

"Nice." He turns away from the laptop. "What's up?"

"I was thinking I might be of more use in Quantico, now that the bomber is in forensics' hands." I gaze up at the screens showing the feather and photos of the plane.

"You think Ailes and his group might make some headway?"

"I think an unconventional approach might be helpful. There are still some things about the Chloe murders that should be pursued."

"The whole thing is nagging me," replies Knoll.

"Yeah. I just think there's some deeper part to this. We've got two victims that can't be who we think they are. The pilot's fingerprint is likely a record switch. Something about the two Chloes . . ."

"You don't think the inferno was to destroy the evidence?"

I shake my head. "I think he wanted an apocalyptic pyre. I think he wants us to think we know what he did. That he just found some girl that looked like Chloe and tried his best to pass her off as Chloe."

"Why?"

I've been going over and over this. "To pull the rug out from under our feet. To get us to build false confidence so he can destroy it."

"Destroy it? How?"

"I'm not sure. The pilot we found is a dead ringer for the one that went missing in 1945. Our two Chloes are indistinguishable from what we can see. But there's only one body to examine, a partial one at that. There's something else . . ."

Knoll nods his head. "And you think Ailes and his geek pack might have a better chance at breaking this than we do in the field?"

"I think it's just as important."

"All right. I'll call you if we need you back here."

An hour later I'm sitting in the lounge at the Fort Lauderdale–Hollywood International Airport thinking about the fact that the men of the Flight 19 Avenger squadron were last seen just a few hundred yards from where I am. It's a strange feeling.

I'm trying to ignore the news on the television hanging over my head. They don't have anything new to add. They just keep repeating the images of the Avenger on the sandbar and the pillar of fire at the cemetery. Even without the image of Chloe climbing out of the ground, it's biblical enough. By now the connection between the two events is obvious, due to their apparently supernatural nature, and "Warlock" keeps showing up on the closed captioning.

I imagine him laughing at us as he sits over his Dungeons & Dragons game board in his Batman underwear.

On my laptop screen is the image of the feather. It's obviously a big, bright, neon clue. Forensics had already identified it as a dove feather by the time I made it to the airport. I'm sure everyone in the conference hall is trying to figure it out.

I'm afraid it's a red herring. And if it's not, it's only going to make sense to us after we see what the Warlock has planned next. It's a clue, but a distracting one. We can't help but look at it and wonder. We're trying to figure out what one hand is doing while the other has already palmed off the aces.

The Warlock's code on the FBI website wasn't meant to be cracked until he was ready. Knowing where the sand came from wouldn't have stopped him. It could have come from twenty miles in either direction. If he'd seen a stakeout, he probably would have dropped the plane elsewhere.

But they're not clues, are they?

They're calling cards.

They're his way of telling us that the next mystery is his creation. He thinks he's too important to write us a note. He only wants to communicate through his miracles.

This is how gods talk to mortals.

Gods speak in symbols too. I'm sure there's a pattern to what he's doing. The airplane may have been a lucky break, but to him it symbolizes something.

Chloe's double was found in the grave. The airplane and body was found on a sandbar in the ocean.

I try to think of how he wants us to see the illusion. The Chloe died crawling out of the ground. The dirt. The "pilot" died in the air.

Earth.

Air.

Classical elements.

I pull up the Wikipedia page on the classical elements. The Babylonians had five: earth, sky, fire, sea and wind. The Greeks were almost the same: air, fire, earth, water and aether.

Aether. The Avenger pilot died from a lack of air. As if he flew into the space beyond the earth. The aether. Or the sky. Either one fits.

I don't know if this means anything, but I send an e-mail to the working group.

Where does the feather fit in?

If the Warlock's using the Babylonian elements, then it's the wind. The Greek, air. Either way, I suspect we can expect at least three more dark miracles from the Warlock. Trying to predict what they'll be is pointless. Never in a million years would we have expected him to make it look as if he ripped a hole in time and pulled an airplane through it.

His imagination has already exceeded our comprehension.

As I think this over, CNN is showing footage from an old movie called *The Philadelphia Experiment*, another of my father's favorites, in which a vortex opens up around a World War II naval ship, pulling it out of time. I shake my head in disbelief.

The media are even supplying movie special effects to help build up his mystery. He's such a goddamn made-for-television-news villain. Everyone, from theologians to fantasy authors, is chiming in with an opinion.

The talking heads are quick to condemn the acts, but all of them have a sense of awe in their condemnations.

Man-on-the-street interviews indicate regular people seem more focused on the illusion than the murdered people. But that's the Warlock's design. If we look at it from his point of view, he's not a murderer. He's a necromancer who gave Chloe life that she used to crawl out of the ground. He brought back a pilot who was supposed to have perished in an aircraft nobody ever thought would be seen again.

The murders are ambiguous. Like a writer who doesn't want to make a character good or evil, the Warlock is trying to have it both ways.

I even see a hint of smiles on people's faces as they offer their opinions on camera. They don't see him as a murderer. Some of them are buying his story. This infuriates me.

I'm about to write another e-mail, this one to Knoll, and demand that we call attention to what the Warlock really is. But I stop myself. Knoll knows. We all know. We can only report the facts. We can't control how people think. Right now the Warlock is winning.

I've been staring at the television for so long I don't realize I'm being stared at by a man in a pilot's uniform. He's sitting across from me, several seats away.

I look over at him and it takes a second for me to recognize him. He's got brown eyes and his face looks rounder somehow.

But it's him.

"Why the long face, Jessica?"

Damian.

Goddamn it.

21

Damian can read my reaction as I start to stand up.

"Please don't get the TSA over here. I haven't done anything wrong. At least nothing that warrants involuntary sexual abuse." He holds up his hands and smiles.

"How about impersonating a pilot?" I think about calling an officer over so I can get a look at his ID.

"It's only a criminal act if I try to fly the plane."

"Well, isn't stealing trains the gateway drug to that?"

"I don't bring up all your youthful indiscretions," he smirks.

"I didn't have any."

"And that explains quite a lot about you. Not having any is the biggest one of all. It makes little girls grow up into authority figures who want to carry guns around and punish men."

I close the laptop on the image of the feather. "Why are you here?"

"Two reasons. One, I don't think you took my warning very seriously about being careful about this Warlock character." In a relaxed gesture, he takes his pilot hat off and sets it in the chair next to him. "I don't need to point out to you that you have the habit of attracting the unstable types." He reaches down into his flight bag and pulls out a *Sun-Sentinel* newspaper and tosses it to me. "And there's this. It's a prepress of tomorrow's edition."

I don't even ask him how he got such a thing. The front page headline is the reappearance of the Avenger bomber and pilot alongside a photograph. There are several stories about the incident covering the history of Flight 19, our investigation and the Michigan murder.

"I've highlighted the item I think you should be most mindful of."

I turn the page. It's an article about the FBI's pursuit of the Warlock. One sentence stands out.

Sources close to the investigation say that the FBI has called in a specialist referred to as "the Witch" to help find the Warlock . . .

I set the paper down and look at Damian. "This is stupid."

"Very. But did you see the photograph?"

"What?" I open the paper again. The image shows several agents standing on the beach looking out at the airplane. I'm in the middle. My black hair flowing in the wind. I'm surrounded by several dozen lighter-haired and balding men.

Damian mocks me. "I wonder which one is the Witch?"

I throw the paper at him. "I don't need this bullshit."

"Well, the good news is you look amazing in that photograph. Seriously. The bad news is I'm sure the Warlock feels the same way."

I want to dismiss his notion, but I know he's perceptive about these things. He's certifiable, but he's brilliant.

Damian is probably the greatest magician I've ever met. And it's for one simple reason; the best magicians are the ones who live or die by their skills. Pickpockets. Card cheats. Damian's whole life is a deception. When he's not harassing me or pretending to be someone else, I suspect you'll probably find him at a card table somewhere, slowly milking the house. Making big losses amid small wins that add up over time.

He handles a deck of cards like nobody I've ever seen. And I've seen the best in the world. Since I know he's not staying practiced to perform at children's birthday parties, I have to imagine it's for gambling.

I've always resisted the idea of asking him for help. I never want to be in debt to him. There's really no bargaining with the devil. I know what he's capable of doing. Still, if there's anyone who can see through a deception, it has to be him.

I give up fighting the question. "So what do I look out for?"

Damian's face changes to delight as he realizes I'm asking for his help. "He's probably not walking around in a cape. Although I'm sure he's dying for them to come back. He probably has one picked out with purple trim. No. He's in love with this idea of the Warlock. It's a character he created. He wants to be him. But he's afraid to actually step into the role—to put himself in public as the Warlock. That's why this is all about ideas. I bet he looks quite normal. Probably tries to use that as camouflage. Buys his clothes at Old Navy. Looks like a square. He'll be hard to find. He blends right in."

"I know the type." I wonder how long Damian had been watching me. He had to go out of his way for me to see him sitting there.

"Ahem, I can't tell you how much effort it takes for me not to stand out."

"Well, just the same. Do it a little farther away. And your profile is about as useless as a fortune cookie." I'm resisting the urge to call one of the airport police officers to detain him. Maybe not press charges, but at least have him held long enough to find out who he really is. Sadly, that would be one more complication I don't need at the moment. I might regret not doing it, but it's not going to help me catch the Warlock right now.

Damian reads my face. "I can tell you're conflicted by my presence. I need to catch a flight anyway. I'll leave you with a thought. And this doesn't come from an amateur. As a person who takes making himself appear to be other people very seriously, it's not hard to see when someone else has stumbled onto one of my secrets."

"What would that be?" It's rare that he ever acknowledges his penchant for deception, much less his technique.

Damian stands up and straightens the crease in his slacks. "I don't choose the role. I let it choose me. At first I wondered if he chose the girl because she looked like Chloe McDonald or if Chloe was murdered because she looked like the second victim. When I saw our fake pilot it became obvious. He's choosing his victims to fit the faces of the already deceased. Both the second girl and our fake pilot were chosen because they looked like somebody else."

"I think we already know this, Damian. Sucks that you came all the way out here to tell me this."

He raises an eyebrow. "Oh. Then you know how as well? It was an old family trick, wasn't it?"

"What do you mean, how?"

"How would you find a girl that looked like Chloe, or a man like a missing pilot?"

I haven't even thought about that question. I've been too focused on airplanes and feathers. "What do you mean?"

Damian's lips form a cocky grin. "Maybe it wasn't a wasted trip. It never is to see you. Maybe you should start by asking

'Who do I look like?' Literally. I'm sure it's a question our non-descript, very bland Warlock once asked." Damian gives me a wink and leaves to chase after what I hope is an imaginary flight.

I watch as he retreats down the moving sidewalk and vanishes into the crowd. He left his hat on the seat. I tuck it into my bag for when I get a chance to ask someone in forensics for a favor.

I hear my flight called. I'm about to put my laptop away and worry about Damian's puzzle later when the answer hits me.

How could I have been so blind?

22

Damian literally spelled it out for me. When he impersonates people, he starts with people he already looks like. He finds someone that resembles him.

I start with a simple Google search: "Who do I look like?" Several sites come up. I click on one called Faceplaced.com.

A website loads with images of people who look very similar. It's not a site that tries to find what celebrity you look like. This is different. The image search goes through millions of publicly uploaded photos, with a lot of weight given to profile pictures. It finds other regular people who look like you. Similar to what law enforcement uses, only this makes use of public records.

I try it with a photograph of my face I have saved on my desktop for ID badges. The site finds several dozen images and ranks them by probability. I notice that it lets you load multiple photos to get multiple dimensions and not just face forward. The site is way more advanced than other systems I've seen. The speed is faster than anything I've used at the FBI. It also has social media profile photos that we don't normally have access to. The results are uncanny.

Of the images on the screen, some of the photos are actually of me from my days in magic and photos friends in college took, others of women who bear an uncanny likeness. This is like looking into a mirror dimension. I see my duplicates getting married, holding babies, doing things I've never done.

I cringe when I see one of the images is my cover of *Magician Magazine*. God only knows how many people already have made that connection. My stomach turns at the thought of the press realizing who the "Witch" really is. There are even more risqué photos out there. I don't need that kind of attention.

I upload the photograph of the man we found in the Avenger. A few similar matches pop up, but nothing that looks like a direct hit.

Nice theory. No dice.

I ignore the PA calling my name.

I realize I'm an idiot. That's not how the Warlock found the match. He looked for a match for the actual pilot, Captain John Kelsford. I pull the scanned photos the Navy sent us of the Avenger crew and load that into the system.

Three close matches come up.

The second and strongest is from a Facebook profile of a man who looks strikingly like Kelsford. It's eerie. Even the hair is similar.

His name is Jeff Swanson. He lives in Oregon.

I log into the FBI telephone database and get his home number. It's a strange feeling. I'm only acting on a hunch. A hunch based on something Damian only suggested minutes ago.

I pull out my phone and look at the keypad. Do I call? Should I go to Knoll or Ailes with this first? What if it's a miss? I don't want to look stupid.

I've done enough cold calling in the paper jungle that I shouldn't be embarrassed by the idea. To hell with it. I dial the number.

It rings.

A woman picks up. The database says the number is shared with his wife.

"Hello?"

What do I say? "Hi there. I'm calling to see if Jeff Swanson is at home."

"Oh my God. Everyone keeps calling. No. It's not Jeff in the airplane!" Her voice is more amused than angry.

"Sorry," I reply.

"It's all right. We've been laughing about it all afternoon." The woman's voice is pleasant. "It's all been a bit of a joke."

Damn. I feel horrible for calling. I'm just glad that she's not taking it seriously.

"Sorry to trouble you."

"It's fine. I'm glad so many of his friends care. Who should I tell him called?"

"Just a friend from work." I don't want to bring the FBI into this.

"Well, thank you for asking. Lord knows what the text messages are costing him."

"Yes. Sorry again to trouble you." I'm about to hang up when I feel my stomach turn. "Pardon me? The text messages?"

"Yeah, from Guam. He had to fly out two days ago to help a friend who got in a motorcycle accident." Her voice is matter-of-fact.

An alarm goes off. I try to sound calm. "Have you actually spoken to Jeff since he left?"

"He texted me from the plane and when he got there. Sent me photos. He tried calling but the connection was messed up. He left a message on my voice mail."

I feel a chill down my spine. Voice mails are generic and

can be copied. Most people don't even change their password. That's how the British tabloids spied on celebrities for years. It could have been left anytime. "Miss you," etc.

I don't know what to tell her. This woman thinks she's been talking to her husband for the last several days, when actually, she's probably been talking to the man who killed him, masquerading as him in texts and e-mails. Even photos.

God knows, he could be sending her Photoshops of him in photos of Guam. He could carry the charade on for months if he needed to. Even have Jeff break up with her or get sick and die over there or vanish in a scuba accident.

His wife would never know.

It's the perfect way to hide a murder; never let anyone know the victim is dead.

I think about how much of my contact with friends outside of work is electronic. It'd be easy to masquerade as me if you had access to my e-mail and text accounts.

I decide it's best not to tell the wife anything right now. For all I know, the Warlock has her phone tapped. I need to make sure we can get to her before he does. I say good-bye as calmly and cheerfully as I can and hang up.

On the surface it's a flimsy premise, yet it makes sense. It's what I would do.

I call Ailes as I race for a taxi to take me back to the conference hall.

I almost shout the name into the phone. "Jeff Swanson."

"Jeff who?" asks Ailes.

"Have one of your people look him up."

"Hold on."

I run out to the taxi pickup zone and flag down a cab. I bark the name of the hotel to the driver.

On the way back to the command center Ailes gets back to me. "Good match, Jessica, but someone already checked his name. He's alive and well."

"Did they talk to him?" I ask.

"What?"

"Did someone actually talk to him? What do the notes say? Did the person following up the lead actually see him in person?"

"Hold on. They said his wife said he was fine. No priors on her. No reason to think she's lying."

"She's not. I think she's been deceived. She's only been talking to him via text message for the last three days. Anybody with his phone could do that. Swanson could be dead. He could be our pilot."

"Shit."

"Yeah."

Ailes lets out a breath of air. "This is major league thinking, Jessica. Let me get to Knoll and the director on this. It changes everything."

A break. Our first real break. Not a planted clue. A genuine chink in his armor. And all I had to do to find it was let one sociopath and potential murderer back into my personal life.

What will taking this all the way cost me?

23

By the time I walk back into the hotel conference hall, the Faceplaced.com image of Jeff Swanson is up on the screens alongside the photograph of the dead pilot we found in the plane and the photo of Captain Kelsford. The resemblance is eerie.

Knoll weaves his stocky body through the tables toward me. He points a finger in my direction.

"You've been holding out on us."

At first I think it's an accusation. Then I realize he's paying me a compliment. I pull my laptop out of my bag and set it on an empty table.

"How did you make the connection?" he asks.

For obvious reasons, I don't go into my complicated personal life. I'll tell Ailes later on about Damian. For now it's best to focus on jumping on this lead.

"Watch." I show Knoll the website and once again upload the Navy's image of Kelsford. Swanson's face comes up as the closest match.

"Well grab me by the balls," replies Knoll. His thick fingers scratch into his bald scalp as he watches the website load. He snaps his fingers and waves several people over. "You see this?" he calls out to the computer forensic team.

An older agent in a light blue polo speaks up. "We tried something similar using our database. No luck."

There are thousands of ways a computer can try to match a face. The crudest way is to try to match images and not the actual structures of the face. The more advanced systems measure distances in multiple dimensions and look for really distinct traits like ear patterns.

Knoll shakes his head. "Our perp isn't using the FBI database. This is probably a totally different algorithm and image pool. Ours is filled with mug shots and missing people." He mutters under his breath, "Probably more modern too. Can we try it with a photo of Chloe McDonald?"

I've been waiting to try it with her image since I left the airport. I use the last photograph taken of her provided by her parents. The website kicks back several hundred images. Makeup and hairstyles make it much harder to find a match.

Knoll groans. "Damn. I was hoping it was going to be easier. We probably already called half the girls here anyway."

"Yes, but did you speak to them or people who said they were fine? Do we even know it was them?" I'm getting more paranoid about the way the Warlock might have electronically impersonated Swanson. "To get a better match we can also add more Chloe photos. I'm betting the Warlock probably used several to find her double. Maybe we try just the images from the media if he didn't kill the original girl. That might be where this started for him."

"Good point." Knoll points to a young woman with red hair. "Morgan. Go double-check these. Mark down the girls we actually talked to."

I shake my head. "We need to send someone by in person to talk to them."

"Why is that?" asks Knoll.

"If this is really true, the Warlock's got Swanson's phone and is pretending to be him to his wife. If I'd called that number instead of the home phone, maybe the Warlock would have answered and pretended he was Swanson to me. If he wants to keep us off the track of the fake Chloe, I'd route the calls to some girl I found on Craigslist and paid to pretend she was her. We can't know until we make face contact with the girl."

Knoll doesn't like this. "That's a lot of girls. Could be thousands if we change the hair parameters. Maybe we could video conference some of them? Just getting phone numbers is going to be a challenge."

I shake my head. "It's got to be face-to-face. You can fake a person on Skype now. It's cutting-edge, but I saw a convincing TED demonstration where a VFX studio took a bunch of photos and made a virtual actress that looked exactly like the original. I don't mean in that squinty almost real way they use in movies. This was dead-on. It took a huge amount of computing resources, but at this point I wouldn't put anything past the Warlock."

Knoll didn't want to hear that. As head of the task force, he's in charge of marshaling all the national and local law enforcement agencies. This could mean involving hundreds of local police departments and field offices. "Crap. We'll talk to our connections at the social networks and see what they can do to help. They've helped us before on terrorism cases and some kidnappings, although I can only imagine the legal minefield."

I stare at the hundreds of faces on the screen that look like Chloe. Each one a ghostly reminder of the body we watched consumed by flame, and of Chloe herself drained of blood and tossed into the river. One of them is our Jane Doe. I impulsively reach out and touch the screen, to try to feel their faces.

"We'll find her." Knoll is staring too.

He's feeling the same thing I am. I look around and see several other agents with the same expression on their faces. We feel closer. It doesn't immediately bring us to the Warlock, but for the first time we feel like we've seen behind the curtain. All our theories have been just that. This is the first test that gives us a little hope. We've learned something he doesn't want us to know.

Knoll's phone rings. He listens for a minute, then hangs up. "We have confirmation of a Jeff Swanson checked into a hotel in Guam. He's visiting a friend in the hospital."

It's the perfect excuse to keep the illusion going that he's still alive.

Knoll shakes his head. "No one has seen him since he checked in. The hotel clerk says the photo we showed her doesn't match the man he saw. Looks like someone went to great lengths to maintain the deception. The Portland field office is sending undercover agents to talk to the wife. We're going to see how long we can keep the fact that we know this from the Warlock. It might give us a little more time."

Dr. Chisholm makes his way over to the table. He gives me a nod, then pulls Knoll aside and out of my earshot. Knoll seems bothered by it. He steals a glance in my direction. I want to ask what's going on, but know I'd be acting out of place.

Chisholm finally turns back to me. "Let's go for a ride."

Knoll is shaking his head. "I think we need to let her get back home."

Chisholm replies. "Yes, but let's get her professional opinion first. It's her life we're talking about."

My life?

24

THE SUN BEACH HOTEL is five stories tall and has the same whitewashed exterior as a dozen other beachfront hotels on the Fort Lauderdale strip. It's several blocks up the highway from the sandbar where the airplane was found, but the rooms at the front have a clear view. This hotel is not the first place you'd look if you were trying to find a sniper or someone following the action.

The crowds along the beach have thinned since the airplane was loaded onto a flatbed truck and driven to a warehouse in nearby Port Everglades. Agents are combing it over with tweezers, looking for more clues.

On the way to the hotel, one of our local FBI escorts in the SUV said forensics had found canvas fibers under the wings consistent with the flotation balloons Lieutenant Droves mentioned. It's a minor thing, but it helps us better understand how it was done. Or rather, how the Warlock could have done it.

So far this entire machination could be the work of one man. It's frightening to think of what one person can do by himself. There's some solace in that he's probably not tied into some kind of terrorist network. But do we really know that?

We exit the SUV and Chisholm briefs us on the location as

we enter the hotel. "We've done a preliminary sweep with the bomb unit and the dogs. Swabs and barks came back negative. Still, this guy could probably make something that will get past that. So be careful." He hesitates in front of the elevator.

He's trying to give me an out to pass on checking the room that raised their suspicions. It's ridiculous. I'm not going to let someone else walk into something I'm too afraid to. Besides, what difference does it make if I'm here?

Chisholm waves to the front desk. "We've checked the registry and already spoken to forty-one guests in the hotel. Nothing stands out. A lot of French Canadians."

We take the elevator to the fourth floor. Interesting that it's not the fifth. I guess the Warlock didn't want to stand out by taking a room on the top floor.

"How did you find this room?" I ask.

Chisholm sighs. "The name. It was registered under A. Baris. Your suggestion about a potential mythological connection gave us some ideas. We pulled all the registrations along the beach and had a computer sift through potential fake names and anything that cross-referenced with something relating to magic or mysticism. Abaris is a rather unusual name. Abaris the Hyperborean was an ancient magician. I know. Sounds like something out of a comic book. Obviously"—he pauses—"it was an intentional clue. He wanted us to find this place."

The police officer standing guard at the door lets us inside. It's not a large room. The bed has been pushed up against the wall to make more space. There's a telescope in front of the large window trained on the beach in front of the sandbar.

I look around. There's no blood. No bodies. It looks like a normal beach hotel room.

"We've had a fiber team in here. Hotel rooms are always

filled with fun surprises." Chisholm points to a spot next to the telescope. "There was another tripod set up there. From the indentations in the carpet we can tell it was a video camera or a digital still camera with some big glass on it."

"Why the telescope then?" It doesn't look like a particularly expensive model. It probably doesn't have anywhere near the image quality of the camera that was there. I walk over to the telescope and have a look. Our footprints in the sand are still visible. Out in the open, part of the show.

Chisholm looks out the slightly open window at the people passing on the sidewalk below us. I wonder for a moment what an experienced profiler like him sees when he people-watches. The thought makes me a little self-conscious. He turns to me, "We think it's him telling us that he's observing us. It's aimed right where we were standing earlier today."

A breeze blows through the window. The Warlock could have taken us out one by one with a high-power rifle from here if he really wanted to. I kneel down to look at the ledge.

Chisholm sees me looking for marks where a rifle may have rested. "We checked for that. No evidence that he placed a gun on there."

I guess that's reassuring. "So he's not trying to tell us he can kill us?"

"Not exactly." He draws the words out. This isn't good.

Chisholm motions me over to look at the ceiling. He points to where a piece has been removed. "We found a slit about a half inch across. We cut it out of the ceiling and sent it to forensics. It was created by a knife with a curved blade. Probably a kris knife. Something with sacrificial implications. Inside the slit we found a sliver of glossy paper. He'd stabbed it to the ceiling while he was here. It was from a cover of a magazine . . ."

Chisholm's voice trails off as he makes eye contact with me. I know where this is heading. I'm already shaking my head. My magazine. The one on Ailes's desk. My cheesecake magician photo. The Warlock knows about me. He wants me to know that. He stood right where I'm standing now, watching me.

Chisholm continues. "Ailes told us where to match the paper right away. Everyone thought I shouldn't bring you back here. But I wanted you to see this. I want you to know what we're up against. I don't think we should hide anything from you. I have to go to some pretty dark places to understand the people we deal with. I don't think sparing you that is going to help you. You need to understand what he sees."

I stare up at the place on the ceiling where he'd stabbed my magazine cover with a knife. I examine the floor. He must have lain there looking up at it. What was he thinking? Was it sexual? Was it just to throw me off?

I think back to the man on the warehouse roof at the cemetery. Was that my first encounter? Did getting close to him make him interested? Or is it the fact that he sees me as a threat because I'm a magician? A challenger to him.

Chisholm points out several spots on the carpet that have tape markings. "He had five candles lit. We also picked up a faint outline of a body. He's about five-foot-seven. Probably weighs a hundred and sixty pounds. Athletic. No semen, for what it's worth."

"Too bad," I reply matter-of-factly. That would give us a DNA profile to run through the database.

"How long ago did he leave?"

"Less than an hour before our forensic team got here."

"An hour? He likes to cut things close."

"Perhaps . . ." Chisholm has a pensive look on his face. "He didn't seem rushed. I think you surprised him at the cemetery when you chased him down, if that was indeed him. This time he's trying to prove he's in control."

"How far is he willing to go to prove that?"

"I guess that depends upon how much of a threat he sees you as. He already knows about your background. Today's little item in the news doesn't help the situation. Although we might be able to use it to antagonize him a little bit. Maybe play up the idea that the FBI's Witch sees through all his tricks. Get him off-balance, make him deviate from his script."

"I don't want to be a distraction from the investigation," I reply.

Chisholm shakes his head. "It's not about that. As we know, this guy is a highly organized thinker. It takes meticulous planning to pull off what he's done so far. We need to get him to mess up."

"What if he's a good improviser?" I ask.

"Nobody is that good. You saw him at the cemetery."

"I saw someone. We don't know who. It could have been anyone," I reply.

Chisholm thinks this over. "This hotel room is proof that he likes to be close to the scene of the crime when it happens. He wants to watch us. He's choosing these locations so he can do that. The piece of memory card wrapper we found back at the warehouse by the cemetery tells us he's probably recording what he sees."

"But now he's told us as much. He wants us to know how close he can get. If there's a next time we're going to clamp down even faster."

"True," agrees Chisholm. "I think he's moving toward more public locations to hide."

"Or to make a bigger spectacle."

"Probably. In the meantime we need to play every card we have. And that means you. It's about catching him off-guard. The telescope is his way of telling us he's the one in charge. Maybe what we need is someone on the other end staring him down and saying they're not impressed. What's it like when you're onstage and see someone sitting in the audience with their arms folded, looking bored?"

The first image is of my grandfather looking disappointed. Chisholm means regular people. "It's the worst thing in the world. It's when you start to slip up. You go out of your way to impress them and that's when you get careless. You forget everyone else and focus on the skeptic."

Chisholm gives me a menacing grin. "Think you can make him slip up? I want to push this weirdo away from his plan. Make him react. Act impulsively. Put our Witch against the Warlock. He's fixated on you. I want you to look back at him and ask, 'Is that all you got?'"

"You mean give him performance anxiety."

"I guess you could put it that way," he replies.

25

DON'T LIKE THE IDEA," Ailes tells me for the hundredth time when I get back.

Neither do I.

At his insistence, I flew back last night on an FBI jet and slept in a dorm on campus at Quantico. I resisted any kind of official protective custody but agreed to stay on the reservation, at least for the next several days while we try to figure out how serious of a threat the Warlock really is to me.

Sleeping here or back in my apartment, it's not like it's going to affect my social life much. Even when I had a boyfriend, work was still my focus. Going through miles of data in the paper jungle isn't the most exciting kind of law enforcement, but it is preferable to being a beat cop telling junkies they couldn't loiter in the bus shelters.

Once I knew magic wasn't for me, it was my goal to join the FBI. Even as a little girl I had a strong sense of right and wrong. The pinstripes and disciplined reputation of the FBI appealed to this little girl who spent half her time as a vagabond. My love of figuring things out lined up perfectly with my image of an agent solving cases. To get there, working as a street cop was a way for me to acquire some practical experience. A lot of the agents I work with—most, in fact—have never had to draw their gun in a dangerous situation. Most of the real work in the FBI involves chasing down leads on the phone and talking to people face-to-face in relaxed settings. As a police officer, I'd sometimes have to draw my gun two or three times a night answering burglary calls or pulling over suspicious vehicles.

Working under this kind of constant tension helps you develop a bit of a relaxed edge with less life-threatening things. I guess that's why I'm not as afraid now as I maybe should be. I've been shoved down stairs, kicked, clawed, and had guns pulled on me. My sense of fear is different than most people's. And that's just the dangerous situations I faced in the line of duty.

The closest I ever came to death was in a magic trick. I tell myself that scrape wasn't why I quit performing. I think I've been trying to prove that to myself ever since.

Ailes is not crazy about Chisholm's idea of using me as bait. So far he and his cohorts haven't come back to me with a specific plan for how they want to agitate the Warlock, beyond using the media. The current idea is to have me do interviews with cable news playing up my own expertise and dismissing him. The goal is to get him to break his silence and communicate with us or a news agency we have good relations with.

I don't know how well it will work. Evidence suggests the Warlock is extremely composed. Ailes even threw the idea back at Chisholm, saying that the whole hotel room was staged to look like he's obsessed with me so all the behavioral analysis skull fuckers (his words) would spin their wheels trying to come up with a scheme like this.

I'm not sure where I stand. I've seen firsthand how obsessive men can be. But then I think about Ailes's point that the Warlock wants to control every facet of the illusion. Registering under the obvious name, the telescope and the magazine are all desperately transparent.

He set up the hotel room so we would find it and have one more thing to distract us while he plans his next move. I think about the kris knife stabbed through my photo and it makes me realize something. Ailes is half right.

"He already won this battle," I tell him.

Ailes looks up from his screen. "What do you mean?"

"You had the director pull me out of the field and now he has everyone arguing about what to do with me. Maybe that was the real goal. Not just tie up Chisholm and behavioral analysis, but you and me too?"

Ailes thinks it over. "Cognitive capacity."

"What?"

"It's the total amount of brainpower you have. We only have so many neurons in our brains. If they're focused on one problem, then there are fewer resources to worry about another. I've been thinking about something. He knew our number cruncher would take seven days to break his code. It's how he knew when we would find the girl in the cemetery. One digit too few and we would have cracked the code in hours. One too many and it would have taken centuries. He knew almost to the minute."

"Inside information?" I ask.

Ailes shakes his head. "You don't need it." He points to his computer. "It's all out there on the Web. There are articles about our main cruncher and how powerful it is. A simple formula would tell you how complex of a code you'd need to tie it up for a certain period of time. The Warlock is looking at this like a math problem. Besides the computing power, he probably has at least a rough idea how many people each division of the

FBI has and how many we've tasked to the case. It's all online and in reports to Congress.

"Once upon a time we thought things like computers and DNA would make quick work of solving crimes. Then we got computer crime, multiple DNA samples in a crime scene, and all the other complications that go with that. Sometimes I fear the next technological evolution."

"Yeah, but it makes catching the dumb ones easier," I reply.

"True. Our overcrowded prisons are proof. But it's the smart ones I worry about."

I think about the telescope and the video camera. "What if he wasn't just recording the airplane and the response, but counting heads?"

"I've thought about that. But how would it change what he does? Does he have a different plan if there are two hundred agents working on the case as opposed to one hundred?" He pauses. "Ah. Of course . . ."

The Warlock may not be a mathematical genius like Ailes, but he's a very logical thinker. "He's doing the opposite of you. You look for the one man out of a thousand who can make a difference."

"Yes. And he looks for the one that might cause problems and tries to figure out how to eliminate them. Only he's getting us to do that for him by putting you under protection and limiting your involvement. He thought he had the upper hand until he saw the FBI has a magician."

"How do you test this? How do we know it's a bluff?" I ask.

"I don't know if it's practical to do so. Better if we're just mindful of the fact that he's doing that."

"There's got to be more we can do. More I can do."

"Jennifer is in Texas trying to talk to the people who run

Faceplaced.com and we're already spread thin here. Thanks to you." He points his thumb to the conference room across the office where Gerald, the tall, lanky math geek in the skinnier than usual FBI tie, is making wild motions in front of a webcam.

The idea that we can't even rely on video conferencing potential victims leads to a heated discussion between Ailes and the assistant director about how far we should go in questioning everything we see. On a practical level, trying to canvass this many people, even with local law enforcement, was going to be a challenge. Especially when the Warlock has gone to great lengths to place Swanson outside our reach.

Gerald told Ailes he could do a feasibility test in hours. He ripped apart one of his gaming consoles and hacked together a motion capture device while we sat around and ate lunch.

"We can't let the Warlock control the case." I'm dying to get back out into the field. I'd made several hints that I could be useful in Michigan. I don't know if that's really true or not, but I hate waiting for something to happen. To me, it seems like there's more to be learned from Chloe McDonald's murder, two years ago. I go back and forth on whether or not she was killed by the Warlock or if he just used her murder as an opportunity. There might be more leads back there.

I stare at Ailes's wall calendar. The Avenger appeared three days ago. There were six full days between the hack and the cemetery. Another six between that and the Avenger. We're all looking at our watches, counting the remaining days. I've got a gut feeling the Warlock may try to surprise us. He doesn't want us to know his rhythm.

In magic, we use a false expectation of timing to catch people off guard. We do things on the odd count. I pull coins from the air and keep dropping them into a bucket until I steal a champagne bottle from there. I create a rhythm as they hit the bottom of the bucket. Clink, clink, clink, smile. Clink, clink, clink, smile. It's after the smile, the relaxed moment between the beats, when I do my dirty work. All eyes are on my face. My hand falls to my side and I steal something. We lull you in with a pattern, then get you.

I've already made clear that I think the Warlock is going to hit either a day early or a day late. Probably early, while we're still preparing ourselves in anticipation.

When not being distracted by my own predicament, I've been trying to help Ailes's team in the bullpen sort through all of the image matches for Chloe. The other agents are tracking down the likeliest matches by requesting server records from various social networks and doing soft inquiries into missing persons.

"I think we'll carefully consider how we deploy our assets. What would you do in Michigan if I can get you out there?" ask Ailes.

Before I can answer him, his laptop makes a ringing sound. "Hold on." He smiles. "I think it's for you." He spins the screen to face me.

I'm looking at an image of myself in the other conference room. Only it's not me.

I look at Gerald through the window. He grins back at me from his setup. Then I look at the screen; the image is pretty good. With a little bit of digital noise to mimic a bad Internet connection, maybe a better image map to base it on than the photographs of me he got behind my back, and it would totally pass. Gerald spins around in his chair and I watch the virtual version of me do the same. There's no appreciable delay, at least none that stands out on video conferencing.

He made a pretty convincing 3-D model of me in just a few hours and figured out how to use the gaming consoles motion sensors to animate it in real time. It's scary to think what the Warlock could have done with years of planning and more resources.

Ailes turns the laptop to look at the virtual me. "Good work, Gerald."

Gerald's voice comes though my mouth. "Want me to work on the voice emulator?"

Ailes shakes his head. "I don't think we need to go that far. How long to make a 3-D map of the director?"

"Twenty for a basic one. He's bald, so I don't have to do the hair. The software side is mostly done. All I had to do was just hack it all together."

"Do it. Let's schedule a video conference with him in a half hour. Maybe we can get a little more love for our image search. With more horsepower, we might crack this sooner."

26

Gᴇʀᴀʟᴅ'ꜱ ᴅᴇᴍᴏɴꜱᴛʀᴀᴛɪᴏɴ ʜᴀꜱ me thinking. Although we don't know if the Warlock is going to that level of deception to hide his victims' identities, it's not worth putting anything past him since we've already seen how texts and e-mails fooled Swanson's wife.

Efforts to trace the messages and calls have led to a firewall of proxy servers. None of them look custom-made. Just off-the-shelf hacks using readily available tools and how Gerald pieced together his impostor software. There was no need to invent anything, just find the tools already out there. They were good enough to get the job done.

The Warlock seems to be very pragmatic. After testing out other image-matching services, Faceplaced.com seems the most likely fit for what he's using. It has a much superior algorithm and a far more extensive database of images to draw from. Before heading out to Austin, Jennifer did a little snooping to see if she could get the code for the site, but the admin had it locked down tight.

Ailes sees me staring at the screen on my laptop displaying the Faceplaced home page. "What's on your mind?"

I point to the website. "The hotel room is planted. But this site is the one place we're sure he's been at least at some point, and he doesn't want us to know about it. It's where he gets some of his magic tricks from, so to speak."

"Yes. Unfortunately, despite Jennifer's best efforts to talk to the owner geek to geek, he's not letting us look at his server logs."

"I know. But I think we want more than that. We want to see all the searches. We might be able to find out who he's after next as well as the identity of the woman in the grave. Maybe even set up a little trap."

Ailes sits back in his chair and shakes his head. "We've asked. We've hinted at a search warrant. But the probable cause is too thin. It could take weeks. He's the anti-authority type that would go public if we made any move. And that would be bad. He also told us the searches get purged nightly. But that could be a lie. We need to keep this a secret from the Warlock. Before Jennifer left, all she could manage was a promise from him to not tell anyone we've been asking. And it's a goddamn lot of data. There are thousands of girls that could look like our Chloe. Swanson was a lucky hit."

The website is important. I don't know Jennifer at all, other than a brief conversation, but she doesn't seem like a people person. Of course, I'm kind of aloof myself. But I know how to turn on some personality. "Maybe we don't need another hacker to convince him?"

"Are you saying Jennifer was the wrong person to send?"

"No. I'm just saying that's not working. Let's try a different route. Let me give it a shot. If we can't get a search warrant, then we need to keep trying. This is our best lead by far."

"It's a potential lead. There might be other ways to make the connection between Swanson and the pilot. We don't know if the Warlock even knows about this website," replies Ailes.

"He does." I can't put my instinct into words.

"Why are you so sure?"

I hesitate. "Remember I told you about the friend who pointed out the website?"

"The guy you ran into at the airport?"

"I didn't tell you everything about him."

FOR THE NEXT half hour I give Ailes the mostly unfiltered backstory of me and Damian. It's uncomfortable, but someone else needs to know. And I trust him. I've only just met him, but he reminds of the kind of father some of my friends had who would ask you how you were doing and mean it.

Ailes thinks everything over, then finally replies, "So you think that if one crazy sees this, others have too?"

"Yeah, I guess that's one way to put things."

"And you're not worried about this Damian character?"

"I think he's manageable." That's a lie. "In any case, the owner of the website is our best lead."

Ailes takes a moment to think it over. "This guy is a bit of a jerk. Abrasive and insulting. He tried to talk down to Jennifer quite a lot."

I'm sure that didn't go over very well with her. "Maybe that's the problem. She threatens him. She probably knows more about his platform than he does. The only thing he could do was cling to his castle and tell her she couldn't play inside it. I don't pretend to be an expert on anything relating to computers. He'll know that. Possibly I can play to his ego a bit."

Ailes gets straight to the point. "And bat your eyelashes?"

"If it gets us his cooperation and access to the servers, then yeah. It wouldn't be the first time I've had to act to get someone to get out of the way." I look at Swanson's image on the screen.

"And it might tell us if he's choosing the victims to fit the scenarios or the scenarios to suit the victims."

Knowing how the Warlock selected his victims would be a big break. Did he want to kill the second girl and look for a previous murder to tie her to? Was it the same with Swanson? Did he just happen to look like a pilot missing since 1945? The odds of that being the case are astronomical.

"Yes. Answering that question could make a world of difference." Ailes's phone rings.

His face freezes as the voice on the other end repeats something.

"No? They're sure?" He shakes his head and hangs up. "Ready for this?"

I can't even begin to imagine what's about to come out of his mouth anymore.

"The lab did a test of what was left of the body from the cemetery. They used a procedure that's not even in the journals yet. They finally found some tissue from which they could extract DNA."

"And?"

"Perfect match with Chloe McDonald. There's no contamination. No ambiguity."

"I don't get it."

"The tests say it's the same girl. They've matched it to the samples the medical examiner took. We even found a sample of the original Chloe's blood in our labs from back when the case first happened and they wanted an outside opinion."

I'm still suspicious of anything that's been sitting on a shelf. "What about to the parents?"

"Chloe was adopted. We can't look for a match there." I can

see Ailes's mind work. "We're going to try to find the adoption records to track down the biological mother . . ."

I shake my head. Of course it would have to be they can't match her to her parents. It's the way the Warlock works. "It's the long burn." I try to calm myself.

Ailes stops typing. "Pardon me?"

I think of an example. "I'm doing a card trick, let's say, and I need to get something out of my purse. But I know that you're watching my hands, that you won't look away from them. You're 'burning' them like I might be a card cheat. So I'll do something suspicious to distract you. I might put a hand on top of the deck of cards completely covering them and let it fall away like I just took something. You're going to focus on that hand because you know it's hot. But while you're looking at it I can switch the deck of cards with the other in my purse or wherever. You'll never notice because you're sure you already caught me. Then boom, I open my fingers and show that my 'hot' hand is empty. You've been suckered all along. You thought I was stealing one card. I stole them all."

I stand up and lean on the table. "The Warlock wants us to think he just found a girl who looked like Chloe McDonald at first and then removed her fingerprints to make it hard to identify her. That's the obvious answer. Why else would he go through all the trouble to hide that? It's because he wants to postpone the big reveal."

Ailes is trying to follow. "That it's the same girl? So what's the Warlock hiding from us by making us think it wasn't going to be a match at first? Why make an impossible illusion look less impressive? Where's the advantage?"

27

I'M TALKING OUT LOUD as I think it through. "He's trying to hide the obvious answer. At least the one that will lead us to him faster. It's also the secret that makes his deception harder to disprove in the minds of the public. Remember, he's not trying to win a court case here. He wants to make history. If he pulls this off, he'll have fooled the FBI in the most mysterious ways imaginable. That's why he's obscuring how complete the illusion is."

"Explain."

"The perfect match is too good to be true. If we knew at first we had a DNA match that couldn't be contested, we'd come straight to the only logical conclusion. Maybe even figure out his method. I know it's convoluted. But he wanted us to think he was hiding something in his other hand. He needed to distract us from the real secret."

"Which is?"

I remember Damian's comment about this being an old family trick. I'd ignored it at the time. Now it makes sense. "My grandfather used to perform an illusion called the Transmitted Woman. He'd call a woman from the audience and have her step into a cabinet that looked like a big metal machine. He'd twist some dials and sparks would shoot out the top. He'd open the door and she would be gone. There'd be an explosion and she would reappear, sitting in the audience."

"Twins?"

"Not for that illusion. But everyone assumed that. Even though the girl was really from the audience, not a plant. He told people to come back each night and see the effect performed again with a different girl. And he would deliver. Reporters would chase the girl down and follow her around to prove she was a plant that worked for us. But they couldn't. She wasn't in on the secret."

"All right. How?"

I feel funny telling him. This trick has been a family secret for a long time. A few people in the magic community know how it was performed, but it's never been published anywhere. It's part of our own Secret Library. "All right. Magic oath time?"

"Sure," Ailes replies seriously.

"Back then, things were different. My grandfather could travel with a much larger cast than my father or I could. He had thirty chorus girls in the show. Women had less variety in makeup, hairstyles, and clothes. Lots of them wore hats. When people came into the theater, my grandfather would watch from the wings and pick a woman who looked like one of his chorus girls. With thirty girls backstage, we were bound to find at least one woman in the audience who could pass at a distance. If we didn't have an outfit that matched, our seamstress could make up something close enough. He'd call the woman onstage and an assistant would lead her up the side steps. That's when we'd switch her for our chorus girl. While the audience is distracted by the machine sparking and making a noise, the usher would bring the woman back to her seat in the dark. The chorus girl would go through a trapdoor and vanish. An instant later the spotlight would reveal the woman from the audience back in her seat. The audience was never the wiser. They didn't realize the switch happened before the woman even got on-stage. She was led back in the darkness with no idea what happened on stage. Afterward, the people around her would teller her she walked into the cabinet and vanished. She'd insist she came right back to her seat. Grandfather would suggest that she'd have no memory of what happened to her, making both accounts fit. It's not a practical trick to try today, of course."

"But what does that have to do with the Warlock if the DNA matches?"

"Twins."

"Twins? You just said no twins," Ailes seems almost agitated.

"Not my grandfather's illusion. But that's not my point. He could do that illusion because he had access to thirty girls. At least two or three were going to be a match for someone in an audience filled with several hundred women. Cheap human labor was the technology of the day. The Warlock is using the cheap technology of our day, raw computation. What's the percentage of births per year that are identical twins?"

Ailes knows this off the top of his head. "It's doubled in the last thirty years because of fertility treatments. Thirty to fifty per thousand births on average. Fraternal twins rises to almost one out of ten for mothers in their forties because they're the ones that use fertility treatment the most. If you just count women who go to fertility clinics, the rate climbs even higher. One out of three births for that group result in twins. Not necessarily identical, but there's an increase in that too." Ailes notices my surprise at him having this stat on hand. "My wife is a fertility specialist."

"So just by looking at birth records and the age of a mother, the Warlock could create a pool of twins. If he compiled a database of every woman over forty who has given birth, he knows that one out of ten of them had twins or triplets. If he cross-references that with death notices in the newspapers, he could create a subset of potential twins split up for adoption. If he had access to other records, like arrests and convictions, or even fertility clinic data, he could find more separated twins. Some of them will be genetically identical.

"The girl we found in Chloe's grave was her twin sister. The Warlock chose them because they were separated at birth and didn't know about each other. He wanted a perfect DNA match."

Ailes takes a moment to think it over. "Low-income parents are more likely to give up twins for adoption. It also skews the percentage of twins who are split up and adopted. There would be tens of thousands of split-up twins out there who never knew."

"Oh my God!" I almost make him jump out of his chair. "It's even easier than that! He doesn't need access to all those records." I point to the face-matching website. "All he needs to do is look for girls who most closely match and then find out their birth dates! He can get that off of their profiles. He uses the website to find exact matches but with different names. He then compares the birth dates they've posted online. You and your twin share DNA, a face and a birthday. Two out of three are probably online whether you realize it or not. All he has to do is send an innocuous e-mail or an @reply to ask if they were adopted and he's in. He looks for twins first, then checks birth dates!"

Ailes is nodding his head. "He could make a program to do that. Technically, he could limit the first search to all girls

born on a specific day and look for matches." Ailes's eyes go up
as he thinks. "Roughly five thousand girls are born every day.
He could canvass tens of thousands of girls in a couple days.
It's a brilliant gimmick. He has the computer sort through
millions of images looking for matches. Computationally, it
may not have even been possible or realistic a few years ago.
Now there are relational databases that specialize in those
kinds of queries."

I nod. "If he comes up with several thousand matches he can
have an automated system hit them with messages or e-mails
from other accounts asking if they were adopted."

It's a scary thought. He could find a large supply of split-up
twins who never knew they had a sister or brother. From a forensic point of view, there's little we could say that would dispute the idea that they're the same person. The DNA would
pass in a court of law. There are other markers, like surface
methylation, but we don't have reliable forensic tests for that.

"What about Swanson?" asks Ailes.

"He doesn't need to be a genetic match. Just an identical appearance. He used the system to find Chloe and her twin by
crunching millions of images. That probably took some time.
For the original Avenger pilot, all he needed was a similar face.
That's as easy as uploading a photo of the pilot."

"Of course," Ailes agrees. "I'm convinced. But . . ."

If we can't prove our twin hypothesis, when word gets out
that the girl who burned in the fire is an exact genetic match to
Chloe, the Warlock wins. People will think he's the real thing.

We can't let him.

"You have to let me go to Texas and talk to the owner of
Faceplaced. We need to find out what kind of data is amassed
on the other side of this screen. We need those server logs. The

Warlock used it to find Chloe, her twin, and a physical double for the lost pilot. I'm sure he's going to want to use this gimmick again. It's too good. It's too damn good!"

Ailes pulls out his phone. "I'll do you one better. This is critical. I think there's a jet ready to go. We can have you in Texas in two hours. And if the director doesn't go for it, then I'll have Gerald pretend to be him to get you permission." I think the last part was a joke. I think.

I slide my laptop into my bag and head for the airfield as the flight gets arranged. We're close. So much closer than the Warlock realizes.

28

AFTER THE JET reaches cruising altitude I call Ailes on the satellite phone. It feels a little weird being on the plane by myself. When I flew back from Fort Lauderdale, I shared it with some forensic people bringing samples back to Quantico. This feels almost excessive. I tell myself it's not a waste. The fuel, the pilots, all of the expense is worth it if we can stop the Warlock. That's to say, this is worth it if I can persuade this programmer to help us out.

Getting the data from that website is now more critical than ever. I'm convinced the Warlock's next victim is in there somewhere. The Warlock is too smart to be traced through there. It only takes a minute to download software that essentially makes you invisible online. It's like a library; even if you don't know who checked out what books, knowing what books were looked at can tell you a lot.

"How did the demonstration go with the assistant director?" Ailes had Gerald video conference Breyer masquerading as the head of the FBI

"He was impressed and disturbed. He knew the NSA and the CIA psy-ops were working on something similar, but he didn't know how to react when I told him one of his agents put it together from a game console from Toys 'R' Us, substituting millions of dollars' worth of government hardware for something that costs three hundred dollars. He asked Gerald to start working on a way to tell when we're looking at an altered image; a sock puppet, as Gerald calls them. He thinks he can do it by dissecting the motion algorithm. It won't tell us if someone is using a different method, but it can spot one similar to ours."

Being able to tell electronically if we're talking to a real person or not is crucial. We may have to track down tens of thousands of people. We have call centers with video conferencing in the FBI where we can do that from if we're sure we won't be spoofed by the Warlock.

Screening this many people in just a few days is a logistical nightmare. Anything we can do to narrow the field would help immensely.

"What are the other departments up to?" I ask.

"Right now the big discussion is with Chisholm and behavioral analysis is how this affects the profile of the Warlock. They seem to think this could make him some kind of super-genius hacker. Gerald and I are trying to convince them it doesn't. There's a difference between knowing how to use a tool someone else made and being the person who invented it. We don't even know that he's made a video puppet. And if he does, all it means so far is that he's very resourceful. People tend to read too much into skills they don't have."

I can relate to that. Some people see you do a simple mind-reading stunt and they think you're psychic. I used to pull the watch steal I did on Jensen on first dates. I stopped doing it when I realized that it might be a reason men were too afraid to call me for a second date. Or at least I think that's the reason.

"What about matching the birthdays?" I ask. The idea of

putting matching faces to matching birthdays to find twins simplifies things. If the Warlock is looking for matching pairs, so to speak, that would allow us to narrow our potential victims by a larger margin. We have computers to sift through the data; the trouble was finding a source for that information.

"Yes. That was very helpful. It gave the director enough reason to push ahead with the Yearbook Project."

I hadn't heard about that. "Yearbook? I don't know what that is."

"It's our own social network database. Unlike some of our databases targeting terrorism suspects, where we need a court's permission to even enter a name, this is a database of publicly available information all cross-referenced and processed by artificial intelligence. If a bunch of people wish your username on Twitter a happy birthday, we can then add a birthday tag to your profile. If you upload a photograph with faces in it, the system uses deductive logic to figure out who they are and then uses a face search similar to Faceplaced to build a profile."

I'd read we were working on a project like this but the Department of Justice lawyers weren't sure of the legality of collecting personal profiles en masse for non-terror cases.

"I didn't know it was that far along," I reply.

"That was sidestepped when an outside contractor did all the heavy lifting and basically presented it to us for no charge."

"I see. That outside contractor wouldn't have been a certain computational mathematician who now consults for the FBI?"

"No comment," replies Ailes flatly.

So he went ahead and built the Yearbook Project on his own dime and just gave it to them. The man's heart is all in.

"I've got some other little tricks we're putting into it," says Ailes. "We can glean all kinds of information from body language in photographs. Did you know that we can tell with eighty percent accuracy whether or not you've had sexual intercourse with someone based upon your posture and expression in a photo of you next to them?"

"I hope you don't mean me personally." My mind immediately thinks of all the photos online of me with ex-boyfriends.

"Uh, no, Agent Blackwood. I admit it's creepy. But this kind of data is everywhere if you know how to collect and interpret it. Online marketers are already using this stuff. You'd be amazed at how much we didn't have to invent. It's shocking the amount of information we put online about ourselves that we'd rather not share with the world."

My magazine cover flashes in my mind. "Trust me, I know. What should I know about this programmer? I'm about to call him."

"Liam Reynolds. He's twenty-eight. Has a degree in computer science from Texas A&M. He makes his living as a freelance programmer. He's done a lot of contract work for different companies. His hobbies are the usual—video games. If you play, don't make the mistake Jennifer did in telling him her online handle."

"Why is that?"

"He found out he was nowhere in her league and didn't take it well. Of course, she also qualifies in the top five percent in marksmanship in the FBI. Gerald says he once watched her hit a perfect series with a blindfold. She was doing it all from muscle memory."

I knew she was scary. "No need to worry about the video game thing. If it's not an app for my phone where I'm trying to solve word puzzles or line up pretty gems, I haven't played it."

"Good. I think we need to play up the other side. Just be

your charming self. Don't intimidate him. Please don't steal his watch. The mere fact that an attractive girl is talking to him will probably be more than he can deal with. Hold on." Ailes pauses. "Gerald just handed me a note. He says that it's a seventy percent probability Reynolds hasn't had a date with a girl in the last three years. For what that's worth."

It feels terribly manipulative, but I got over that while learning how to do undercover work in the police academy and then in the FBI. I haven't done a lot of it in the field, but you realize that most of the people you're going to be lying to aren't actually the ones you want to arrest. With Liam Reynolds, I have to pretend that I don't think he's a power-mad creep standing in the way of us stopping the Warlock from committing another murder. I just need to be an attractive woman asking for a favor.

Sometimes it works. Other times it backfires badly. I've seen some girls embarrass themselves trying to flatter men into letting them have their way. If a guy is just happy for the attention, then it doesn't matter. If he's really insecure and starts to feel manipulated, he will shut off entirely. Reynolds strikes me as the insecure type.

When I was ten I watched another child sweet-talk her father into buying her something in a store. I tried the same thing with a video game a few days later with my father. He just looked at me and asked, "When did you become a baby-talking moron?"

Sharp, to the point and brutally honest. He wasn't as cruel as Grandfather could be, but his words could cut just as deep.

I hope I have better luck with the hacker.

29

Liam Reynolds is squished into a booth at TGI Fridays in suburban Austin, leaving almost no space between his gut and the table. When I approach the booth, he's looking out the window into the parking lot, through a pair of aviator-style glasses. He takes them off in dramatic fashion as I sit down. I can only guess he's trying to make some kind of impression. But it's not the one he intended.

Close to three hundred pounds, he's wearing a Dallas Cowboys jersey that hangs over his body like a collapsed tent. Short, with almost blond hair that's spiky, he has a face too pasty for Texas and a roll under his chin probably related to the basket of onion rings he devoured while waiting for me to get there.

"Mr. Reynolds? I'm Agent Blackwood."

He gives me a suspicious nod. I shake his soft and clammy hand. I'm not bothered by heavy people. The big guys I've gone out with were the type that learned to compensate for their genetics with a quick sense of humor and a likable smile. But Reynolds possesses none of these qualities. He's turned whatever rejection he's received throughout his life into a layer of smugness. He knows he's smart, so it's the thing he tries to hold over people. I can see right away why Jennifer may have been the wrong person to send.

"Thank you for agreeing to help me. I know someone had some technical questions for you before. I'm here to ask if you can help me build out the profile." I take a folder from my bag. It contains one of the questionnaires Chisholm helped behavioral analysis create. I figure the best way to get at Reynolds is through his vanity.

It's an old interview technique taught to me by a police captain. We all want to demonstrate competence, even to our enemies. While Reynolds isn't an enemy, he's shown us hostility. His sense of righteousness overwhelms any urge he has to directly cooperate by granting access to the server. But if I ask him theoretical questions, he might soften his stance.

The way to work on smart yet insecure people is to challenge their intelligence in a nonthreatening way. We can't walk away from an unanswered question. Especially one that relates to us. Like my friends in college, and sometimes me, who couldn't pass up a women's magazine with a sex quiz or an article on cheating, these insecurities rule us: "How well do you score in bed? Is your man cheating on you? Five ways to tell . . ."

On the phone from the plane, I'd told Reynolds I wanted to talk about building up a profile of a programmer who might do what the Warlock did. I imagine Reynolds might see him as a kind of equal. With the right prodding, he might even see helping us take him down as a worthy task.

"You took an FBI jet here?" Reynolds says this almost as if it's not a question.

"Yes." Ailes was insistent that I have some backup, and had a field agent meet me at the airport and drive me here. An older agent, Mark Ross, with a polite Texas gentleman twang, he offered to wait in the car and do some paperwork while I talked to Reynolds.

Reynolds shoves a cheese stick into his mouth. "I tracked an IP address on your e-mail that came from an FBI router. The ping time took a little long. I figured you guys have some fast fiber, so it must have come from a satellite, which meant an airplane."

"Interesting. I didn't think about that."

"You can tell a lot from data." He says it like it's a profound statement.

He seems to want to flaunt the fact that he has access to such information. I resist the urge to take the bait. "I don't know much about computers. Figuring out how people work is enough for me."

"So you're not going to ask me about my server?" he asks.

"Not really." I notice that he has a hard time looking me in the face, even when he's not staring at my breasts. I'm wearing my normal office attire, a suit and a blouse that's not very revealing. That might be what's tantalizing him, figuring out what I look like under it all. "We can talk about the server if you want. But I think you made your case pretty clear to Agent Valdez." I flip to a page in the questionnaire. "Do you think someone else could copy what you've done with Faceplaced?"

He smirks. "Not my code. It's locked down. There are other systems out there, but I think mine is the best. Part of the strength of the program is that it looks for images that aren't just straight-on shots. It'll take profile shots and make data points for that as well. That's how you get better nose and cheekbone maps. I got the idea working on a face scanner for a security company. They just wanted something that worked head-on. I tried to explain that if the image only works like that, then you can fool it with a photograph. It's like the face recognition they put into phones. You can trick it with an image of the person you took on your own phone. Stupid. Absolutely stupid." Reynolds wipes his greasy fingers on his shirt and shakes his head.

"That does sound stupid. So your system is the only one that does this?" I'm not trying to play dumb, just overemphasize what I'm not clear on to keep him talking.

"That I know of. I'm sure the NSA, CIA and probably you guys have something like it. But not for the public. Probably not as clean code. Definitely not made by one person. Most of the face-matching sites are designed to be intentionally sloppy and skew toward better-looking matches. People upload their photos for fun to see what celebrity they look like. The more famous and attractive, the better. If they were accurate, nobody would ever use them."

Reynolds takes a lot of pride in his work. He's the type of person who has to denigrate what everyone else has done to feel better about his own accomplishments. That being said, he's definitely intelligent. While he may be socially awkward, I don't want to underestimate his analytical skills.

I drop a compliment. "I guess that's why yours is the best."

He rolls his eyes. "Uh, yeah. So what's it like being famous?"

"Pardon me?"

Reynolds glances at me, then quickly looks away. "I pulled up your image from the newspaper and found some photos and videos of you online. Your real name is Blackstar? Right?"

So Reynolds decided to research me? I shouldn't be surprised. I Google everyone I meet as well, especially guys I meet. To Reynolds, it's his way of trying to get the upper hand.

"Actually, it's Blackwood. My grandfather changed it to 'star' to sound famous. He also wanted to show up Harry Blackstone, I guess."

"I watched a torrent of a Japanese television special. You looked young then."

He has no idea how to talk to a woman. "I was seventeen."

"The tiger thing was kind of cool. I figured out how you did it, though."

So could a ten-year-old. "Yeah, analytical people can see through magic."

"Why did you stop?" he asks.

"Because I wanted to help people. Magic wasn't my thing. I had enough as a child."

Reynolds nods. "Do you miss dressing like that?"

30

LIAM REYNOLDS is deliberately provoking me. He's obviously watched television shows where the detectives try to corner the suspects, only to have the tables turned on them. He thinks this is what smart people do. They show the dumb cops how brilliant they are. He probably pissed himself with delight when he made the connection between me and my past life. It's a little piece of information he wants to hold over me.

I can think of a thousand unkind things to say, but none of them will get me what I want. "Yeah, I didn't care for the outfits myself."

"I didn't say they looked bad . . ." He's trying to be flirty but only knows how to be creepier.

"It paid for college."

He raises an eyebrow. "I bet. Those Japanese guys loved you."

So much so, they even made a pornographic manga comic featuring a girl who looked just like me. Jesse Magicstar. Reynolds is the last type of guy I'd want finding out about that. I look for another question to ask him. "You ever come across anybody who's acted suspiciously? Maybe asked you for the code?"

"Lots of people. I get asked for it all the time."

"Could you provide us with some names and contact information?"

"Isn't that your job?" he says snarkily.

"What?" I ask.

"Finding this guy?"

"Mr. Reynolds, this is how we find people. We ask people like you to help us."

He waves a hand in the air. "And if we don't, you violate our rights and throw us away in some hole."

I don't know if there's a hole big enough for this jerk. I reply calmly, "Has anyone from the FBI made a threat to you about that? If they did, I'll report them. Short of a court order, your cooperation is voluntary and nobody should be coercing you."

Reynolds scoffs. "I get it. You're the good cop. That other . . . woman was the bad one. This is how it works."

He's a sad little man who wants to play an important role in all of this. He thinks he's another Edward Snowden, standing up to the man, when all he's doing is stopping us from getting a killer. It's a game for him.

I set the questionnaire aside and pull a photo from my bag and drop it on the table. It's a crime scene photo of Chloe. "We're all good cops. We want to get the guy that killed her and the other man and stop him from doing it again."

Reynolds ignores the photo. "What makes you so sure anybody was murdered? I'm not convinced that this guy has done anything wrong."

His eyes are fierce, as if he's being personally challenged. He's much more obsessed with this case than I think we realized.

"Mr. Reynolds, do you really think he can raise the dead or make an airplane travel through time?"

"Anything is possible. There's already a discussion thread on Reddit explaining a quantum universe theory for this. Wormhole bubbles. Maybe that's what this Warlock is. A scientist who's showing us what he's capable of."

So Reynolds sees his idealized self in this monster—an unrecognized genius who has to show the world how brilliant he is. "Seriously? You believe this?" I can't hide my surprise. Reynolds should be smarter than this.

"I've seen a lot of crazy things. Not everything is a trick, Miss Blackstar. But maybe you can't see that." His voice is condescending, like a frat boy who just came down from a hit of LSD and thinks he's seen the secrets of the universe.

"Maybe. But we've got two dead bodies and your website is the only connection. And you're stopping us from finding out who may be involved."

Reynolds holds up his hands again. "I'm just protecting my users' rights. Don't get all high-and-mighty on me. They have an expectation of privacy. Have you read the Constitution?"

To Reynolds, anyone with a badge is chomping at the bit to violate his civil rights. "Yes. Several times. I even swore an oath on it. That's how you become an FBI agent."

He sneers. "Maybe you should read it again. The part about unreasonable search and seizures."

"Nobody is trying to seize anything from you. All we've asked for is information."

He sits back and folds his arms. "Private information that belongs to my users."

"Your website doesn't have a privacy policy that covers this. Our lawyers checked."

"That's how it starts. A little here. A little there. And the next thing you know I can't even fly in an airport without the gestapo stopping me. Of course you wouldn't know about that on your private jet."

We do step over bounds, and people are right to be suspicious. Our country is supposed to be a free democracy and not a police state. I'm a bit of an anti-authoritarian myself, but I understand the idea of law and order.

This conversation is not going where I wanted it to. "I fly commercial all the time. I have to put up with the same inconvenience. I may not agree with it. But it's the law. I answer to the Constitution and the people you elect to make the laws and interpret it. My job is not to pick and choose which laws I'm going to enforce based upon what I agree with. Congress, elected by the people, gives us directives telling me what to do according to the Constitution."

"They're a bunch of crooks bought out by the corporations," replies Reynolds.

"Maybe so. The FBI has put a number of politicians in jail. Between you and me, it's a source of pride for us." I pick up Chloe's photograph and bring it to his eye level. "Political arguments aren't going to help us get her killer."

"Neither does being a good little Nazi who only says she's following orders." The words come out of his mouth too neatly, like something he's rehearsed over and over in his head.

It's such a sophomoric conversation. The kind of thing I went through in college when guys with Che Guevara shirts found out I was a criminal justice major. To them, anybody who was in authority who wasn't them or on their narrow bandwidth of political thought was a thug.

I pause, then speak as calmly as I can. "I have a pretty clear idea of what right and wrong is even when things are gray. Do you?"

"Yes. Giving in to you guys would be wrong. I don't care how many photos of dead girls you try to scare me with. Maybe you'll start calling the Warlock a terrorist next. Then you'll get to do anything you want. That's why people have to stand up to you." His cheeks are flushed. For him, this is his moment. I'll bet anything he's recording our conversation to share triumphantly with the Internet later.

"Recording me without my permission is against the law," I tell him.

His face goes white as he stumbles, "I don't know what you're talking about."

"Would you mind showing me your phone?" I ask.

"I don't have to," he replies.

"No, you don't. I was just making a point."

"What's that?" His eyes flicker to his pocket. A clear tell that he's been recording this all along.

I decide to let the recording drop for now. He knows that I know. Confronting him on that won't get us what we need. "We're not asking you to do anything wrong. Sometimes you have to make judgments. If I walk by your door and hear you screaming for help, I have to decide whether to kick it in or not. I don't know if some killer has a knife to your throat or your girlfriend has you tied up in bed and you're playing a game. I have to make a choice."

"You knock first. It's that simple. How does your imaginary hypothetical sound now?" He looks proud of his comeback.

"You get those hypotheticals all the time when you're a cop, Liam," I use his first name in a friendly manner, like we're old pals having a philosophical discussion. "Only they have real consequences. In a few days you might know what I mean. I hope not."

"What if you kick in the door and it's just me and my girl-friend? How does that make you feel? How often do you get to use the murder excuse?"

"Every time we kick in a door we have to answer to twelve people who decide if it was the right call or not. That's how it works. Checks and balances."

He shakes his head petulantly. "Sorry. Can't help you." He checks his watch. "I got to go take a call. Maybe if you're in town awhile we can talk about something else later?"

This guy is unbelievable. "I don't think we're getting any-where."

"Hey, you guys should be thanking me," he replies.

"Pardon me?"

"I wrote a blog post about all this but haven't published it yet. I could blow your bungling wide open. I even wrote about you after you called me. Photo and everything. I've documented everything."

I have to breathe slowly. Posting this online would ruin the one lead we have. "Why would you do this?"

"I haven't published it yet. Relax. What do you have to fear about transparency?"

"Transparency? You're the one who won't let us look at the server logs."

"That's different. It's totally different."

"Please don't publish that. It could make things much worse."

"I'm still thinking it over. Call me later and I'll give you my answer." He squeezes out of the booth and waddles away.

I stare at his sweat-stained back and don't know what to do. I've been in Texas less than an hour and managed to ruin the best lead we have.

I could chase him down and bully him over the recording, but I don't know what good that would do. It would just make things worse. And right now they already feel as bad as they can get. I regret second-guessing Jennifer.

So much for me and my delicate touch.

31

I GET DROPPED OFF at the hotel and call Ailes. I explain Reynolds's threat to go public with what we've asked him, despite our warnings.

Ailes can tell I'm frustrated; he's calm and soothing. "We'll figure out how to handle this. We might have to elevate things a bit. Get one of our attorneys to talk to him again. We'll manage."

"I don't know if it will work. He wants to be a martyr. I think he's hoping we'll arrest him. I wouldn't be surprised if he's already got the post set to go up on a website. He's the kind of guy who reads about hackers getting busted and wants to be a celebrity."

"I know the kind," says Ailes. "That could be dangerous for us."

I've let everyone down. "I'm sorry. I'm so sorry." I'm sitting on the edge of my bed with my head in my hands.

"Easy, Jessica. He made up his mind before you got there. At the very least you may have bought us some time. He probably wrote the post after Jennifer left, just to prove how smart he is."

I know Ailes is trying to make me feel better. But I screwed up. I thought I'd get here and pout my lips and Reynolds would fold over. I'm stupid. So stupid. I fell for his little argument. Any minute now he could send out his post explaining how we're interested in his website and how he imagines we're trying to roll over on him.

The Warlock would most likely see this and know we've figured out one of his secrets. He'll change his tactics and make it harder for us to catch him.

I'd like to think the heat might stop him from his next victim, but chances are he already has them. Swanson went missing days before he showed up in the airplane. We have no idea how long he held Chloe's twin sister captive. The scars on her body suggest he had access to her for a long time.

Every time you deal with a difficult witness, a light bulb goes on in your mind. What are they hiding?

Part of me wants to think Liam Reynolds is the bad guy. It's a normal reaction. The last asshole you meet is the biggest asshole in your universe.

Ailes's and Chisholm's people profiled Reynolds as soon as we found the website. He's not a killer. They never would have let me near him if they had any doubt.

Reynolds is just an asocial jerk on a power kick. So deluded that he asks me out after he turns down our request. He's the kind of guy who sits around in his apartment reading books on how to pick up girls by putting them down and then stutters once he gets a conversation going.

Before I hang up with Ailes, he tells me again not to worry. "If he does anything stupid we can get into his system and get some of what he may have. It may not be admissible in court. But that's something we can sort out later."

Ailes is hinting to me one of his geek friends can hack

Reynolds's whole server, which without a court order would be illegal. Hopefully they can get one before then, although I'm afraid that Reynolds is smart enough to see that coming and too dumb to get out of the way.

He's an okay programmer who makes a living as a free-lancer, with his one claim to fame being some code he probably lifted from one of his clients. This is his ticket to nerd stardom. He doesn't see himself as standing in our way. He's the wise hacker trying to show the jackbooted FBI thugs the noble path. He thinks cooperating with us is worse than what the Warlock is doing.

More disturbing is the idea that he's trying to protect the Warlock. Asshole or not, he genuinely surprised me when he said he thought it might not all be a trick. The news is filled with idiots entertaining the idea the Warlock is legitimate. Seeing someone with an IQ in the triple digits think that is scary.

Having failed this task, I have a few hours in the hotel before the plane heads back to Quantico. I place my clothes on hangers while I take a bath. I keep my gun on the toilet seat and close my eyes as the hot water pours past my toes and around my body. Normally it's relaxing. I have to take myself to that calm place I'd go when my family would argue or I'd be stressed out on the road.

I messed up. I know I did. My stomach clenches and my skin burns from the shame of it all. I try to just give myself a moment of peace in the bathtub and listen to the water. It's hard. I see Chloe's face. I hear Swanson's wife.

We only have two or three days left until the next crime.

The primal part of me wants to take my gun and go shove it in Liam Reynolds's fat gut and make him cry. That's one of the hard parts about being a cop. You're taught how to use force to solve problems and then admonished to never actually do it. I'd put a gun to his mouth if I knew, absolutely knew, it would save a life. I wouldn't pull the trigger. Not for being an asshole. But I'd let him know I'd consider it.

The hotel phone rings.

I ignore it. If anybody with the FBI was trying to reach me, they'd call me on my mobile. I pull my hair up higher and dip down into the tub so the water can soak my neck. I get cramps there when I'm stressed. Right now there are a ton of them squeezing like vise grips.

The phone rings again. Whoever it is, they're not giving up. If I want any peace I'm going to have to answer it. I lean out of the tub and grab the handset from the wall.

"Yes?"

"Hello, darling. Having a bad day?"

Damian.

I don't even ask how he got the number.

"Sounds like you're taking a bath," he says.

"What do you want?" I steal a glance through the open bathroom door, afraid he might be sitting on the bed.

"It's not what I want. Other than to make you happy."

I crane my neck to look in the hallway closet mirror. The room is empty. "Then stay away."

"I am. But that's not why I'm calling. I understand you had a difficult time today with a rather difficult individual with bad hygiene."

"I don't know what you're talking about." He's not in my hotel room, but has he been following me? I took an FBI jet. There's no way he could have known or even made it here in time. I didn't even know I'd be here four hours ago.

"Of course you don't. We all have our secrets. You might want to call on him again, though. He might be a little more cooperative."

I've seen what Damian has done to men who get in my way. I stand up in the bathtub and almost slip. "What did you do?!"

If he threatened Reynolds, that could be very, very bad. I feel like I'm about to throw up. Images of the jack of spades in the dead pimp's pocket fill my mind. It's hard to breathe.

"What did you do?" I ask again forcefully.

"I appealed to his sensibilities and higher logic. I think he's going to be very helpful."

"Damian! What did you do?" I shout it out loud. I'm frantically trying to towel off and nearly fall over. I don't know how I'm going to explain things if he threatened Reynolds, or worse.

"Relax, sweetheart. He's fine. Trust me. He wants to help you."

"Why?" I ask.

"Because I bought his company."

32

Damian was the call Liam Reynolds had to take when he left the restaurant, and he couldn't refuse. Damian made him an attractive offer, then wired the money into his bank account.

Mark Ross, the Texas field agent, picks me up from the hotel and takes me over to Reynolds's condominium. On the way I call up Ailes and try to explain to him what Damian did.

"Where did he get the money?" asks Ailes, surprised.

"I'm afraid to ask. He wanted to put the company in my name, but thankfully he didn't. It's probably registered to some offshore shell company."

"I kind of wish he had. I'd love to see the accountant's reaction when you put it on the expense report. What did he pay?"

"He didn't say. I'm sure Reynolds will tell us if we ask."

Reynolds was now expecting me and would turn over all the passwords and provide us with any help we need. The next step is getting Ailes's team access so they can download all the data and put whatever they need on the server to trap the Warlock.

Even if the Warlock is covering his tracks, there are ways to work around that if you know someone is going to be visiting a specific site. Instead of tracking the source of a connection, you can make his computer send out a burst of requests, kind of like a fingerprint. With the cooperation of local ISPs, you can look at their traffic and trace the pulses.

We get to Reynolds's condo after dark. It's in a nice suburb of Austin. He gives me a big grin at the door as he lets me and Ross inside. He reeks of cologne. He's just as creepy as before, only this time he's trying to be charming.

The interior is sparsely furnished. There's a black leather couch in front of a giant flat-screen with a couple of game consoles and a workstation off to the side. Books and magazines are piled up in the corner. The place smells like pizza and sweat.

Reynolds is all smiles. "You didn't tell me you had rich friends."

Yeah, asshole. You didn't mention your integrity came with a price tag. The professional side of me keeps my sarcasm in check. "Lots of people are very concerned by this case and want to do what they can to help."

He leads us over to his computer. "The website and back end is run off of a remote server I rent. I'll provide your people with access to that. As part of the arrangement, I'm supposed to provide you with any help you need for the next forty-five days."

An hour ago he was staring down the federal government in a defiant political act. Now he's giving us tech support. Agent Ross sits down to look at the website.

I'm polite and cordial. "Thank you, Liam. Dr. Ailes will have some more intelligent questions for you. One of his people will be calling in a minute or so." The real reason I came over, other than to make sure Reynolds hadn't been strangled to death, was to ask about his blog post. "Um, about that blog post you mentioned?"

"Deleted," he replies as if he was doing a charitable act. "Part of the agreement is that we make this change in ownership a stealth transaction for now. I'm dying to tell my friends I've been bought out. But I agreed to wait until the end of the forty-five days."

"Thank you. I appreciate that. I assume that if you had made any recordings, those would be deleted too?"

Reynolds hesitates. "Yes. Of course. So what do you guys plan to do next?"

He seems eager to help now. "The computer forensics will be handled by Quantico. They're going to want to look for suspicious IP addresses. Anything that stands out. Like how you discovered I accessed the site from the FBI jet. If you can think of anything else offhand, it would be a big help." I only tell him what we've already asked him for. There's no reason to risk our plans for setting up a honeypot by sharing them with someone whose loyalties can change so quickly. Especially given the Warlock's loyalties.

"I'll take a look." He still has that grin on his face. How much did Damian pay him?

Once again I decide to play to his ego. "If you have any ideas, we'd love to hear them."

"I'll think about that. Um, by the way. I'm sorry if I was a little abrasive earlier. That was just business."

Business? I thought I was investigating a murder. Silly me. "I understand. We all have to live by our convictions." And know their price. I'm sickened by the idea that all it took was a dollar sign marked across the face of Chloe's photograph.

Reynolds realizes how his sudden cooperation looks and tries to backtrack. "I stand by what I said before. But if someone else owns the site, then they can do with it what they please. It's a property rights thing, really." He's trying to rationalize his flip.

"Understood. Again, we appreciate your help." I don't want to debate him. We got what we need. We get the data and the asshole gets his blood money. Part of me wants the check to bounce. But that's not Damian's style.

That's the other thing I have to worry about. Damian knows he just did me a huge favor. He's bought himself some slack.

It compromises me.

First the lead on the site, now this. He's making me more indebted to him. Given his history, that puts me in a difficult situation. He wants my attention more than anything. Now he knows he has it. There are also things I withheld from Ailes about my relationship with him that could make me look very bad.

The only way for me to deal with the complication is to talk it over with Ailes and take it up to the assistant director. I've disclosed everything I've needed to in the past. Within a narrow definition. But I need to make sure I look beyond clean on this. Any omission can become a noose around your neck. It will be painful to explain how he fooled me. There's no other choice.

Reynolds picks up a shoebox off his desk. "Hey, do you remember how I told you guys that the system purges user-uploaded photographs after twenty-four hours?"

"Yes?" We'd hoped he was lying and there was a log of them because that would make the search a lot faster. If the Warlock used the website, then he uploaded photos of his victims. If we can find those photos and tie them to a specific IP address, that could tell us who's next. Most sites get rid of the data because they don't want to be held accountable if someone uploads a naked picture of their girlfriend or worse.

Reynolds nods toward the box. "It seems, uh, it seems there was a glitch in the system . . . Turns out that one of our hard drives was caching all the photos. I was going to manually wipe them and destroy the data. There's some, uh, racy stuff in there. But it has over a million uploads inside that it didn't erase because of the glitch."

Yes, a "glitch." I don't ask him if the glitch has anything to do with the box of tissues next to the hand sanitizer by his monitor. "Thank you, Liam." I take the box from him. There are three hard drives inside. Looks like a lot of glitches.

"Yeah, happy to help, since I guess this all belongs to you now." Something tells me Damian may have used more than money to influence Liam.

I leave Reynolds to Ailes and his team when they conference call. Ross drives me back to the airport, with the box of hard drives sitting in my lap. The victims' faces could be in there, as could the identity of the next potential ones.

I have a thought—what did I do when I first found the site?

I uploaded my own picture.

What if the Warlock did the same? What if his photo is somewhere in here? It's a chilling thought to think his face could be somewhere on a hard disk I was holding.

Ross speaks up as we head to the airport. "One million."

"What?" I ask.

"He left his bank account open on his computer. One million dollars. That's how much your friend paid him. Must be nice to have that kind of money lying around. We have to keep our work cars parked one day out of the week just to fit the gas budget."

Who knows what the Web site was worth or even if it was making Reynolds much money. Most of those ventures fail. Damian offered him a magical number. *Say yes and you're a millionaire right now . . .*

We all feel the crunch of government budgets. It's half of the paperwork Ailes talked about.

Ross continues, "Of course, your friend probably made a wise bet. Once this blows over and everyone hears about the website, it'll probably be worth millions more. Smart. Very smart."

Goddamn you, Damian. You don't miss an angle.

33

ASSISTANT DIRECTOR BREYER has his fingers steepled as he stares at his desk. I've just told him everything I know about Damian. Intimate things. Ailes and Chisholm are seated on either side of me. Chisholm is there to provide some kind of analysis of Damian. Ailes is there to provide what I guess is moral support. All of these men are old enough to be my father. Not that I'd ever tell him any of this. I feel so exposed, yet in a way, I'm relieved.

"Why didn't you bring this to my attention sooner?" Breyer finally says.

I take a deep breath. "When I went through background checks here, I explained everything." Not quite everything. I didn't tell them about some of my assumptions . . .

Ailes tries to defend me. "Agent Blackwood mentioned this man to me before she left for Austin. I don't think she's done anything intentionally to hide or obstruct information about him."

Breyer looks agitated. "Then how did he know she was there? How did he know what we were trying to accomplish there if nobody leaked it?" He looks me right in the eye as he says this. I can tell he thinks I may have whispered it to Damian on a phone call or made some kind of seemingly innocent admission. He's wondering if things are really over. He still doesn't know what to make of me.

"I didn't," I reply. "As I explained to Dr. Chisholm before I left, it was Damian who led me in the direction of the face-matching website. I think he knew which one the Warlock was using."

Breyer's voice has a touch of condescension. "And that didn't set off any alarm bells?"

"Every single one. That's why I disclosed that to Ailes and mentioned Damian in my notes to the case supervisor, Agent Knoll. After Damian bought the site, I made it clear that we needed to bring this to your attention."

"Do I need to remind you that Dr. Ailes is not career FBI?" replies Breyer.

Ailes calmly interrupts. "Blackwood was assigned to me by your order. And like it or not, the director gave me a badge and a gun." He pauses for a moment, "And all the authority that goes with it."

Breyer waves off the comment. "Yes. Yes. It's not the point."

Ailes is trying to protect me. I respect him for that. Everyone in the room knows he's the one with the most political power if he chooses to use it. I get the feeling Breyer doesn't like being reminded that Ailes can call the shots when he wants to. But to his credit, Ailes is reluctant to do that.

I just wish it didn't come down to him having to stand up for me. I've tried to dance this line as carefully as possible.

There's an expression in the bureau about covering your ass with a blizzard of paperwork. If you're worried that something might make you look bad, you don't hide it. You just file a bunch of reports about anything and everything. When I was a cop there were guys on the force who'd complain about everything they were asked to do, so just in case something blew up on them, they could pull out an e-mail where they said it was a bad idea to begin with.

I never took that approach with Damian. I reported the facts as they happened. I just left out my suspicions and my off-the-book attempts to find out who he really is. Breyer knows I did everything right technically. In my write-up about Faceplaced.com, I mentioned Damian as a source. I didn't red flag him. But he's right there in the notes.

"Where does he get his money? What do you know about him?" asks Ailes.

It's just as embarrassing as the intimate details. For as much time as we spent together, I can't say I really know any more about who he was before there was an "us." Damian never spoke about parents or family. He'd be on first-name basis with every bartender at a popular nightclub, but I don't think he had friends. One night we might go out to eat with a handsome older couple with a yacht in Biscayne Bay, people we'd never meet again. Damian had met them earlier that day at a wine store. It was like that all the time. He knew lots of people, but nobody "knew" him.

He always paid in cash. I'd asked him casually about money. He mentioned investing and something to do with the Internet. But that was the extent of it. Given Damian's charm and ability to connect with people at every level, anything is possible.

My ex-boyfriend, Terrence, had a friend who made his money as a deal broker connecting people he met at country clubs to businesses looking for capital. If you know people with money and you're clever, it's not hard to get into the game.

I tried to ask Damian on a few occasions about his childhood. The impression I got was that he wasn't a happy kid. I suspect he'd been living on his own since he was a teenager. His ability to fit in and make people like him seems driven by a need to survive.

I'd never had another lover like Damian. I suspect the reason was because lovemaking for him was more about making me happy. I think he really was after my mind. Our relationship was sexual, but his attachment was something else.

I could be in a restaurant filled with gorgeous South Beach models, but never would his eyes stray. He could charm the hell out of a waitress in front of me, yet never appear flirtatious. He made me feel I was the only woman in his world. I still wonder if that's the case.

Breyer looks over at Chisholm. "What do you think about this character?"

Chisholm has been absorbing this with his normal clinical detachment. It's unnerving. I catch him watching me out of the corner of his eye.

"He sounds a little like Abagnale if he never wised up," replies Chisholm.

Frank Abagnale was the teenager who masqueraded as an airline pilot, a doctor and a dozen other fake identities before getting busted for counterfeiting. He was the inspiration for the movie *Catch Me If You Can*. He's now a respected businessman and a visiting lecturer at the academy.

Chisholm continues his thought. "Frank Abagnale was an aberration. A sharp kid who got caught up in a game that got out of hand. Nothing sociopathic about him. Damian is different." He turns to me. "Do you think he believes he's these other people?"

Chisholm is asking me if I think Damian is delusional. "I don't know. When I catch him, it's like he snaps back to himself.

Or at least himself as I first met him. He knows what he's doing most times."

"Interesting. Multiple personality disorder is a mostly imaginary condition. The best treatment is to send a patient to a facility where they don't acknowledge it. The condition tends to go away. This situation sounds a lot like what some of our undercover operatives go through. The CIA has an entire program for helping agents who have been in the field for prolonged periods of time deal with the shift back. Most of the criminals we've dealt with who've used assumed identities for long periods of time are in constant fear. They never forget. The curious thing is that usually the best undercover cops are the ones who test on the edge of being a sociopath. That makes treatment even harder."

Breyer waves his hand in the air. "I'm not worried about what makes him what he is. I want to know if he could be our Warlock." The question is directed at me.

I knew this was coming. "No. It's not him."

"Why do you say that?" asks Breyer.

I don't have an answer other than a gut feeling. I choose my words carefully. "I've never known him to be capable of hurting an innocent person."

Chisholm's eyes light up. "Innocent? Care to clarify that?"

Damn. He pays attention to everything. "It's an expression," I explain. "We're all trained to use force. But only against the bad guys. Like any man, I'm sure Damian would defend himself." I almost add, "Or someone else," but keep my mouth shut.

"Got it," replies Chisholm flatly, neither agreeing nor challenging me.

Got what?

Ailes makes an attempt to change the direction of the

meeting. "Whoever Damian is, assuming he hasn't doctored the Faceplaced data, we may have some answers in a few hours about past and potential victims. Maybe even a photo of the Warlock. All thanks to his generosity, I might add."

Breyer is still skeptical. "Assuming. That's a big assumption from where I'm looking. Right now he looks like our biggest suspect. Blackwood, when you get a chance, I want you to sit down with one of Chisholm's people and go over everything. I'd also like to send a forensic team to your home."

"Yes, of course." I don't have a choice. "I also have a hat he left behind. But I think it's another one of his games."

Chisholm looks like he's trying to decide whether to say something. "Agent Blackwood, you've admitted this man has fooled you before."

"Yes?"

"I know it's difficult to look at this objectively. But have you entertained the idea that the Warlock could be a separate personality? Maybe something he keeps locked away while he's around you?"

A thousand times since he showed up in my apartment a few days ago. "Yes. And I know the stories about wives who never realize their husbands are serial killers. I understand all this. The difference between them and me is that they've been ignoring little details. Bloodstains. Late hours. Weird kinks. I look for them."

"Look for them?" asks Chisholm.

"Ever since I saw what he was, I've tried to find out if he could be dangerous to me. There's not a day that goes by that I don't think about that." Or if he killed the man who attacked me . . .

34

Aɪʟᴇs ꜰᴏʟʟᴏᴡs ᴍᴇ into the hall while Chisholm stays behind to talk to Breyer. I can only imagine what little details Chisholm picked up from me that he's now revealing to Breyer. I feel guilty for not telling them about Damian and the pimp. I know it would put the entire investigation into a different light. Damian would become their focus.

I know he's not the Warlock. I'm positive.

I keep telling myself this. Each time I grow a little less certain.

I've known two incredibly strong personalities in my life. My grandfather and Damian. My own father was a shadow in the presence of my grandfather. Even when we lived on our own, Grandfather was still the patriarch of the family. My father always felt like acting on his own was being defiant to his father. I transfer a lot of paternal feelings and rebelliousness toward my grandfather because of that. I wanted to pull away from his influence more than anyone else.

With Damian, it's the way he sees right into me. I'm still that awkward teenage girl he met at the magic convention. He knows the woman is an act. I've never known anyone who could read me as well as he can. And it's scary because he's the most unpredictable, impossible person I've ever met.

Unpredictable. Impossible.

These are the same words people are using to describe the Warlock.

They're also the same words you could use to describe my grandfather if you didn't know him like I did.

I guess that's what's nagging me. Unlike everyone else in this building, I know men like Damian and my grandfather. My life is filled with unusual, impossible men. Men from the same world as the Warlock.

When we're inside the elevator, Ailes notices my frustration.

"Something on your mind?" he asks.

"I've told them everything I know," I say defensively.

"And?"

Ailes has proven he's earned my trust. "Well, not everything I suspect. I just don't want to send us off into any wild-goose chases."

Or expose Damian for the thing he did to protect me.

"If you're sure it's not relevant and it's only speculation, then keep it to yourself. I don't need to know." We reach the bottom floor. Before we exit, he turns to me, "On the other hand, you better be damn sure he doesn't have anything to do with this."

The thing I'm dying to know, if Damian did it, was under what circumstances he killed my attacker. The coroner's report said there was a struggle. Bruising on his knuckles and signs that he fought back. The bruising suggests that Damian came at him head-on and not from behind.

Did Damian just try to talk to him and it escalated from there? Was Damian acting in self-defense? The forensic evidence doesn't dispute that. It also doesn't say that's the way it happened either. Damian could even have provoked him into a fight, knowing he was going to kill him. Or Damian could have just arranged it from hundreds of miles away. Anything is possible with him.

By the time I reach the bullpen, I know the right thing for me to do is to cooperate as fully as possible. If someone pushes me about my suspicions, which nobody did, I'll tell them that I think he may have acted in self-defense in a crime I have no proof he was ever involved in.

Gerald and Jennifer are waiting for us when we walk into the room, with grave expressions on their faces. They're standing in front of a video projection of an image of Chloe. It's a photograph of her I haven't seen before.

"This is Denise Lewis," says Jennifer. "Same birthday as Chloe, and as you can see, an identical match. She grew up eighty miles away from where Chloe's body was found. Her family moved to Ohio when she was twelve. She went to Ohio State and majored in biology with an intent to go into veterinary medicine."

I remember Chloe volunteered at an animal shelter.

Gerald clicks to another image. Denise is on a horse against some sparse rocky mountains. "Six months ago she updated her Facebook status to say she got an internship to work in a village in Mongolia teaching English. She's made sporadic updates since then. Even uploading photographs." He shows another photo of her. This one shows her nuzzling a horse by a yurt.

"Nice photo?" He brings up another image. It's the same exact photograph, but a different girl. This one is Asian. "The Warlock modified these photographs with her image." He points to the skin on her cheek. "These aren't Photoshops. He actually rendered the entire image using a 3-D model. The light bounce is perfect. A fake made in two dimensions wouldn't quite get the shadows right. The only giveaway on this image is that he used a blurring tool with too low of a randomness. I don't think anybody would catch it unless they knew exactly what they're looking for."

Ailes shakes his head. "Do her parents know?"

Jennifer's face drops. "No. They think she's still alive. We told Knoll. He's preparing for what to do next."

"Goddamn this asshole." Ailes is visibly shaken.

As with Swanson's wife, we don't want the Warlock to know what we've learned. If he's still trying to maintain that Denise is alive, he might stay in contact with them so nobody ever makes the connection.

But what's his endgame? Tell the families they died overseas? Send back a cigar box filled with ashes?

He could theoretically keep this going for years. If we didn't realize the twin connection, it'd be one of those unsolved mysteries you see on television. Only one writ large with a baffled FBI in the middle of it all.

"What else?" asks Ailes.

Gerald shows an image filled with hundreds of small photographs. "In the hope that the Warlock uploaded his own photo, we theorized some parameters and found four thousand uploaded images that appear to fit. We're searching the IP addresses for potential masking, etcetera to look for matches. We've also sent them to behavioral analysis. They're going to run them through VICAP and do a search through the images we collected in Fort Lauderdale of the crowd at the Avenger site."

If we can tie one of the uploaded photos to someone who was there, that could be a big lead. It'd give us a face to put on the news. It would show we were doing something besides waiting for the next murder.

I walk over to the screen to look at the faces up close. The frames are tightly cropped around their heads. There's a range of human emotion. Any one of them could be the Warlock. Ailes stands next to me and squints. He's having the same thought.

"What about the next victim?" I ask. "Do we know which search was done first? Did he look for Chloe's twin or Denise's?"

"Chloe," says Jennifer.

Interesting. That means that he selected Denise because she looked like Chloe. If it were the other way around it would suggest he had nothing to do with the Chloe's murder. This, on the other hand, suggests he killed both of them and had been planning this several years back.

"What about Swanson? Did he find him after he found the plane?"

"Probably. The logs show a high-resolution image of the original pilot was uploaded eight months ago. He was looking for a match to Kelsford and that's how he found Swanson."

Eight months? Assuming he was looking for a match for the pilot because he'd already found the plane in the ocean, that's at least how long he waited on the discovery of a lifetime. A secret so big that it would change history. But he just kept it to himself. At least it supports the idea that he went looking for a victim to fit the crime and not the other way around. The odds of the other possibility are incomprehensible. It's some comfort to know he's not that lucky.

At least now we know his big secret, or at least one of them. The Warlock is looking for lost identical twins or look-alikes of previous deaths. I hope there's a way to use the data to stop the next killing. Somewhere in the stream of photos is his next victim.

We spend the rest of the day going through the data. Ailes

has persuaded the FBI's computer forensic lab to let him use one of its supercomputers to process the images through the Yearbook system. But it's not enough. There are too many images and correlations to connect. We're playing another numbers game, like we did with the code the Warlock planted on our website.

Ailes and the director have been on the phone with the NSA, pleading for them to grant access to one of their unofficial databases. From the sound of the yelling, it doesn't sound like it's working.

Sometime past midnight I pass out on a couch in a conference room with my laptop still on my chest after I'd finished a write-up explaining the Warlock's trick to the working group: He used social networks to find two girls who were lost twins. He murdered one of them almost two years ago, leading to a high-profile investigation. A few months after she's buried, he digs up her coffin and steals her body, leaving the coffin open with a pipe running down into it so he can place sand or a clue inside later on. He then murders the second girl a week ago. Probably by burying her alive in a nearby location and then moving her body to Chloe's grave. To throw us off the path he removes Denise's fingerprints and booby-traps her body to explode into an inferno, destroying most of the physical evidence.

It's an incredibly complicated trick, but that's the point. This is killing as performance art. The result is the public thinks a murdered girl came back from the dead and then burst into flames like something out of the Bible. And all of the evidence supports that idea.

Brilliant. Horrifying.

An hour after I fall asleep, Gerald runs into the room and knocks on the door.

I sit up, almost spilling the laptop onto the floor. "What? You find something?"

His face is red. "We got the third victim."

"That's great!"

He shakes his head. "No. We're too late. We think she was just killed twenty minutes ago."

I feel like I've been punched in the stomach. I want to puke. "What? How?"

Gerald is speechless. "It's impossible . . ." He motions for me to follow him.

We run across the campus to the operations center. Gerald tries to dry his eyes before we enter the room.

35

IT'S PAST 2 A.M., but there's easily a hundred people in the special operations center at Quantico. Many of them look as tired and exhausted as me. This case has become a source of professional pride. The room is a large office floor that's been retasked for the Warlock case. Everyone is gathered at one end of the room looking at several large video displays on the wall. Gerald and I spot Ailes and work our way over. He's listening as Knoll waits for somebody to give him an answer on the other end of a phone.

I can't see the video through the crowd. Too many bodies are blocking the screens. Lots of people are making phone calls and asking questions I can't quite make out.

Everyone's expression is somber. It's the kind of reaction you see here when there's been a terrorist attack or a national tragedy like a mass shooting. Ailes waves me and Gerald through the throng.

His eyes are red and his voice is low. "We tried, Jessica. Maybe just a little more time and we could have stopped this." He shakes his head.

"What?" I try to get a look at the screen. Two agents are

sipping coffee and blocking the view. I tap one of them on the shoulder. He sees who I am and lets me through.

I turn to Ailes. He shakes his head again.

The image is too much to take in at one glance.

There's a young girl. Blond hair, maybe between seventeen and nineteen. She's naked and lying in the middle of a street. Her head is turned sideways and there's a pool of blood around her.

White feathers surround her. White ones like the one we found in the airplane. Some of them are poking through the skin in her back. They appear to be growing out of her. Like wings.

She looks like an angel.

A fallen angel.

The image changes to a different view. More of the street is visible. Hundreds of people are looking at her lying there. I recognize the intersection. It's one of the most recognizable ones in the world. I've been there a dozen times. I've had dinner with Terrence a block away from that very spot.

Times Square.

The Warlock's latest victim is a dead angel in Times Square.

Another screen shows headlines from websites and television news. The image is self-explanatory. But the headlines spell out what the Warlock wants us to think anyway: An angel has fallen to earth.

Knoll holds the phone to his chest and quiets the room. "NYPD says almost all the bones in her body appear to be broken. There's an indentation around her head and shoulder—it looks like from a fall. They're checking the nearby buildings, but it doesn't seem possible that she could have jumped that far." He puts the phone to his ear and listens. "They've got some cell phone video from witnesses. They're going to transmit that to us in a few minutes."

Someone asks if the feathers match the dove feather from the Avenger. Another person says they appear to match visually, but there's no chance to do physical tests. We haven't released that feather clue yet to the public in order to prevent a copycat from spoiling the investigation. I don't know if there's much point now.

I step closer to the screen. There's no sense of terror. Almost peaceful. The feathers in her back are carefully placed. They look organic, like they belong there. I imagine that every devoutly religious person who sees this is calling friends, asking if it's some kind of sign.

Ailes is trying to take it all in like the rest of us. I'm waiting for the other shoe to drop. As striking as the image is, there's nothing supernatural about it. The feathers are well-placed, but for all we know, she could have been dropped from a helicopter. There has to be something else there.

Her right hand is curled under her head. It's clenched in a fist. I call out to Knoll. Maybe he already knows. "What's in her hand?"

He sets the phone aside for a moment. "One of our New York forensic people is looking at that right now. We're going to get an image in a moment."

We all wait for the image on the screen to change. The Warlock has our full attention and that of everyone in Times Square, plus the millions watching the various Internet feeds being streamed for phones. The image of the fallen angel is horrific but captivating. The blood around her body, the white feathers. It's like something out of the book of Revelation.

"Claire Nelson," Gerald says to me. "I'm pretty sure that's her name. I found her photo in the Faceplaced data. We're trying to contact her family. We knew this an hour ago. If we'd been faster . . ." His voice breaks up.

I try to console him, "Gerald, he already had her then. I don't know if there's anything we could have done. The recent victims were killed hours before we found them."

I tell myself this is true. I cannot bear to think that while I was sleeping on the couch I could have done something to stop this from happening. It's a horrible thought. If I'd managed to persuade Liam Reynolds sooner before Damian had to step in. If only I'd noticed things that I'm not seeing yet. If I wasn't distracted by the illusion. I look at the room full of faces. We're all thinking the same thing. Maybe if I'd worked through my lunch break. Maybe if I'd taken more time to look at the evidence. It's the way cops see things.

Somebody shouts for everyone to quiet down. "Video coming through!"

We all hush as the image of the girl changes to a frozen frame of video. An Asian girl smiles at the camera. The video plays and she makes a peace sign in front of a huge video wall. A loud noise cuts out the audio and there's an explosion in the street behind her. It looks like a jet of smoke. Hundreds of feathers float in the air. The person holding the camera zooms through and we can see a grainy image of the angel on the ground. Feathers rain down all around her. The camera jerks upward. The buildings are all brightly lit. There's nothing but emptiness beyond their glow.

It's a perfect illusion. It looks like she has fallen from the sky at an incredible speed. The person controlling the playback is rewinding and trying to freeze-frame it to see where she actually came from. It looks as if she just appears out of nowhere. Hopefully we'll get more video.

Knoll calls out from the phone. His boxer face looks sad and confused. "Forensics is sending us a photograph. They say she's holding on to a ticket. Just a second . . . It's a ticket to the Empire State Building observation deck."

What?

Knoll puts his hand on the mouthpiece. "The time stamp on the ticket was ten minutes before she fell."

The Empire State Building is a mile away. Someone could walk the distance in that time. She certainly couldn't jump that far. It doesn't add up. It's incomplete.

Ailes feels the same way. "What do you think?"

There's more. This is all part of the deception. "Without the ticket, it's straightforward, I guess. I'm not sure what he wants us to think. It's just a visual image right now. A mystery inside a mystery, maybe. I don't think we've seen all of it. There's another part to this."

Knoll quiets us down again. "New video coming online. NYPD just got this from security at the Empire State Building. They're streaming it to us."

The screen cuts to a live feed from inside what looks like the security center of the Empire State Building. Several NYPD officers are standing around a monitor while a detective and a security guard roll through recorded video. The person holding the camera brings the lens closer to see what they're looking at.

"You getting this, D.C. and Quantico?" asks the detective in New York.

Knoll confirms over the phone.

The detective has the security guard play back a video. It's from a security camera showing the corner of the observation deck. We all crowd in for a closer look. We know something is going to happen. It feels like we're watching live.

A blond girl, our angel, is wearing an overcoat. She steps to the edge of the deck by the fence and waves at the camera. She smiles. A bright, big smile. She starts to glow. For a moment the screen is filled with a blurry rainbow. There's a flash of light and then she's gone.

She vanishes in plain sight.

The time stamp on the video is five seconds before she appears a mile away in the middle of Times Square.

Five seconds.

One moment she's waving to us. Another and she's an angel falling from heaven.

Gerald is shaking his head. "That's faster than the speed of sound."

"Wheels up in forty minutes," shouts Knoll. "I need everyone who is going to New York to be outside and on the shuttle in twenty minutes."

I look at Ailes and don't ask. I tell him. "I'm going."

36

Times square is a madhouse in the middle of the night. The NYPD has set up screens to block the body from onlookers and shut down the entire block to foot traffic. Not that there's much point now. What happened has already been photographed and recorded a thousand times over. Late-night cable news programs are playing a clip of the angel's fall. That's what they're calling it on the news. We watched it while we were in the air. Hundreds of camera phone photos of the victim's naked body are already online. Word about the Empire State Building ticket clutched in her hand and the security camera video still haven't leaked yet, for what it's worth.

Twenty of us took the jet to LaGuardia. With the intersections blocked off by motorcycle cops, I don't think our driver ever did less than eighty miles an hour. A paranormal feat of its own in NYC. A caravan of FBI Suburbans escorted by police cars with flashing lights rushed us down the Brooklyn-Queens Expressway and across the Queens Midtown Tunnel in under ten minutes. The trip from the tarmac at Quantico to Times Square was under forty-five minutes. Most of the witnesses are still standing around being interviewed by the FBI, the NYPD and the several dozen news crews that are filling the streets and sidewalks outside the barriers.

Our driver had to honk at a reporter doing a live feed in the middle of the road so we could get past. Inside the taped-off area, it's just as much pandemonium. Every law enforcement agency in New York is here. The New York FBI office, the largest division outside of D.C., is out in full force. They're already canvassing the crowds and have set up a mobile command post a hundred feet from the body. Men with flashlights are on the roofs of buildings searching for clues while helicopters are flying overhead with their spotlights scanning from above.

Somewhere in the middle of this chaos the Warlock is watching. I know it. This city is the center of the world. Almost a century ago my great-grandfather became a household name just a few blocks away.

Half of our group has gone to the Empire State Building. Knoll pulled me into the Suburban with him to go look at the body while the scene was still fresh.

A New York field agent walks us past the barricades and across the street to an opening in the screen around the girl.

She's just like the photograph. Amid the already bright lights of Times Square, work lights make the scene feel like day. I can see my own reflection in her blood.

It was hard to tell from the two-dimensional photograph, but I can clearly make out where part of her face has been caved in from the impact. The asphalt is also dented. It appears as if she hit the ground hard.

All the evidence makes it seem like she really did fall from a tremendous height. But how is that possible?

A tech with a portable ultrasound unit is checking her bones as a fingerprint tech clears an area on her outstretched hand.

The ultrasound screen shows hundreds of fractures. Her left shoulder is pulverized.

After taking it in for several minutes, Knoll turns to me. "What do you think, Blackwood?"

I'm not sure what I think. I can only say the obvious. "It looks like she fell. But I guess the question is where and when?"

He kneels down to examine the body more closely. "You don't think here? It's been planted?"

"I don't know. There's just not enough information. We know what he wants us to think. What happened is a different matter."

A local agent introduces the deputy police commissioner to Knoll. Dressed in khakis and a T-shirt under his coat, Floyd Greene looks like he was just pulled out of bed. In his fifties, with gray hair and sharp features, he resembles an Irish cop out of an old movie. He gives me a polite nod before talking to Knoll. "Any observations, Special Agent Knoll?"

Knoll cranes his head and looks at a helicopter overhead. "No copter was overhead at the time?"

Greene leans in to say something privately to Knoll. He looks at my FBI ID around my neck again, then includes me. His voice is low, almost a whisper. "We've had five surface-to-air missile batteries around this island since 9/11. We've got radar that'll tell us if a mosquito takes a piss in Central Park. Nothing gets past it. We didn't see a thing." He nods to the body. "Either our little angel here fell from heaven or someone planted her body here. There's no way she got here any other way. Radar would tell us."

Knoll scratches his head. "Balloon?"

"Anything big enough to carry a person is going to show up on radar."

"What about a train of them?" The words sound stupid as I say them.

Greene gives me an intense gaze. "Explain?"

I only think of the idea because he said a balloon would be too big. "Instead of one large one, a few dozen smaller ones all tied to a long rope. Each one no more than a couple feet across."

Greene turns to Knoll. "Who is she?"

"Agent Blackwood is the one we bring in to figure this kind of stuff out. Kind of an outside-the-box thinker. Real outside-the-box." He says the last part matter-of-fact. Nowhere near the skepticism when we first met.

Greene nods his head. "Oh. I heard of you, now. Well, in the umpteen million meetings I've had going through every scary scenario that could happen in this city, nobody ever mentioned the possibility of sneaking in a large object, like a bomb, using a series of low-radar-profile inflatables hooked up like that."

My cheeks turn red. "Sorry. Just asking a question." I feel like I'm ten and interrupted my grandfather in the middle of one of his stories.

"Don't be sorry, Agent. I'm paying you a compliment. We try to imagine the unimaginable. Now I got to go yell at somebody for not thinking of that. Hopefully he'll tell me that our radar would catch it."

Knoll rolls the idea around in his head. "You think that's it?"

I shake my head. "No. I don't. I don't think she fell here. At least not from that high up. I don't think the Warlock would chance setting off a hidden missile defense system. I was just thinking around things."

Knoll makes a kind of grunt. I'm not sure if that means he gets what I'm saying or is just frustrated.

The girl's eyes are looking right at me from the reflection

in the pool of her blood. It's as if they're telling me something.

We're missing a clue.

It's got to be an obvious thing, like the feather or the sand.

Oh my God!

"What?" asks Knoll.

"Just a second!" I hold up my finger and pull out my phone to call Gerald back in Quantico. He picks up after three rings. "Gerald, you told me the girl's name. How did we find it out?"

His voice still sounds hurt. "I found her photo in the database. But she doesn't have a twin. A lot of close matches. But nobody with the same birth date."

Knoll steps closer to listen. I explain to him and Gerald at the same time. It's the Transmitted Woman effect. "He doesn't need a genetic match. Just a girl who's close enough physically. Like Swanson and the pilot. We're meant to assume there was only one body. He picked two girls that look alike. This girl and another. That's who we saw on the observation deck."

"What do you mean?" asks Knoll.

"Chloe died almost two years ago. The Warlock used her and her twin because he needed to make it look like she only died hours before we found her. But this is different; the Warlock knows we'll find out the identity of this girl. The other girl, the one who vanished from the Empire State Building, she's not a twin. Just a double. The moment she vanished, this girl was planted here. Two girls."

"I think I get it. But how?" asks Knoll.

I shake my head. "That's not important right now. The other girl, she might still be alive! He knows as soon as she sees her face on the news, she's going to talk to someone. That's if he doesn't already have her. We can still save her!"

"Christ!" Knoll radios the head of the field office and the

NYPD to broadcast the image of the girl on the observation deck to the news. Hopefully she'll see her face and call in. That's if she's not in on it or being held captive. I hadn't thought about that until just now.

I bite my lip trying to think around the problem. The Warlock had to have thought about that situation. He's still several steps ahead. He's already got a plan to get rid of the girl from the Empire State Building.

I interrupt Knoll. "Check all the international flights that left in the last few hours from LaGuardia and JFK. She might be an out-of-town tourist. Maybe from another country. For all we know, he could be waiting on the other end to kill her."

If the Warlock was in Manhattan when the angel fell, he could have sent the other girl unwittingly away so she'd be out of the city by the time this broke on the news. If he wanted to meet her at the other end of the flight, it'd be as easy as routing her through some extra destination. He could fly direct and pick her up at the other airport.

Knoll relays my instructions. As soon as he's done we climb back into the Suburban and go downtown to the Empire State Building. I give the angel one last look and pray we can save the girl who vanished.

This murder has to be the last.

If he kills again it will be my fault.

37

Hᴇʟɪᴄᴏᴘᴛᴇʀs ᴏᴠᴇʀ ᴛʜᴇ ᴄɪᴛʏ hover like wasps beyond the protective barrier around the observation deck on the eighty-sixth floor of the Empire State Building. The NYPD copter searchlights paint the city with disks of light. News helicopters, told to keep a safe distance back, patrol in wide circles, covering events with their long-range cameras.

The size of the police presence makes me think of newsreel footage of World War II battlefields and the more recent coverage of cities in the Middle East under siege. All this hysteria, created by one man.

Knoll has been circulating the image of the girl right before she vanished as widely as possible. While the manhunt for her plays out, we've come here to look for some kind of clue as to who she was and how she vanished.

None of us know what we're searching for, other than some kind of explanation for what we can only describe as paranormal. A girl vanishes in plain sight from the top of the Empire State Building. Seconds later, her angelic twin crashes to the earth in the middle of Times Square. How do you begin to investigate something like that? I know part of the trick; at least I'm sure there are two girls. But that doesn't explain how it happened.

Dawn is still a few hours away, but the city is wide awake.

People who were up late to see the news called friends to tell them to turn on their televisions or go online. No official connection to the Warlock has been announced yet, but they already know. The media have been going crazy. The tourist videos and the photo of the fallen angel strike the same chords as the mysterious reappearance of the Avenger and the graveyard body consumed by flames. I remind myself her name was Denise. I've got to remember her as well as Claire, and not fall for the deception. There were two girls there, just like here; only this time, one could still be alive.

When we left Times Square, piles of flowers were being laid next to candles. I'm glad some people realize there's a victim in all this spectacle. At least I hope they see her as a victim. We passed hundreds of people lined up on the sidewalk trying to get a look at what they saw on television. Their faces were filled with awe and wonder. We spotted several people holding signs declaring it the end of days. A street preacher was perched on a trash can giving an impromptu sermon.

On the elevator to the observation deck, I try to imagine how the public will react to this latest deception. Those people in the streets still haven't seen the video of the girl vanishing. The fallen angel is the tragic and strangely beautiful conclusion; the vanishing is the first all-out magical miracle that people will be able to watch over and over again.

The Warlock keeps escalating things. First it was something in a remote location. Next it was a public beach, predawn. Now he's committing murder in full view of hundreds of people in one of the biggest cities in the world. No one could imagine how big this murder would have become. I'm afraid to think about what happens next.

We're waiting for the NYPD to set up a remote monitor in

the observation deck lobby to show the video from the security system. This is to help us better understand how she vanished. Our FBI team is up on ladders checking the cameras, looking for some kind of electronic trickery. I know they won't find any. He's never left behind any obvious proof of his deception. The last thing he wants is physical evidence showing the event was anything less than divine.

The city is a vast jungle of sparkling lights below me. Photos can capture some of the view. But it's so much more than that. A thousand different sounds float up here. Police cars, squealing bus brakes, the ever-present sound of construction.

I walk over to the spot on the deck outside where the girl vanished, careful not to touch anything. The forensic team has already swept the area for clues, but it's always good practice to be safe. I look up at the camera that is trained on where she stood. It's a stubby black box locked inside a plastic dome. There are four cameras watching the outside perimeter. They keep track of tourists as they file out of the metal and glass lobby onto the narrow walkway around the building. Fishhook-shaped barriers curl over the top of the fence, preventing people from climbing over the edge. Over the years it's been a temptation some found too hard to resist. There were five attempts in three weeks alone in 1947 before they put in the safeguard.

I push my arm between a gap in the metal bars. The distance is too narrow for even a small child to slip through. Knoll sees me and walks over.

"I don't think you're going to make it through, Blackwood."

"You'd be surprised by the tight spaces I used to crawl through," I reply. Part of being a stage illusionist meant shoving yourself into very small spaces in apparently empty boxes.

"Having a six-hundred-pound white tiger only inches away can be a hell of a motivation."

Knoll's eyes widen for a moment. "You're an odd woman."

"Yes. People keep reminding me." I don't think he meant it as a dig. It was just an observation, perhaps a little too accurate for my liking.

"It's a good quality." He turns to the security camera. "They keep a pretty good check on who comes out here. They have to go through a screening. Look for parachutes, Uzis, the fun stuff. Unfortunately, they're not as concerned about people leaving, as long as they don't do it over the side. We'll have the videos ready in a second to do a head count. So far, they haven't found our girl going back into the elevators or the stairs. Of course, if she took the stairs, she could still be walking down them and won't be too hard to find. Every public inch of this building is under observation from the time you enter to the time you leave."

I pull away from the ledge. "Is it? No blind spots? The cameras look more concerned with people as they get closer to the edge than if they stick close to the side walls. But there could be cameras I don't know about."

"I'll check again. They might be a little overconfident."

A field tech leans his head out the door and waves us inside to the table where they've set up the monitors. Several dozen NYPD detectives, FBI agents and other officials are already gathered around waiting to watch the high-resolution playback from multiple angles.

The tech seated in front of the playback controls explains that he's put together a video sequence of the girl up until the point she vanishes. There were ninety other people in the lobby and on the deck, he cautions, making it difficult to follow her at some points.

He starts the video with her entering through the

ground-floor lobby by herself. The view is from the high-ceiling looking down on the wide marble floor. The next shot shows her paying for her ticket in cash. We then see her get in line for the elevator. The elevator camera shows her riding to the eighty-sixth floor. Another shot shows her walking across the observation deck lobby and out onto the observation deck. Another camera follows her as she walks around to the opposite side. The last camera catches her as she steps into the corner. We all lean in because we know what happens next.

The girl smiles, then vanishes in a flash of light. After that, she doesn't reappear on any of the other cameras. She never steps back into the elevator. She never takes the stairs.

She's gone.

The tech rolls back to the moment she vanishes and replays the video frame-by-frame. Everyone crowds in closer to look for some kind of clue, as if in slow motion the flash of light will reveal her secret.

I'm skeptical. It's like a magician's puff of smoke. The flash isn't an artifact of a miracle. It's there to hide something.

Behind us, an NYPD detective steps from the elevator and walks behind the table. "So far we've tracked down fourteen people who were on the observation deck when it happened. None of them recall seeing the girl."

"What about the flash of light?" asks Knoll.

"Two of them think they may have seen a really bright camera flash, but nothing for sure."

Interesting. Everyone was too busy staring down at the city. None of them saw the Warlock's greatest trick.

One of our agents, a woman with short brown hair and an FBI jacket, rushes in from outside holding the glass dome from a camera. "We may have found something."

38

THE AGENT HOLDS up the dome in her gloved hands for us to see. "We noticed a thin film over this. Like a kind of spray. It may be the same kind of material they use on glass to allow you to project images onto its surface." She pulls out a small flashlight and aims it at the dome. A bright glow appears around the point at which the light passes through.

"She was a projected image? Like a hologram?" asks one of the techs sitting at the table.

Knoll starts giving instructions. "Check all the cameras in the building and be careful about fingerprints. Check with security and the manufacturer to see if this is standard."

The head NYPD detective gives orders to his subordinates to assist. Agents and field techs fan out to inspect the cameras in the lobby and elevators using the flashlight test. Just a few feet away from me, an FBI agent aims his penlight on the bubble over the camera aimed at the lobby. A glow appears on the surface when he brings the light closer.

The agent holding the first dome nods her head. "Just enough for a bright light, but not enough to be noticed. We should check the cleaning closets in case he slipped the material into the custodial supplies."

One of the IT techs sitting at the table starts digging into an equipment case. "I can set up a video projector so we can see if that works. Maybe replicate the effect."

They're excited to think that they may have figured out his trick.

It's a wonderful theory.

It's wrong.

I don't say anything yet because I don't know what else they should be doing. People assume magicians use far more sophisticated methods than we usually do. Most of the time the explanations are mundane, nothing like holographic projections and sophisticated lasers. Those elements might be part of a trick, window dressing, but they aren't the method.

When put on the spot to perform as a young girl, I'd sometimes just take a strand of my own long black hair and use it to make a napkin or a dollar bill float. Against the right background, it was invisible. People thought I was using magnets or wind currents. They never guessed my own body was the gimmick.

The film on the domes theory has enough credibility to make it plausible, but it's too complicated. To create the image of the girl entering the building and going all the way to the observation deck, the Warlock would need projectors all over the building. It's the kind of thing out of a movie. It would also betray his methods. It has to be one of his fake-outs.

I ask the woman a question. "What about the dome over the camera that was watching the corner? Did we check that one yet?"

"They're taking it down now."

I know exactly where this is going. I hate to be the one about to burst her bubble.

A tech comes in from the deck and sets the globe on the table. We watch as she takes her flashlight out and flashes it on the surface. The beam passes straight through with little reflection. It's nothing like the other domes we've checked.

She tries the light from a different angle to no effect. "I guess he must have wiped it down."

I shake my head. "I'm sure he never touched it."

The woman looks at me with a hurt expression. I just took away her moment. I'd feel bad, but this isn't about egos. There's no time for politics. It's about getting to the truth as quickly as we can. The film is just a big time-wasting ruse, typical for the Warlock. The critical proof isn't there because that's not how he did the illusion.

The spray decoy is there to buy him time. To convince us that the first girl never existed, that she's some kind of phantom. He wants time so he can kill the other girl. If she was an accomplice, this stunt wouldn't serve much of a purpose. It only buys him a few hours if we keep chasing the theory.

His deception took a lot of planning. I think about how I would create this distraction. The spray could have been applied at any time from a hidden sprayer, maybe even by an unwitting accomplice. I doubt we'll ever find out when it happened or exactly how, probably months ago. It doesn't matter right now.

The Warlock left this one dome clear to tweak us. After we've wasted time and manpower on the theory, he wants us to know that's not how he did it. He wants us to think he would have done it that way if he were merely a stage conjuror. It fits with his need to make us believe he's the real thing. I think he hopes we're going to be sending people all over the building searching for hidden projectors next.

I've seen projecting devices as small as a lipstick case for sale in catalogs. Given the fact that forensic techs can spend weeks looking for a bullet hole in a small room, searching the entire Empire State Building for something like that is an almost impossible task. It's a devious way to tie us up and send us down the wrong track.

Knowing why he did this still leaves the question of how he accomplished the deception.

"Quiet please!" Knoll is holding his phone and motions everyone back to the table. He asks one of the techs if they can get Internet access. The man nods and pulls up a browser. Still on the phone, Knoll relays a link for him to go to.

"It seems the Warlock couldn't wait for us to release the observation deck footage," says Knoll. "The news just got ahold of a video uploaded to the Web. It shows the whole thing from someone's camera phone up here."

The tech plays the video. Same girl, same effect, different angle. The "miracle" happens in the background as the person taking the video films the city at night.

Knoll calls over to the NYPD detective and the head of the FBI field office. "We need to find out who uploaded that ASAP."

While we were sitting on the observation deck footage we could control part of the message. We were denying the Warlock his full effect. But he wasn't going to let that happen. He wants the world to see the entire illusion in all three parts when they wake up. The vanish. The descent. The revelation of the fallen angel. The whole miracle he created before we have a chance to explain it away, assuming we can. He wants us to explain it away with talk about holographic projectors and not have any to show.

We'll look clueless.

He'll win.

I get an idea, but it's just a notion.

I need us to dismiss the phantom-girl concept if we're going to put all our energy into finding her now. I have to go out on a limb to do it. I'll probably look like a fool. But I don't have a choice.

I turn to Knoll. "Mind if I try something?"

"What do you have in mind?"

"Better if I just show you. Give me a minute. Can we get a live feed from the camera outside where she vanished?"

The tech at the table nods.

"Just start recording in a minute," I explain. "It'll probably look dumb. But I just want to see something."

I step outside the lobby and walk around the back of the observation deck to the spot where the girl was last seen. I feel like I'm about to make the biggest ass of myself in front of everyone. My grandfather would yell at me for trying something like this without practicing first. Every second counts here.

But this isn't a show. This could be life and death.

TWO MINUTES LATER I walk back into the lobby. Everyone is crowded around the monitors.

"Did it work?" I ask, afraid I made a complete ass of myself.

They spin around to look at me. They're all shocked.

I guess it did.

Knoll is searching for the words. "You . . . you vanished." He's clearly shocked.

I hear someone mutter in the background. "She is a witch."

My body relaxes, but my mind goes into overdrive. This only means that we have that much less time to save the girl who vanished. She has no idea what happened or what's coming.

39

Everyone is waiting for an explanation. I think about the right way to describe what happened. I have to explain this clearly, but I also need them to remember the moment they were fooled. The trouble with telling someone how a trick is done is that after they hear the simple solution they decide the secret really isn't that big of a deal and assume they were on the verge of figuring it out anyway. Most of the time that's not the case.

I also need to present it so that they won't just dismiss what I did as nothing like what the Warlock did once they see the differences. That's the difficulty with trying to debunk psychics and people who claim they have magical powers. People who secretly want to believe will dismiss any deviations as proof that the psychic is real because you didn't replicate what they did exactly the same way. I had two minutes to plan my little illusion. The Warlock had years.

To walk them through my thought process, I start with a story. I need them to get my point. "When Harry Houdini died, he left behind the plans for what may have been one of his greatest illusions if he performed it, the Flight of Venus. He wanted an illusion that didn't use cabinets, trapdoors, or anything else that people were using back then. The curtain would rise, revealing two men holding a large plate of glass, like a table. Houdini would help an assistant up onto the glass, have her lie down and then throw a cloth over them that hung a few inches below the edge of the glass. He'd then whip it away and she would be gone. It would have been done in full light. Even with people all around the illusion. It probably would have been his most deceptive effect ever."

The lobby is filled with people waiting for me to reveal the mystery. I still feel guilty explaining how these methods work. Like I'm a little girl telling my family secrets in school to impress the children I want to make friends with. Revealing the Secret Library.

"The method was simple. My grandfather thinks Houdini got the idea from the old Chess Master illusion. Um, never mind." I catch myself getting too particular. "The point is, the girl never really disappears. The audience just doesn't recognize her. One of the men holding the glass sheet is a hollow dummy. When the cloth is covering the assistant and the men, she climbs inside the robes of the dummy. She then walks off the stage holding one end of the glass. In plain sight." I point to the monitors. "We shouldn't be looking for the blond girl, or holographic projectors, for that matter. We need to look for a girl, or maybe a guy, leaving the Empire State Building whom we never saw go up it. It could be a wig, glasses, lots of different things. Simple changes can change our perceptions." As I say this, I think of Damian and his gift for disguise. It unnerves me to think that this is the kind of illusion he could create. Was I right to dismiss him out of hand?

Knoll shakes his head and points a finger at the monitor, paused the moment right after I vanished. "Agent Blackwood, I think we understand that part of the explanation, thank you."

He's frustrated and impatient. "How the hell did you disappear? We watched you hold out your hands and vanish in a flash. One moment we're watching you there. The next you're standing behind us."

"Agent Knoll, I did it the easy way," I reply. In any other situation I would have enjoyed the fact that I fooled him.

"The easy way?"

"I walked."

"Walked?" He raises an eyebrow. I get similar reactions from the others gathered around the monitor.

I point out the window. "There's a blind spot about five feet in front of the corner. Right under the other camera trained on the other side of the building. The cameras are meant to keep people away from the ledge. Not watch them when they're nowhere near it."

I can see he's agitated by the way I'm explaining the illusion. I need him, and everyone else, to understand each part so the whole thing makes sense. Everyone else is staring at me with folded arms. A room full of cops hates to be fooled. That's why it's extra critical I call their attention to everything before I destroy the mystery.

"To get to the blind spot it took less than a second, but I needed a way to distract the camera. So I did this." I point to the monitor, now back on the live feed, then snap my fingers. The screen flashes white.

The tech at the station lifts his hands from the keyboard as people stare at him. "I didn't do shit." He angrily pulls up a window showing IP addresses for the camera feeds.

People turn to me with open mouths. Frustration is turning into anger. I'm not trying to piss them off. "Bear with me a moment, please."

"Did you jack the system? Use some kind of signal disrupter?" asks the tech.

"No. Nothing like that. I can't imagine how I'd even do that. I did it the low-tech way." I point out the observation lobby window to a uniformed NYPD officer smiling back at us. "I asked Officer Malloy to aim a green laser pointer at the camera." We keep several of them in our field kits.

Out on the observation deck, Malloy flashes the laser through the window and splashes it across our chests, then up at the camera dome, causing the screen to go all white.

"The light is so bright that when it hits the lens it overloads the sensor. Somewhere out there the Warlock was watching through a telescope with a laser aimed right at the camera lens. Or he managed to pre-mount it weeks ago." I point out to the twinkling lights of the city. "It could be hidden on any of a thousand buildings that are in the line of sight of here. No spray. No hologram. Just a ten-dollar toy. All it took was a second for her to go from the corner to the blind spot. One bright flash."

"So she's an accomplice?" says Knoll. I'd already considered and dismissed this.

"I'd bet against it. At least not knowingly. She looks like she's playing a game, having fun. It's hard to see her ears, but maybe she has a Bluetooth and he's giving her instructions. She probably has no idea of what's going on. The film on the other camera domes is a ruse to give him enough time to kill her so she can't explain her part in all this. He wants us to be chasing after phantom projectors."

They still look unconvinced. "All he did was shine a bright light right at the camera lens to make us blink. On the security video, with the low frame rate, it looks like she vanishes. He could see her from the telescope, or be on the phone with her and know when she moved. That's it. He could have triggered the laser from anywhere by sending the telescope feed to his phone. The point is, two girls. One is dead, while the other, the one who may have unwittingly helped him, might still be alive and in danger."

The real question is if we can find her in time. Knoll pulls out his phone to check how the search for her is going. I step into the corner and call Ailes to see if he and Gerald have made any progress.

Ailes sounds pessimistic. "We checked the airports. Nobody has been spotted who matches that description. Five international flights already departed. We've sent photographs to the other end as well, asking gate personnel to ask passengers if they were at the Empire State Building. But there's another thing we need to consider, Jessica."

I know what he's about to say. I realize my theory that she's a girl from out of the country whom the Warlock is going to kill when she gets back home is only half right, if at all.

"He may have just sent a car for her and found someplace around here to kill her straight away. She could be dead by now."

I can't believe that just yet. My gut tells me she's still alive, but not for much longer. I look out through the lobby windows at the lights of the city. She could be out there right now with just minutes to live.

40

A GIRL'S LIFE IS on the line. Chloe and Denise were killed before I was on the case; now two more people have already died. That's too many. It's got to stop. I can't just think of myself as a bystander. This may be Knoll's case, but it's my responsibility. I'm supposed to be the expert. I have to see through the tricks. I have to be a step ahead of the Warlock.

I shout to one of the techs sitting at a laptop, "Pull up a map of the city!" I trace my fingers down the path from Times Square. He could have been there at the moment the angel fell and then taken Broadway to Thirty-fourth and picked her up in front of the Empire State Building. From there it's just a few blocks east to the Queens Midtown Tunnel and off Manhattan and to any airport in the area.

Damn it. If he had decided to linger for a while, which he's done previously, we could have passed him and the girl on our way to Times Square. Just a few hundred feet away from us as we rushed past! I want to throw up. We were so close. This isn't right. I hate that I've taken this long to see through his lies.

Knoll asks the NYPD to find out what camera footage we have of cars near the Empire State Building's entrances and Times Square around the time she vanished in the hopes that we can put out a highway alert, but it's been several hours since the descent. He could be out of state with her by now.

Would he be with her? I think about the idea that first struck me, that he's getting her to leave the city voluntarily. I came up with an airplane because that would get her away the fastest. But flights are delayed all the time and airport lounges are filled with televisions. Many flights, especially international ones, have televisions onboard. The Warlock didn't waste any time uploading the footage of her on the observation deck. He must know she won't see it. Either because she was dead or because she was not around a television.

Would he drive her away from the scene of the crime and risk being caught on a camera with her?

No.

After his illusion is in play, he wants to be in a place where he can just watch. Maybe he would use an accomplice, but that still leaves another loose end. The really highly organized killers are solo acts. Or they use people in ways they don't know. And he likes to be in control.

The warehouse by the cemetery. The hotel in Fort Lauderdale. He needs to be at the scene and take in the aftermath. He was probably there when Claire appeared in the middle of Times Square. Hell, he's probably on someone's camera phone.

How could he get the other girl out of the city without anybody noticing? The subways are filled with cameras. Bus stops won't keep her isolated. A private car or a taxi leaving near the building means a driver with a radio and her in plain sight of the rearview mirror.

He likes things that are automatic. Self-working solutions. Simple.

He wants her in an anonymous place and isolated. But he

needs to be able to get to her when he's ready. Local public transportation is out. She could get off a city bus or a train at any time.

I should be able to figure this out. I've spent most of my life traveling on almost every form of transit imaginable; planes, cruise ships, tour buses . . .

A tour bus.

A private tour bus.

A bunch of strangers locked in a box and driven from one spot to another.

"Agent Knoll!" I run over to him. He's on the observation deck talking to an NYPD captain.

"Yes?" He's taken aback by my urgency.

The words come out in a rush. "A tour bus. One that leaves here, then heads for somewhere else, like Niagara Falls. Some of them don't have televisions. And the driver probably won't turn them on this late at night. Even if she does sees herself, she's stuck there until they get to the next pit stop. That's where he will pick her up!"

If the girl from the Empire State Building was following the Warlock's instructions, maybe against her will or, more likely, not knowing what was really going on, he could get her to run toward the camera, put on a disguise in the blind spot, and then go catch a tour bus nearby right as it leaves. This would isolate her from the aftermath. She'd have no idea what she'd just helped do.

Knoll vigorously nods his head. "Maybe. Maybe." He looks to the NYPD captain. "Can we get on this? Treat it like an escaped felon and not a kidnapping? Assume she doesn't want to be found?"

The captain pulls out his radio and sends out an alert to the state police, then the assistant commissioner. He opens the glass door and calls to the techs at the workstation. "Find out what she looked like when she left. ASAP. For now we'll just send out the photo from the deck camera. Let's not let this one slip through our fingers."

Knoll phones the head of the New York field office to start calling all the tour operators and find out if any left within a few blocks shortly after she vanished. I just threw out Niagara Falls as an example. She could be on an overnight bus anywhere. That's assuming I'm right and she's not dead already.

The techs scan through the video footage of the visitors as they enter the elevators going down from the deck. Out of ninety people, at least seven women look like they could be her with blond hair.

There are lots of different hairstyles. Some have hats and glasses. Dark hair, red hair, short, long, curly, straight. Put a blond wig on any of them and you could have our girl.

"Which one?" asks the confused tech.

Oh God.

The motherfucker.

I see what he's done.

The cunning bastard.

All of them.

He arranges for at least half a dozen girls who look alike to be here. But only one has the wig and is told where to stand. The others are there to distract us, to make us chase after taxis, Town Cars, buses, everything.

My voice is almost a shout. "All the girls! Send all the photos! He might have them taking trains, buses, anything that moves.

But the tour bus is the one we want. I think that's where we'll find the only girl he plans to kill." I pray I'm right. Being wrong could get someone else murdered.

There's no telling what the truth is. His illusions involve layers of deceptions that go so deep, there's no way of knowing what we've missed.

 CALL AILES to update him on our situation. He and Gerald are trying to make a map of probable stops for the tour buses. Jennifer is going through the images we pulled from the Empire State Building security footage and trying to match them to the database of photos we got from Faceplaced.

Claire Nelson, the girl we think is the fallen angel, was the first one uploaded into the database. The other choices are close enough to fool the security camera. They're the ones he picked to show up. How he got them to do so we don't know yet. It probably wouldn't be hard: a free trip, a contest—anything. Some of them appear to be with friends, so our angel's double is one of the few who appears to arrive by herself.

Gerald conferences in to tell us about the Warlock's latest deceit. Minutes before the double vanished, the Warlock sent out a status update on Claire Nelson's Facebook and Instagram. It was a selfie in front of the Empire State Building.

"On my way to the top!"

The message was meant to be cute and ironic. It's disturbing because we know who really wrote it.

I go with Knoll and the rest if his team back to the Times Square crime scene. Despite my interjections, I'm still just an adviser. I sit in the back and try to keep my mouth shut. There's a hierarchy here, and I don't want to pretend that just because I've had some clever insights I get to move to the front of the class. I've ruffled enough feathers already. Besides, none of them has been proven correct yet. And if I'm wrong on any of this, I could not only set the case back, people may die.

The NYPD has brought in three scissor lifts to allow us to look down on the scene from above. Knoll motions for me to join him on one. I climb under the railing and the operator takes us up thirty feet. A photographer on a separate lift is using a camera with an infrared lens to take pictures of Claire's body. We have no idea what other clues or taunts the Warlock may have left behind.

"Good work with your little stunt. We could have been chasing all over the building," says Knoll as we ascend.

"We'll see. I could just be making things worse." The lift comes to a stop and I have to grab the railing to keep from losing my balance.

"I ask myself that every five minutes," replies Knoll. "But that's why we work as a team. If one of us says something stupid, somebody else can point it out."

"Well, don't hesitate with me."

"I won't." He says this with a half smile. It's the first time I've seen his boxer face break into anything other than different degrees of serious around me.

I could tell how much he resented my presence when I was first pushed onto this case. I now realize it's not a matter of ego for him. He just wants to get the job done right. He felt I was being maneuvered onto the team out of politics. Which was true. For the first time he's acknowledging that I may have some value here yet. I hope I don't blow it.

Knoll's face tightens as he looks down at the body. "You have any kids, Blackwood?"

I'm sure he knows the answer by now but is making a polite inquiry. "No. I'm not sure if I'd make a good mother."

"I think you'd make a great one."

"Really?" I've had men tell me I was too detached, too cold. This surprises me coming from a hard ass like Knoll.

"It's the people who worry the most about being a good parent that do their best. At least I'd like to think so."

"You have kids?"

"Two girls and a boy. My oldest daughter is almost ready for college," he replies.

As he looks down on Claire Nelson I can only imagine what's going through his mind. He's a good cop and a thoughtful person. I can sense the fear he has about not being able to protect his own children from the evil in the world. His feeling of loss has to be greater than my own.

I've avoided long-term romantic attachments for one reason or another all my life. I've been in love, but never so much so that I was willing to take the kind of emotional risks that go with getting married or having children. I tell myself that someday I will when I meet the right guy. Someday. That seems like a thousand years from now. Unfortunately, biology isn't as patient. Beyond that, I wonder if my own analytical nature and mixed-up childhood have made it impossible for me to make that leap beyond logic and just go with my feelings. I could have met the right guy a dozen times for all I know.

My feminist side hates to acknowledge it, but when some women turn thirty they really do change. Maternal instincts, the urge to nest, go full bore. In a way I kind of hope these feelings will change me and my way of seeing things. Would I have given Terrence another chance? Will I open myself up to other opportunities? Will I let people in?

On some level I deeply understand the desire to turn off the rational part of one's mind and follow emotion. Sadly, this is also why so many people want to believe the Warlock is real. To them, he's the proof of the supernatural. He's evidence that there is such a thing as fate and that God or the universe has a plan for us.

But this is all just a trick. An illusion of mystery. The murdered girl, bleeding on the asphalt below us, is just a prop in the Warlock's twisted play.

In this moment I think I understand something about him. He's analytical. He's logical. He's not a believer in anything other than himself.

He wants to believe. He envies that ability for others to let go. He wants to embrace emotion and religious belief. He may even have convinced himself on some level that he does believe these things, but deep down he doesn't. He's manufacturing evidence because he sees none. God isn't a living entity for him, so he's trying to pretend he is God.

It's an unsettling insight for me. I call myself religious and go to church from time to time, but I know deep down, I'm not really a believer. Although I keep trying.

"Haven't found the right one?" asks Knoll, breaking me out of my thoughts.

"One?"

"Partner," he replies, using the politically correct term. Does he think I might be a lesbian? Wouldn't be the first time.

"Not yet." I should be thinking about Terrence. He's probably no more than five miles from here. But when Knoll said "partner," the person who comes to my mind isn't one I'd like to admit. It's Damian.

Forensics is about to move Claire's body. They've picked up the feathers and placed white chalk marks around the ones close to her.

"So how did she get here?" Knoll says, turning his mind back to the present.

I knew this question was coming the moment I saw the still image on the live feed back at Quantico. "She was dumped by one of the cars that passed by. Maybe a hole cut in the trunk." It's my only theory at the moment. I know it's weak. But it's all I've got.

Knoll nods as he tries to puzzle out what I just said.

The glittering lights are surreal. Broadway marquees, corporate logos, giant video screens and, in the middle of it all, a naked angel who appears to have fallen to earth. I shake my head as the news ticker rolls by, describing what just happened. Then I notice something new. They attribute it to "the Angel Killer."

I ask Knoll, "Angel Killer?"

"Our choice of words. Dr. Chisholm decided it's time we shifted the narrative away from the Warlock and take control of the message. We've never officially called him 'the Warlock.' I think this is better."

I like it a lot. "I agree. It puts a face on the victims. Maybe it adds to the mystery if we call her an angel, but I like the idea of making all the victims angels." I catch another headline out of the corner of my eye. I try to read it again before it changes.

I turn to Knoll, confused.

His voice is apologetic. "The tabloids decided to run with that. We've asked them not to. But it's too late. I'm sorry. The press got some pretty good photos of you when we arrived here. People have already made the connection."

There goes any hope of anonymity. There are thousands of people around us in Times Square. It feels as if half of them are looking up at us on our platform. I see the long lenses of professional cameras taking photographs of me. I want to shrink and hide. I know it's too late. It was too late before I even got here.

The ticker crawls by again. "FBI Agent Hunting Angel Killer Revealed to be Jessica Blackstar. Daughter of the Famous Magic Dynasty. Will the Witch Catch the Warlock?"

So that is how they're going to describe this game? Me versus him? My stomach wrenches. This is not the kind of attention I wanted, nor the responsibility it puts on me in the eyes of everyone watching.

Directly in front of me, a cable news channel screen just flashes a tour poster of me in leather pants, a diamond bustier, and a twenty-year-old's idea of a come-hither look.

Knoll watches the screen, then turns to me. "If you want to know what goes on in people's heads, ask Chisholm. But I'll tell you this. I'm glad this is out there. Maybe it's a little embarrassing. But that's not how people see it."

I shake my head and pretend to be calmer than I am. "I don't see how it helps. I'm just an adviser. It detracts from what we're doing. You're in charge of this case. Hundreds of people are working their asses off. Putting me up there is just a distraction."

"Only if you let it be. You've got to look at the big picture. People want to believe this guy is real. Sick as he is. They want to think he can bring back the dead, travel through time. Now he wants them to think he can open the door to heaven and yank an angel down from the sky. We're cops. We can find evidence and try to catch him. But when it comes to helping people see what he's really doing, he's winning. I think that's why we need you out here in front."

"Why?"

"Because you're one of the good guys. Forget the witch part. All people see is a good-looking woman from a famous family who gave it up to be a cop. That makes you a hero. And right now we need to remind people of the difference between good and evil when they get caught up in all these bullshit miracles. We got our own magician to take down this asshole."

He sounds a lot like Ailes. Part of me wonders if he has been talking to Ailes and Chisholm about leaking this to the press. It's cynical, but I wouldn't put it past them. The hero stuff sounds a lot like Chisholm's psy-ops babble.

It's frustrating. It's the last thing I want. I've had enough of the spotlight. I gave it up for a reason. I just want to help people. People like Claire, Denise, Swanson, and even Elsie.

But then I look down at Claire and realize I'm being selfish. She'd give anything to be where I am. Alive. Maybe Chisholm is right.

Forget about my personal issues coming to the foreground. I need to do what I do best: figure things out.

It's all about the trick.

The trick . . .

I see how the Warlock set this up.

I know what he did.

"Baking a cake in a spectator's hat." I say the words out loud.

"What?" Knoll gives me a confused look.

42

A GOOD MAGIC EFFECT plays upon the things you take for granted. It takes place in a situation in which you think I have little control. We're sitting in your living room with a deck of cards. I ask you to pick one. I rip off a corner and hand the piece to you. I then take the remainder of your card and set it on fire in the fireplace. After you watch the ashes finish burning I point to the drink in your hand. You notice that one of the ice cubes in your glass has a folded card frozen inside it. It's the card you picked, minus the corner you're holding. You've been holding the drink all along.

It's your house, your glass, you even poured the drink. You understand how conceivably I could fold a card and freeze it inside an ice cube, but not how I could have done all of that while we're sitting on your couch chatting.

Instead of a sealed envelope in a safe standing onstage, I've done this in a natural setting. There were no trick boxes or smoke machines. I did this in your environment. Putting a dead girl in the middle of Times Square required the same kind of misdirection as getting that ice cube into your drink. Only the scale was different.

Getting it there also involved something that looked natural.

The method reminded me of the trick I just mentioned to Knoll.

I watch the street beyond the barrier blocking the bystanders from the crime scene. Cars pass and try to see what's in plain sight. What's right in front of us? Lots of yellow flashes by.

"A taxi," I explain. Half the cars here are taxis. If I wanted to be invisible, I'd use a taxi. "Probably a minivan. Hollowed-out floor. There's an old trick where you'd bake a cake in a spectator's hat. Never mind. I think that's what he used. A taxi. Not a hat. Sorry. She was dropped from underneath and then concealed in the middle of the street for a few seconds."

Knoll looks at the cars on the other side of the barrier. "What about the explosion? People swear they saw her fall. And the dent in the ground?" He points to Claire. "Her face sunk a two-inch hole in the pavement."

"Are potholes rare in this town? Maybe he used a shape charge. Or he could have made the hole himself a few hours before by soaking the asphalt with gasoline. I made that mistake once trying to fill the lawnmower. That would soften it up."

I'm about to ask to be lowered down to see another replay of the first tourist video when I notice that it is playing on a loop on one of the monitors in Times Square.

My college media professor would flip his lid at how meta all this is. I'm in the middle of a crime scene, in the middle of one of the most famous tourist spots on the planet, and I'm surrounded by news images of what just happened.

The video shows several cars, most of them taxis, passing in front of the camera. A taxi minivan drives by, and a second later there's an explosion behind it. White feathers fall to the ground and the camera pans down to discover Claire's body. It looks like she falls, but we don't actually see her fall, just the aftermath, an explosion of white.

Knoll is squinting, trying to catch the drop. "I don't know. The closest cab was at least five yards away. It doesn't look like she was dumped. People would have thought he ran her over."

The video is grainy and out of focus. All of the ones we've seen so far have been. Nobody was pointing their camera directly at the street while it happened. There are no cars behind that last cab, so we don't have a witness to tell us what they saw from behind.

This is one of the most public locations in the world. Yet, like a theater stage, nobody is looking where they should be until after the illusion happens. To get past the misdirection I have to think of method. I have to stop for a moment and ask myself how I would do it. Not how he did it.

There are two parts to the deception: dropping her body and then creating the illusion she fell. The feathers in the air could be propelled by an explosion. A small charge could send a bundle into the air where it would explode. Wrapped in black tissue paper, done fast enough, none of the cameras would catch it.

"Did forensics pick up any explosive residue?" I ask.

"No. The NYPD bomb squad was on the scene in minutes. They swabbed everything. Negative."

I rap my fingernails on the edge of the metal rail and try to visualize the explosion as it looked from where I'm standing. For some of my pyrotechnics, I'd use an air cannon powered by a cylinder of CO_2. Obviously, nothing like that was found around her body. The bomb squad would be all over it. Was it hidden somehow?

Most performers paint their little boxes of flash powder or smoke black. Grandfather taught me to always keep a couple of cans of paint on hand to match the color of the stage. This helps them blend in. It hides the fact that the smoke comes from a physical prop. It makes it magical.

What if he hid Claire's body and the cannon long enough to create a sense of distance? Time can be used to create an illusion. If my empty left hand grasps thin air, then makes a tossing motion toward a glass in my right hand and you hear a clink, it sounds like I made a coin appear. Your brain connects the action with the sound, but the coin was hidden in my right hand all along, holding the glass. If you'd been watching my right hand, you'd notice the fingers were at an odd angle, possibly hiding something. Maybe the Warlock used a kind of camouflage that only needed to work for a few seconds?

I direct Knoll's attention to what I'm seeing in my head. "Look at the area where she appeared and then the street on either side. Notice that she's in between two crosswalks? They're nice and bright while the unpainted street she's on is dark in comparison. He could have dropped her off behind the cab, but have her covered by some kind of fabric that looks like the asphalt. It only has to be there for a few seconds. In the video it looks like his exhaust is kind of thick too."

"What happened to the covering?"

"A long roller blind attached to the cab. After the cab goes, say, fifteen feet away, it retracts. Probably has an air cannon at the end of it. That gets pulled into the underside of the taxi. We get our explosive-free explosion and our revelation all at once."

Knoll scratches his bald head. "Sounds complicated."

"Imagine if I covered you in a black cloth and threw you out of my moving van onto a dark street in the middle of the night. Only the cloth has a cable running back to the van. After a few yards I yank it back up. If someone is walking their dog, what would it look like?"

"Like I just appeared in the street. But this is a brightly lit intersection. Someone would have noticed . . ."

"Would they? We have thick exhausts, steam grates, almost black asphalt, and a thousand bright objects above us. All the people here are either looking up at the lights or at each other. All of the video we have is amateur footage that wasn't aimed where we wanted to see."

Knoll's eyes look up as he tries to visualize what I'm describing. "I don't know."

"Well, I think it's a better explanation than she fell from heaven. She got here somehow. Besides, the mechanics of this method I mentioned have been used for hundreds of years. If a clockmaker could build this into a mechanical magic trick two hundred years ago, I don't think the Warlock would have a problem. All the elements for distraction are here." I think of how we'd use masking tape to map out a stage on the living room floor, marking out curtains, props and where to stand. The Warlock must have done something like this, dry-running the effect hundreds of times. "He only needs a second or two."

The video replays again on the screen above us. I think Knoll is watching it this time with my explanation in mind. It's of such low quality it's hard to tell for certain, but my theory fits the facts. And that's what we really need now: an explanation. Something consistent with the evidence, which gives us a place to start searching for clues and allows us to say we aren't fooled.

Knoll is beginning to get the idea. "I guess we need to look for phantom cabs now. He had hours to ditch it. It could be hard."

My bet is on it being impossible. He's not going to leave us a piece of evidence that helps us prove how he did it. Part of me wonders if he was even in the cab when it happened. He could

have hired a driver and rigged it with remotes. Maybe use an accomplice who has no idea what they're really doing? Would he
want to be in the driver's seat or somewhere out here watching?

Was he already on his way to kill the girl from the Empire
State Building?

43

WE HAVE THEM lower the lift so we can get out and take a walk around Times Square. A young girl, maybe sixteen, too young to be out this late, leans across the police barrier with her camera and shouts to me, "Can I take my picture with you?"

It's embarrassing. I give Knoll a glance. He steps over to the girl and takes the camera from her. "Agent Blackwood would be happy to." He motions for me to stand next to her.

I try to smile as he takes the photo. He hands the camera back to the excited girl. She shakes my hand and blurts out, "You're my hero! Go get this asshole!"

I give her a polite nod and turn to follow Knoll. "That wasn't what I was hoping for," I reply, not hiding my frustration for feeling so ridiculous.

"It's what we need. You're already a hero in my house."

Knoll takes a phone call from the state police, then fills me in on the search for the other girls. They stopped seventeen tour buses headed in different directions on the map. They found two girls who match the description. One of them at a highway rest stop a half hour beyond the Pennsylvania border on her way to Canada.

A thin smile forms on Knoll's face as he gets the news. "I think we got her."

KATYA VOLNICK, a pretty blond nineteen-year-old Slovenian girl who can speak about ten words of English, was very upset with the troopers when they stopped her. She was waiting at the rest stop for the man with the contest to give her the next clue in the scavenger hunt she was on, and was angry that they might ruin her free vacation. The police tried to explain to her that she did not want the prize the man was going to give her.

It took them a half hour to find a native speaker of Slovene. Through the interpreter, Katya confirmed that she was the one in the video and following instructions from "Mikhail" via a cell phone that had been provided for her. She still had the wig in her purse.

It was a game for her. Recruited back home by an e-mail, she followed the instructions on the cell phone she was given and got to see New York. All of it for some American reality show or Internet thing, or so she was told. All she cared about was the money she was promised and the free trip to the United States.

KNOLL GIVES US the details in the conference room at the FBI field office in Tribeca. Police tried to stake out the rest stop, but "Mikhail" never showed up.

I kick myself for not thinking of looking for tour buses sooner. We could have caught him if we hadn't had to stop the bus at the last minute. The troopers did the right thing, but it burns me. The asshole was close. Real close. Knoll and everyone else are jubilant that we caught a break and just saved a life. I guess I am too. But we almost had him. Damn it.

After the briefing I call Ailes with the news. He'd been

sleeping on a couch in the bullpen waiting for an update. I can't remember when I had a full night's rest either. I look like a zombie in the reflection as the tinted window exaggerates the circles under my eyes.

"That's great news. But you sound angry, Jessica," he tells me.

I pace the New York FBI room trying to sort things out in my head. "We could have got him. He was probably following the bus. The creep got away again." He's always a step ahead.

"Jessica. I think you're missing an important detail. We saved the girl. If it hadn't been for you, we'd never have known about her. He would have killed her and she would have vanished from history. We stopped him. That should make you feel good."

"I know. But we didn't save Claire. We had the information, but we couldn't put it together in time." I stop pacing to sit on the edge of a table and stare at a wall full of missing-persons photos. The faces look back with happy expressions, unaware of what fate has in store for them. There's a map next to the photos with pins at locations where each of them was last.

Ailes continues, "We're getting closer. Close enough to save at least one person. He knows the noose is getting tighter. And he probably still doesn't know about our ace in the hole, that we're inside the website he used to track down some of his victims. This information is putting us closer. If he tries to kill again, we might be able to be there this time."

"If?"

"Some of Chisholm's people think this may have been the final murder. At least for a while. If we only count them as miracles, this is the third one. Like a trinity. The first one was in the ground. The second was in the sky. The third was in heaven. It has a nice kind of symmetry to it. Doesn't it? The Bible loves threes."

"I think it's wishful thinking," I reply, perhaps a little too tersely. "I think he's saving the best for last." I still can't get the five classical elements out of my mind. I used to build my show around a five-part structure. Three may be a holy number. Five offers a sense of completeness. "I think there's going to be at least two more."

I can hear Ailes sigh on the other end of the phone. "Yeah, maybe I do too."

Symmetry. I roll the thought around in my head for a moment. The Warlock wants to show everyone how clever he is. Even going as far as planting little Easter eggs like the sand and the feather. Nothing is left to chance. The last two murders were revealed in carefully chosen locations. The plane appeared near where it was last seen in 1945. Claire was supposed to have died in the most public place in the world. A taunting gesture if there ever was one. The one part that doesn't fit is the graveyard. It got our attention, but it doesn't have the narrative of the others. It was just a cemetery. Sure, it was where his real first victim was buried. But why her and why there?

"Dr. Ailes, can you hold on a second?" I set the phone on speaker, put it down and grab some of the pins stuck to the side of the map. There's something about the cemetery that's odd.

I stick a pin in the town in Michigan. I push another in Fort Lauderdale and a third in New York City.

A triangle.

"Dr. Ailes. The last three murders form a triangle if you look at them on a map."

He lets out a small laugh. "Jessica, any three points on a map will make a triangle. It's getting late. You need some sleep."

I look at the triangle in front of me. "I know. I know. But this is a pretty nice triangle." I'm embarrassed I can't remember the mathematical word for it. I rummage through the top drawer of a desk and find a ruler and a marker. I trace the lines of the triangle on the map. Two sides look perfectly even. "What's the distance from Manhattan to the cemetery?"

Ailes asks me to hold and calls out to Gerald. A minute later he has the answer. "One thousand and sixty miles."

"What's the distance from Fort Lauderdale to Manhattan?"

There's a long pause.

Ailes clears his throat. "Damn, about one thousand and sixty miles! Give or take. Curious. Real curious. You know, Jessica, you're talking to three mathematicians who didn't notice this. You may have missed your real calling. That's a perfect triangle!"

"I'm sure one of the FBI computers would have picked it up sooner or later." And remember what an isosceles triangle was called.

"Maybe. But only if we ask it to. Usually we only use the Data Integration and Visualization System computer when we think someone is dumping bodies randomly and can't find a connection. Gerald is going to put these coordinates in and see what we come up with. Could be something. We might have the next location in here somewhere. Now that you've schooled the math teacher, go get some rest. And feel good. You saved a life today." I sense a touch of pride in his voice.

I take a van with the other agents to the hotel where we're checked in. We're all tired. Some of them seem a little excited about the fact that we saved Katya. I guess they're right to. We showed up here expecting to pick up the pieces of a murder, but we got lucky and saved someone. Barely. Still too late for Claire.

I put the keycard into the lock and kick the newspaper in front of the door across the hall. Above the fold is a high-resolution photo of Claire. In a smaller box is my photo and a headline about me, "FBI Magician on Hunt for Angel Killer."

I can't get away from this bullshit. I have to resist the urge to throw the paper down the hall.

Too tired to even take a bath, I just set my alarm, undress, crawl into bed, and shut my eyes. I'm still too wound-up to sleep, but if I can keep my eyes closed long enough . . .

A minute after my head hits the pillow, the phone on the nightstand rings. I answer without thinking. I should know that only one person ever calls me on actual hotel phones.

"Hello, beautiful. Seen the paper today?"

44

▎ BOLT UPRIGHT. Damian's voice stirs up memories of the conversation in the director's office about him. My reaction to Knoll asking about a "partner" makes me blush when I hear his voice. "Where are you?"

"Too far away for a cuddle, if that's what you're asking for."

"Go to hell. Where are you?" Still holding the phone, I get out of bed and grab my mobile off the desk.

"Why do you care so much all of a sudden?"

"Because you're our number one suspect after that with Faceplaced stunt you pulled." I try to keep the conversation going as I send a text message to Knoll and the ops dispatcher in Quantico.

Damian Knight on my hotel phone. Can u trace? Room 2032.

"Can't a citizen help out law enforcement without being made a suspect?"

"Not when they're you," I reply.

"I see that we were too late for that poor girl in Times Square."

We haven't released information about the girl we think we saved, so I keep my mouth shut.

Damian senses my hesitation. "Ah . . . I'm glad to see my

money wasn't totally wasted. He knows you're getting close now. You probably came within just minutes of catching him. Better to save the girl first . . . I suppose."

"How do I know this whole thing is not one of your stupid games?"

There's a long pause. "Me? Murder is too boring. And, you know, morally wrong. I do have my version of morals. I'm also not the type that likes the attention. This Warlock, well, we all know he's got a god complex. But gods do hate it when mortals mess with their plans."

I speak calmly. "Damian, how can I know it's not you?"

I have to be objective about this. Despite my gut feelings, Damian is clearly the most suspicious person in this whole thing. My stomach feels queasy at the thought that he might be playing me along, deceiving me again. That he could be a cold-blooded serial killer is too much to handle.

I regain my calm. "Damian. You've lied before. There's no reason to trust you. No reason for me to trust you."

"Are we still on that? Fine. Before I hang up I'll give you all the proof you need. Of course, I think you're probably already working on that. To be honest, I called this number because I was sure they'd be tapping it. Transparency, eh?"

Tapping my phone? I catch a glimpse of my naked body in the mirror and suddenly feel vulnerable. Would they bug my phone? Of course they did. I would.

If Damian is our only person of interest and Chisholm could tell I was being evasive, why not? They know it's only a matter of time before Damian calls me again. And now here he is on the other end of the line.

"Why are you calling?" I ask.

"A few reasons. I had an interesting chat with a man from

Tulsa who brought up some curious things. A churchgoing man, he saw the news on a bar television and all of a sudden felt the urge to get good with the Lord. He ran to the nearest church. I tried to tell him nobody is home. I don't know if you're aware of this, but late-night masses are starting to fill up everywhere. Who knows what tomorrow's going to look like. This angel killing stunt is darkly brilliant. This country is experiencing a religious revival because of the Warlock."

I was afraid of this. Right now when you say the word "miracle," the first thing that comes up is the Warlock. Good or evil, he's made himself the center of religious discussion. Each deception elevates him in people's minds. He's created something bigger than all the people watching Times Square.

"I doubt people see anything godly in what he did," I reply.

"Maybe not. I think what he's really trying to do is challenge God or at least our notion of him. And that might be enough."

"Enough for what?"

"He wants followers. He's waiting to make sure he's proven himself. Then he's going to give us his real message. Unless he's already sent you something?"

I'm silent. There's nothing I can say, but I don't want anyone thinking that I'm feeding Damian information. I'm under enough scrutiny.

"I think he'll do it in a public way. He doesn't want you hiding the message. Unless he wants to give it to you first and then reveal the fact that you were trying to suppress it. That's the first step to creating a religion—show the people that the authorities are trying to hide the truth. I think you've interfered with his plans, however. I suspect he's going to step up the timetable a bit."

"That's obvious."

"Of course. This is just a friendly reminder. Remember what I said before about him having his sights set on you? I think that's still true. But now there's another problem. He may not have to do anything to hinder you. The kind of fervor that sends people to midnight mass is also the kind of thing to inspire the more unstable parts of our society. Proud as I was to see your face in the paper, I think you may have more admirers than you can handle."

This is a repercussion I do not want to think about. It's one thing to deal with Damian and the Warlock leaving vague threats in hotel rooms. It's another to have to worry about every psycho out there waiting for a sign who might see my face in the news and get an idea.

"Don't worry, Jessica. I'm sure after you catch him, this will die down and then I can go back to being your number one fan."

That's unsettling. "You may be the worst of them."

"You know that's not true. Anyhow, how's the next clue going? I have to assume he's been leaving calling cards."

We haven't found one yet. As I went to sleep forensics was still going over the body. But Damian's voice sounds like it's a certainty.

"What clue?" I ask.

"Really?" Damian sounds genuinely surprised. "I mean, it seemed obvious to me. Of course I don't have the whole picture. Just the direction, so to speak."

He's being cryptic. "What do you know?"

"Fine. Make me explain everything. First off, the media has it wrong. Typically, of course. She's not an angel."

"We know this, Damian," I try to keep the frustration out of my voice, remembering that others may be listening.

"No. I mean in the Christian Bible, angels don't have wings.

This girl does. In other mythologies, like Babylonian, they do. Of course, that's academic. What they can all agree on is that winged beings are either messengers or, as the Babylonians described them, watchers. Messengers or watchers, take your pick. If she's not here to tell us something obvious, then logic would dictate she's watching something. What was she looking at, Jessica?"

She was looking at something? Damn. I spent over an hour at the crime scene and never bothered to think about this. I even stared down at her haunted eyes. I was so focused on figuring out how he did it, I didn't bother to ask why. None of us did. We forgot the Warlock is trying to tell a story.

The angel herself is the clue.

A text message comes up on my phone from Knoll with a Las Vegas phone number.

Damian sighs. "I can see this didn't dawn on you and your friends. I'm sure you were all tired. Maybe I'm wrong. But we know I'm not. Either way, if you go have a look to see what your angel is watching, don't go alone. I think I'm going to have a nap myself. I've been up for three days straight. If you call this number, just ask for Mr. Smith. I won't be here, though. But you'll get all the proof of my innocence you need. And one more thing . . ."

"What's that?" I ask.

"Put something on. You'll catch cold."

He hangs up, leaving me staring at my naked reflection. He's thousands of miles away, yet he knows me. He knows me better than I know myself.

45

A MINUTE AFTER DAMIAN hangs up on the hotel telephone, Knoll calls me on my mobile.

"We traced it to the Bellagio casino in Las Vegas. We're sending some uniformed police to pick him up."

"He won't be there. He knows you're coming," I explain with a sigh.

"It's worth a try," Knoll replies tersely. "We've told security there too."

"Yes, of course."

"Kind of sloppy of him to use a landline like that."

Knoll doesn't know Damian. "No. He wants us to know where he is. Call the number back and ask for Mr. Smith."

"We're checking on that. See you downstairs in ten," Knoll says before he hangs up.

I get dressed while I wait for Knoll to call back. I have to see what the angel was looking at. I'm exhausted, but I need to know. I send an e-mail to Ailes describing Damian's insight, then go down to the lobby to get a cup of coffee and wait for the rest of the team who were in on the phone call.

Three minutes later he steps from the elevator flanked by two of our forensic people from Quantico. Knoll sees me and shakes his head. "Security at the Bellagio said he left right after he hung up on the house phone. They're going to double check their security footage, but they're pretty sure the man who made that call is the same person they've been watching for the last three days at the poker tables. He only gets up to use the bathroom. Other than that he hasn't moved more than a hundred feet for seventy-two hours. Nuts."

"Yes. Insane. That would be Damian." Leave it to him to figure out how to give himself an airtight alibi and still stay out of our reach.

"They ran his image through their own database. Nothing came up. The casino also says he broke even after three days of solid play. That's a trick in itself."

That would be Damian making a point.

Fifteen minutes later we're back in Times Square. NYPD still has the street blocked off, but the body has been moved to the medical examiner's office. There's an outline of tape marking where the body had lain. Three techs in hard hats are using a saw to cut the asphalt out of the ground where she appeared to have landed. A road crew is standing by with hot gravel to patch it after them. In a few hours it'll be like it never happened. This city seriously never sleeps.

One of Knoll's agents has brought a large printout of a photograph documenting the placement of Claire's body on the ground. It looks like it was taken from the overhead lift. The woman sets it on the sidewalk a few yards away from where Claire was found and rotates it to match her position.

We step back and take a look across the street in the same direction Claire was looking. The buildings are covered with electronic billboards. One of the agents, a tired-looking man with uncombed hair and an FBI jacket like mine, starts taking photographs of everything in front of us. I'm sure we already have this shot uploaded onto a server in Quantico by now, but it doesn't hurt to be thorough.

Knoll takes a sip from his coffee cup and surveys the array of fashion models displaying clothing, perfume and watches. "So which one didn't Leonardo DiCaprio date?"

There are a million things in front of us. Everything around us is demanding our attention. Anything could be a clue. The time on a watch. The image on one of the giant televisions. The models. The information overload is overwhelming. Somewhere back in Quantico, a room full of analysts will pore all over these images for hours or days trying to find something.

Maybe we're being too literal? I remember something about a fingerprint on a cornea leading to a killer. "We ever have anything left on someone's eyes before?"

"Dust, metal fragments. Sometimes fibers. Semen." Knoll has another drink of his coffee in the absentminded way cops deal with the morbid.

We're facing west and the sun is rising behind us. Rays of light start to shine through the streets. I once read an article about Manhattanhenge, a phenomenon that occurs two times a year when the sun is exactly parallel to the streets and sends shafts of light straight through the buildings like an ancient monolith. I look at my own shadow and think of something.

I call Ailes.

Gerald answers. "Hello?"

"Gerald, is Dr. Ailes there?"

Knoll raises an eyebrow.

"He's sleeping on the couch. His wife said she'd kill me if I wake him. Can I help you?"

"Do you have the crime scene photos location-mapped on

the DIVS computer?" Every time we take a photograph we record the position and angle and then upload it into the computer to make a virtual crime scene in 3-D we can go back to later on. For outdoor crime scenes, it's useful to plug in GPS data so you can see where everything is in relation to the world. The position of a body in a ravine can tell you the direction in which someone walked down it. Sometimes that can lead right to one house out of a hundred and narrow your search for clues like hair and fibers.

"Yeah. I'm pulling it up now. What do you need?" I can tell he's tired, but like me, he's eager to chase down whatever clues we can.

"Looking at it from overhead, can you extend a virtual line from the victim's eyes into the horizon?" I ask.

"One second. Let me create a vector at her eyes. What's our margin of error, given the angle?"

I don't know how precisely the Warlock was able to drop the body. This experiment could be way off or have nothing to do with this at all. "I don't know. Is there some other way to make it fuzzy?"

"If you have other data points, yeah. We can approximate it."

Other data points. I think about the push pins in the missing person's map back in the Tribeca office. "What about the GPS coordinates of the other two murders?"

"Maybe . . . I see if anything fits nicely."

"Imagine there are five points and we know three of them. And they're either the same distance as New York and Fort Lauderdale or the cemetery and Fort Lauderdale." I hope I have my geometry right.

"Got it."

I can hear him type away at the keyboard faster than I can

even think of letters. I have no idea where Ailes found Gerald. I get the impression he snatched him out of some genius startup company. The relationship feels like a professor to a prized grad student.

"Huh. That's spooky. I think I got the pattern and the angle right."

"Gerald, what is it?" My heart begins to pound and I get that tingle on my body.

There's a long pause. "Let me just text you the photo."

Knoll watches over my shoulder as the image loads onto my screen. "Holy shit."

No kidding.

If we follow where she's looking and assume there are five locations, she's looking at the bottom of a star.

It's a pentagram.

One of the most occult symbols there is. The Warlock is etching one across the United States. The Sumerians used it, so did the ancient Chinese. For the Greeks it was a symbol of the creation of the cosmos. In early Christianity it symbolized the five wounds of Christ. Turning it upside-down made the symbol into a satanic symbol. It's not just any pattern; it's the pattern of all patterns. And right in front of us.

So far three points are murder scenes. The remaining two aren't. Yet.

Our angel is staring at a town in south Texas.

I'll leave the mathematical permutations of how he managed it to Ailes and his geniuses. However he did it, the warlock got the result he wanted. One more "Fuck you" in the middle of everything else.

The angel is watching a town called Santa Lucia.

Saint Lucy, patron saint of the blind.

46

Back in quantico, ten hours after we left Times Square, Agent Johnson—one of Knoll's task force members, a man with a slight build and curly blond hair who resembles a wise elf—is pointing at a molecule on an overhead screen.

While I was grabbing a nap in the dorm after we got back, they made a lot of progress. They have found more clues. Not the kind the Warlock left for us intentionally, as far as we can tell. Telltale signs of how he pulled off the illusion.

Based on my conversation with Knoll, New Jersey police spoke to a supervisor at a welding supply shop in Hackensack who said a man in a taxi van picked up a cylinder of CO_2 the day before. He had a vague description: medium build, goatee. He said he'd recognize him again if we had a photograph.

After being unable to find any signs of ligatures or bruising on Swanson's and Denise's bodies our medical examiners expanded their toxicology search. In a kidnapping case, presence of certain chemicals is a clear sign that someone was drugged. However, screenings for the usual suspects, like the date rape drug Rohypnol, didn't show anything.

Johnson circles the molecule with his laser pointer. "A search for scopolamine and some of the more obscure tropane alkaloids used to incapacitate someone came back negative. We were about to move on when we decided to do a screening for any substance with a tropane ring. That's when we found this. The nitrogen bond is in a different place, suggesting this is some kind of synthetic. We're reaching out to pharmacology experts and doing a search of the literature to see if this has cropped up before. Our assumption is that it would have the same effects of scopolamine, but break down faster. A synthetic that the Warlock could expect our screenings to miss.

"This drug in its original form, ingested through an injection or even a spray, would render someone in a somewhat zombie-like state and leave them with little memory. We believe our suspect is using this substance to help subdue his victims and keep them under control until he kills them. They would be docile and have very little motor function. He could administer the drug with something as simple as an aerosol. One spray and you're under."

One of our early assessments was that the Warlock might be involved in drug trafficking or manufacturing. This gives that theory a whole lot more credibility. He might not just be a chemist working with known drugs, but an inventor of new kinds of drugs. Nothing about him would surprise me at this point.

Knoll takes the podium. He looks like he hasn't slept since we returned from New York. "Thank you, Agent Johnson. A few hours ago our friends in the DEA brought something to our attention that may be a major break. Five days ago, in cooperation with Brazilian authorities, they raided a pharmaceutical company thirty miles outside of Rio. The company was under suspicion for supplying compounds on the black market used in the manufacture of a variety of narcotics, including the kind that would be used to manufacture the drug Johnson just mentioned. In searching through their shipping records, DEA found a shipment two weeks ago, of something I can't pronounce, to an address of a hotel approximately twelve miles away from where the first victim was originally found.

"We've obtained a copy of the signature on the receipt from the courier company. The name is 'Jose Doe,' obviously an alias, Handwriting analysis suggests the same person who signed for it also signed for the CO2 canister in New Jersey. It's circumstantial, but we think it's the strongest lead we have so far. We know this man is involved in the illegal drug trade, is probably wealthy, has access to boats and aircraft. Behavioral analysis is working with the DEA to check our profile against their database of known offenders and suspects. We're also checking the signature against FAA records and Coast Guard certification."

It's a tenuous link, yet our best one so far, only discovered because I thought the Warlock may have needed a CO2 canister to cause the explosion. One of those wildcard, stab-in-the-dark leads that hit pay dirt. In this case, a link to our Michigan crime that would have gone ignored. As Knoll makes the connections, I allow myself a small smile. The Warlock is human. He's making mistakes.

When he was in Michigan preparing to kill Denise, Chloe's twin sister, he made another batch of his knockout drug in a portable lab. I've seen suitcase-sized kits capable of producing small batches of everything from LSD to meth. Little did he realize that his signature on a FedEx form there would connect him to a welding supply shop in New Jersey. Different names. Same man. You can change your letters, but it's hard to change the shape of your hand and your unique way of drawing curves and lines.

Knoll clicks the remote and shows an image of Claire in Times Square. "Forensics has found dust fragments on the victim's body that suggest the traumatic impact that broke her bones took place somewhere else, which we already suspected. We don't have a geological match yet, but we believe we've found traces of volcanic ash. This suggests he dropped the body somewhere on the West Coast. We're talking to volcanologists to see if we can place that more approximately, although our current priority is stopping the next murder and apprehending this man."

The Warlock drops the girl in the middle of nowhere to break her bones, then brings her to New York to make it look like she falls from the sky. If he flew his own plane, avoided the major traffic corridors and landed at a private airfield, he could have done the trip in a few hours.

Knoll introduces an equally tired Dr. Ailes, who tells us that his team made a big leap with the Faceplaced image data once they got more computational resources from the NSA. A slide of a petite brunette appears behind him. She can't be more than sixteen. She reminds me a little of the girl who asked for my photograph last night. "We think this is our next victim," explains Ailes. "In going through the data, this girl's photograph has been accessed five times from IP addresses that lead to anonymous proxies, similar to the other victims. We don't have her name yet, but our computers think the trees and landscape behind her suggest somewhere in south Texas. We've got agents calling high schools in the area to try to identify her. All of the previous victims were killed within twenty-four hours of their discovery. Last night's murder is still only less than a day old. We have every reason to think she's still alive and we can get to her before the Warlock does."

Knoll returns to the podium. "We're setting up a covert outpost outside of Santa Lucia and working with Texas law enforcement to create a dragnet to apprehend the Warlock. It's a good bet that he's already headed to or in the vicinity. Let's catch him, folks."

What does the Warlock have planned for her? Is this girl going to be the assumed public victim like Chloe or our angel, Claire? Or is she going to be a double for another victim, like Katya? Is she even the fourth victim?

I stop Knoll before he leaves. "What about the fifth point in Colorado?"

"We're sending a team there. It's in the middle of nowhere, though. I can't see what he'd want out there."

"A little town in south Texas isn't exactly Metropolis either."

Dr. Chisholm walks over to us. "Second thoughts, Blackwood?"

"I just don't know. Everything is meant to get bigger. Are we missing something?"

"You seemed certain he wouldn't realize how far we've come," replies Chisholm.

"Yes. But I'm sure he knows we'll pick up on the pentagram sooner or later. He has to be aware we're going to be looking in these places. There's something missing," I explain.

"What about this girl?" asks Chisholm. "A wild-goose chase?"

"No. I still don't think he realizes we know his Faceplaced gimmick yet. I'm sure she's a real target," I reply. He's counting on us proceeding at our normal pace with our standard procedures.

"Then let's focus on saving her," says Knoll. "If it's all we can do right now."

I agree, but I'm still uneasy. I notice Chisholm seems a little unsure as well. We're interrupted by a young agent handing me a slip of paper.

"This came in through the main switchboard," he says.

I read the note:

324 Cascade Lane, Derry, MI. They haven't paid their water bill in two months. Love, D.

I hand the note to Knoll. He reads it over and looks up at me. "What does this mean?"

I type the address into my phone and pull up a map. The pin drop on Google Maps is about eight miles from the cemetery where we found Chloe's twin. "I think it's Damian giving us a clue."

"There's not much we can act on there," says Chisholm. "Maybe at best a stakeout. But it hardly seems worth it. He might just be vying for attention. Although that only makes him more suspicious in my mind."

"He's plenty suspicious, but I'm sure it's worth looking into. Damian has been on target so far," I reply.

"Yes, he has," Chisholm replies with a touch of suspicion in his voice.

Knoll's face contorts. "I think your friend has been doing his homework. Back when I was a police detective we were looking for meth houses in a neighborhood block. We had it pinned down to fifty units, but we needed to narrow things down even more. No judge would grant us search warrants for all of those houses. Instead, we just needed to know which ones weren't the house. To eliminate the houses that weren't likely to be the meth house, the DA came up with a clever gimmick. He got the mayor to deputize us as Water Commission inspectors to walk on property and look at water meters. We could search the outside of all the houses when we looked for the meters."

"I don't see how that's admissible," replies Chisholm.

"It was," says Knoll. "We had probable cause that one of those fifty houses was the meth lab. After we searched the premises of forty-nine of the fifty and found nothing, only one house stood out as suspicious. No evidence that we found as Water Commission inspectors was used in court against the lab operators."

"But you already knew by then which house was the meth lab," insists Chisholm.

"I could smell it in their backyard. But our warrant didn't mention that. We just testified that forty-nine other houses were ruled out. The judge ruled that it would have been unreasonable for us to stake out the other houses if we lawfully knew they weren't the ones we were looking for."

"That's clever," I reply. "We could see if this address is worth investigating."

Knoll nods. "I'm going to send you and Danielle there. I'll check in with our field office and the Michigan Bureau of Investigations."

"What about Texas?" I ask.

"We'll hold down the fort there."

Chisholm has a pained look. "I don't like this. We don't know what's in there. It could be a trap."

"I don't think the Warlock knows we're coming," I reply.

"I'm not sure if it's him I'm worried about." Chisholm still doesn't trust Damian.

Neither do I.

I express my own doubts. "I find it scary too that he's the only one who seems to know how the Warlock thinks."

Chisholm looks me in the eye. "I'm not sure he's the only one."

I was beginning to warm up to him. This sends a chill down my spine.

47

THERE'S A LIGHT RAIN as we stand outside the metal fence surrounding the property. Thunderclouds rumble in the distance. The local FBI office has staked the place out per our request for the last twelve hours while Danielle and I traveled here and Knoll cleared things with the local authorities. Agent Shannon picked us up from the airport and gave us the rundown on the way over.

"We flew a sheriff's helicopter overhead. We didn't see any cars or evidence of recent activity. Thermal imaging didn't show us anything either. We're pretty sure nobody is there."

On the satellite image, the property looks like a large warehouse with a few smaller buildings on the lot. Most of the land appears to be a junkyard. Property records show it was purchased two years ago. Around the time Chloe was murdered. It's not proof of anything, but it's a meaningful coincidence.

The title holder is a company called JTC Investments, incorporated in the Virgin Islands. The D.C. bureau is trying to get to the bottom of it. Unlike the Warlock's Fort Lauderdale hotel reservation under an attention-getting name, this was not meant to be discovered.

Danielle has her arms crossed as we stare at the fence. Solid aluminum panels make it impossible to see into the lot. Our four sheriff's department escorts and five field office agents look anxious as they wait for us to decide what to do next.

The local water meter inspector we had to bring with us is staring down at the lock on the gate, not sure what he should do. In a normal inspection he'd make two calls to the premises, then ask the sheriff's department to serve a notice if there was no response.

I gently push him aside and look at the lock. It's a simple barrel lock. "Would you ask Agent Reed what she thinks?" I tell the inspector, sending him over to Danielle.

She gives me a funny look. I give her a wink. The inspector begins to walk away and I grip the lock. Five second later it falls to the ground. The inspector spins around and stares at the lock resting in the dirt. "I guess it was already unlocked," I reply innocently.

Shannon shakes his head. "I'm not sure if this is procedure." There's a trace of a smile on his face. "But I guess it's legal if it's unlocked."

I reach for the gate to push it open. Danielle's hand snaps out and grabs my wrist. "Hold up there, darlin'. We don't know what he may have on the other side."

"We checked it from the air," replies Shannon.

"She's right." I pull my hand back. I lost my head in the moment. "We don't want him knowing we're here. I wouldn't put it past him to have some kind of surveillance system in place. The moment we walk in the door, he'll know we found his secret spot. And if there's a chance he might come back here, we don't want to ruin it."

"So what do we do? Got a trick for that?" asks Shannon.

Another thunderclap booms in the distance. "Yes. I think so. If he has this place under surveillance he's probably using an Internet connection. If we cut power to the whole block when there's another lighting strike, it'll shut that off."

"Then what? I'm sure he has a backup plan," Shannon points out. "This guy is clever. Real clever."

Shannon is right. Cutting the power won't be enough. I'm sure the Warlock had thought about the possibility of this place being discovered. Who knows what kind of booby traps he could have set up here. If he has something to hide, he might want to take the whole place out. We saw what he did to the body in the cemetery.

"Hold on," I say. "Maybe we need to get some of our own geniuses on this."

I call up Ailes for the thousandth time and explain the situation. We go over a few scenarios and decide that the Warlock would probably not have a bomb connected to a motion sensor, but that he would use a motion-sensitive camera to tell him if someone was on the premises. He could watch the feed on his phone anywhere in the world and react if necessary. If he sees some homeless man digging through the yard for scrap metal, he isn't likely to set off a ton of C4 explosive. If half a dozen FBI agents come marching in through the front gate, that is a different matter.

"Gerald and Jennifer are doing a search of IP traffic in that area. We're going to search for satellite signals too. Do us a favor and set up a laptop with a wi-fi card near the gate as well. We'll give you some software to install."

TWENTY MINUTES LATER Ailes calls back. His team has got a map of all the Internet connections in the area. The FBI field office has a cellular sniffer to use as well, so we can monitor any signals sent over EDGE, 3G, 4G and LTE.

Using a periscope, a tactical unit spots three video cameras on the building. Two of them are aimed at the front gate. We can't find one on the street, so that's some relief. He'd probably get too many false positives out here every time a car drove by.

"I think we got it, Blackwood," Ailes says. "We found three computers on the network. One is controlling the cameras and motion sensors. The second seems to just be sitting there as a backup."

"What about the third?" I ask.

"We're working on it. We're doing a port scan. It seems to be plugged into several control circuits. Not cameras or other sensors. The kind of thing that would turn on your sprinklers at home."

"A fire suppression system?"

"We don't know. We can temporarily block outbound signals to all of them and interrupt the feed. But I can't shut it down for good."

"We'll have to just make do."

"I can guarantee you ten minutes of blackout. After that, he'll know something is up if he's half as smart as we think he is," says Ailes.

I turn to Shannon. "It should just be you, me and Danielle. We need a small team. If something goes wrong, I don't want anybody else in harm's way."

"I agree." Shannon turns to explain the situation to the rest of the team.

Danielle pats me on the back, feeling for my body armor. "Just checking."

I think about her family. "You know, you don't have to go in there."

She gives me a smile. "Three pairs of eyes are better than two. And besides, don't you think it's time the girls run the show?"

Having her with me makes me feel better. She's smart and very observant. Knoll insisted she come along because there are no better field forensic technicians in the bureau.

Once we're all set, Shannon gives me the thumbs-up.

"Are we a go, Dr. Ailes?" I ask.

"Blackout in three . . . two . . . one . . . Go!" he replies.

48

Y OU NEVER KNOW who or what is on the other side of a door. A routine stop for me as a rookie cop ended up getting me kicked down a flight of stairs and my nose broken. Some might say that's getting off easy. The Warlock is capable of anything.

It's a junkyard. But we already knew that from the air. On the ground the piles of crushed vehicles and machinery take on a different meaning. I see three broken-down yellow taxi vans in a heap. Danielle taps me on the shoulder and points to a pile of wings and small airplane fuselages. In another section is a carved-open city bus.

Shannon steps over a huge steel wheel that belongs to a locomotive. Everywhere we look we see things that could have been used in trial runs for what the Warlock has done before. Or they could just be junk. A thousand other salvage yards in this country could have the same broken-down vehicles and parts. Their presence here means nothing.

We walk around a metal building with open sides. A heavy winch sits in the middle with an engine block dangling from the chains. It swings slowly in the wind. The creaking of metal is unsettling in the quiet yard.

Just beyond the shed lies the fuselage for a 757 passenger

jet. The tail section has been cut cleanly off. The wings are no-where to be found. It resembles the aftermath of a plane crash.

We steal glances at each other, acknowledging how fucked up this all is.

Danielle has a video camera in her hands to record every-thing. She scans the piles of broken machinery and debris. The large main building stands before us. Rust-colored steel walls support a slightly pitched roof. There are two massive rollup doors and three smaller ones on the front. Off to the side is a doorway. Shannon heads toward it.

"Wait," I whisper. "I don't think we want to go through there."

"I was just going to have a look through the window. Legally, I don't think we can go inside," he replies.

Danielle and I exchange glances. "Do you see a water meter on the outside?"

"I'm sure we will if we walk around the back," he replies.

"I didn't hear that."

Shannon shakes his head. "We can't play that game, Black-wood. There are rules."

"I agree. The county DA said we could search the premises for the meter."

Shannon is intent on being even more rigid than just by-the-book. "I don't think he meant inside."

"Wait," says Danielle. She pulls out her phone and types something. A few seconds later her phone buzzes with an in-stant message. She looks back up at us. "We're good to go."

"How's that?" asks Shannon.

Danielle points to the airplane missing its tail section. "No aircraft numbers and improper storage. That's a violation of FAA regulations and a federal offense."

"You can't be serious," says Shannon.

"I just texted my husband. He's a lawyer for the FAA. We're acting with their blessing now too. Any more questions?"

She gives me a wink. Professionalism keeps me from hugging her.

"Fine. How did the ladies become the macho kick-in-the-door alphas and the man the shrinking violet?" replies Shannon. I can tell he wants to play it safe. He's not invested in this like Danielle and I.

"It's a changing world, darlin'," says Danielle.

"I just hope there's room for me." Shannon shoots me a sideways glance. It's the first time I realize he's actually threatened by me.

I walk over to the middle of the three smaller rolling doors. "We should go through this one." I scan the door and frame for any sign that it has been tampered with. There's a small piece of tape at the lower corner. I point this out to Danielle. "Can you replace that after we come back out?"

"No problem. All the doors have them, by the way."

The tape is a low-tech way of detecting entry into a building by whoever owns the building. It could belong to a legitimate business for all we know. The taxis and planes are just circumstantial in theory. But my gut tells me this is his place.

Danielle kneels and carefully pulls away the tape in the lower corner using a pair of tweezers. I pick the lock and set it aside. Shannon suppresses a smile at how quickly I manage to get it off. I point to the bottom handle so he can lift the door.

"Glad I can be useful in some capacity," he groans as he lifts the edge of the door a foot.

I place a cinder block from a heap underneath to keep it open, then lie flat to peer inside the building.

My eyes take a few moments to adjust. Light streaks in through vents in the ceiling. The entire structure appears empty. Shannon and Danielle squat down next to me.

Danielle gets out her flashlight and scans the interior. There are a few benches and tables. Tool chests and machinery lie around, but there's nothing else inside the cavernous space.

I'm not sure what I was expecting, a giant mechanical tyrannosaur? I wriggle myself into the warehouse. Shannon is about to protest but stops himself short.

I use my flashlight to illuminate the inside. I splash the light around looking for any kind of clue. There's a small box of a building in the corner, probably an office. I walk over and shine my light inside through a window. There's a desk, a chair, an outdated calendar on the wall and an unplugged mini fridge in the corner.

Danielle has made her way over to me. "Not the smoking gun we were hoping for?"

I shake my head. "Not enough. No. Not really."

We walk across the interior of the warehouse while Shannon keeps watch at the door. Danielle looks down at a workbench. Pliers, hammers and drills sit on top of it among piles of metal shavings.

"This could be his workshop," says Danielle. She spins her beam around, hoping it hits something. "What were we expecting?" she asks rhetorically.

I aim my light at the floor and walk toward the back, searching. For what? Blood? Photographs of Times Square? A wall covered with clues and pieces of string linking all the crimes together?

"Five minutes," comes Ailes's voice over my earpiece. We have five minutes until the blackout ends and the Warlock knows we're here—assuming this is really his place. But is it?

We're only here because of the clue Damian sent me. Everything outside is suspicious, but not conclusive. Did he send us down a blind alley? On the surface it was a pretty good guess, but that's the extent of it.

"Has your mystery friend ever been wrong?" asks Danielle.

"No. Never." My voice is defensive.

"I don't know what to say. Maybe it's right in front of us and we're too dumb to see . . ."

I turn around. Danielle is staring at the concrete floor.

"Well, aren't we two silly geese. Walking all over it," she replies.

It's the markings. Stripes of white paint for crosswalks and streets. Gray outlines. Even the manhole cover has been painted in.

We're standing in the middle of Times Square.

49

Mʏ ɢʀᴀɴᴅꜰᴀᴛʜᴇʀ'ꜱ ʜᴏᴜꜱᴇ in the Hollywood Hills had a theater in the basement. He would put on private shows there occasionally, but its real purpose was for rehearsing. The entire back wall was covered with curtains; when you lowered them, they revealed a wall of mirrors in which you could watch yourself performing.

When my father and I would drive there from our Venice Beach apartment to visit Grandfather several times a week, I would leave them in the library and sneak down into the theater to play. The whole place smelled of dust and cigar smoke.

Without the lights on, the only illumination came from an ancient exit sign powered by a dim bulb. I'd push the musty crimson velvet curtains back and stand in the middle of the stage. If I gazed out across the upholstered seats I could see a faraway girl who looked just like me.

We'd dance together in the red light and take turns racing back and forth on our stages, trying to see who could make it to the other side first. I'm not sure it was always a tie.

Sometimes I'd sit on the edge of the stage and just stare across the theater talking to the other girl. I'd ask her questions about her life. Surprisingly like my own, but with some differences.

She lived in the mountains north of there. She went to a friendlier school and had brothers and sisters. The biggest difference of all was that she knew her mother. Hers never ran off, too young and too unprepared for handling a child.

The girl on the other side of the mirror talked to her mother every day. And they looked exactly alike. When she grew up she wanted to be just like her mother. "A magician?" I would ask.

She shook her head and said magic was the furthest thing from her mother's mind. "She helps people. She helps little girls in trouble. She's the bravest person in the world."

As I grew older I tried to understand what my visits there meant. Embarrassed as I was of my overactive imagination, I understood the need for a space where your mind could see the impossible and could tell you what's really deep down inside.

Standing in the Warlock's play space, it's an unsettling memory. Alone in the dark, he didn't imagine a better version of himself. He imagined how he could use his intellect in the most twisted way possible.

Shannon is using swabs on the section of the fake Times Square where the angel appeared, in the hope that we find some traces of blood. Danielle is taking photos of the tire tracks crisscrossing the Times Square layout. He'd must have driven a taxi van back and forth thousands of times to get the timing right. From one end of the building to the other is almost half a city block.

I walk to the far left corner of the warehouse when my nose picks up a musty odor. The concrete comes to an abrupt end where it's been chipped away. There's a rough ten-foot square of dirt.

"Three minutes," says Ailes in our ears, reminding us that time is running out.

I try to make sense of the dirt. What purpose did it serve? In the corner I see where the ground has been disturbed and there are several deep furrows, each as wide as a hand. Exactly as wide as a hand.

My blood runs cold.

This is where Denise died.

He buried her here.

She really did die crawling out of a grave.

"Shannon, get a sample here quick!" We need to see if there's blood in the dirt. That could be the proof we need to connect the Warlock to her murder.

Shannon comes running with a sample kit and starts scooping up dirt. He knows time is running out, so he doesn't question me.

Something penetrates the back of my mind. It's an uneasy feeling. I close my eyes and listen. It's a humming sound. Danielle notices me concentrating.

"Do you hear that?" I ask. I walk toward the source of the sound and end up standing next to the side wall of the building.

"Something outside?" she asks.

I shake my head. There is nothing on the other side of this wall except piles of junk. I look up at the air vent. Faint light streams from outside. It's supposed to just be a wall, but what if it's not?

I touch the metal surface. There's the faint echo of a chamber. There's something inside. I think he's built an entire passage here. I walk along the wall trying to find a gap.

"Two minutes," says Ailes.

"GO!" I shout to Danielle and Shannon. We still have to make it out of the yard.

Shannon grabs his kit and they take off running for the exit.

I can't let this go! I keep trying to find the secret passage. The wall doesn't want to give up its secret.

Danielle and Shannon reach the door and slide underneath. They look back at me from the gap. I'm not going to make it.

"Ailes, how long before you can pull this trick again? I'm not going to make it out before the cameras turn on!"

"What? Hold on. Twelve hours at the earliest. That's how often his backups sync. But if you're in there he'll see you."

"Only if I move."

Across the warehouse Danielle nods to me. She understands. The only way we can keep our discovery a secret is if they close the door and make it out of the yard while I stay here.

I shut off my flashlight and watch the crack of light from the open door fade as they lower it back down and run back to the front of the property.

"I'm going to shut off my phone so the battery will last," I tell Ailes.

"Understood."

I reach into my pocket and power it down. There's a whir and a clicking sound inside the warehouse as the systems come back online. I can see the red lights of surveillance cameras twinkle on in the dark ceiling like red stars.

I take the first of what will be several low and shallow breaths to avoid setting off the motion sensors. I sit here in the dark alone and wait.

Somewhere at the other end of the darkness I imagine the little girl from the theater looking back at me.

50

Spending twelve hours by yourself in the dark without moving is difficult. If my head moves or my arm twitches, the motion sensors will catch it. The Warlock will get a text notification on his phone and a live feed will show him what the infrared cameras are seeing: me sitting here by myself.

If he sees me here it will burn this location at the very least. He won't come back and we won't be able to nail him.

My worst fear is what's sitting on the other side of the wall. I keep my eyes shut and try to identify all of the different smells and sounds in this warehouse. I found the grave because of the musty odor. I found the wall because of the sound—which I'm pretty sure is a refrigerator.

He'd need one to keep the chemicals he uses in his knockout drug. This one sounds big, like it has a freezer. I can only think of one thing he'd need that much space for behind a secret wall: a body.

Chloe is probably just a few feet away from me. Pulled from life, then dug from the ground so she could be stashed away for her twin to take her place, she's now shoved into a refrigerated cabinet like some kind of lab specimen.

Did the Warlock put her there so he could go look at her

body? Is it some kind of sick thrill for him to walk over to his secret room and stare down at the body of his first victim?

Did Denise know when she was dying, trying to climb out of the ground a hundred feet away, that her twin was already here?

Underneath the smell of wet dirt, concrete and rust is an acrid odor. It's not machine oil or the thousand other scents you find in a garage. This is a fuel smell, like a high-octane propellant. The scent of dragsters and jets.

There's also the slightly rotting odor of fertilizer . . .

Jet fuel and fertilizer. A less lethal combination took out half of an Oklahoma federal building. Behind me is enough space for a hundred trucks' worth of bombs.

How much would the Warlock need? The purpose of the explosion wouldn't be just to kill any investigators, it would also be to remove any trace of evidence.

During our briefing Shannon explained that on one side of the property is a factory where women toil away at making police uniforms. On the other is a machine shop where a dozen blue-collar men and women work every day. They're at work right now, with no idea what's going on next door.

A bomb this big would leave a crater the size of a block. They'd all be gone. How many people? Fifty? A hundred?

My mind races with all of the disturbed possibilities. I try to keep my pulse down so my chest doesn't start heaving and set off the sensors. If he sees me here, I'm not sure I'll make it to the rollup door before he can press a button.

To some, the lives we've seen lost so far don't seem as consequential in the devil's arithmetic. I have a new reason to remain motionless: It's not just my life, it's everyone around me.

On the other side of the fence, Danielle, Shannon, and all the agents and police who are waiting for me would be taken out in the blast.

One twitch, one sneeze and the sensors go off.

My heart starts to race again. I concentrate on slowing it down. My left hand is still in my pocket on my phone. I left it there in case I need to turn it on to make a call.

Do I tell them to pull back and clear the area? I think I can make the call without moving more than my thumb. But what about sound?

With a metal roof and thin walls, I'd think audio surveillance would be pointless. Or is it? Wiring the place with microphones is fairly easy. Should I put anything past him?

I decide to wait.

The sunlight coming through the vents begins to fade. I don't dare check my watch. I just stare into the darkness and keep my mind as clear as I can. In some ways it's easier than I would have thought.

I've always been a solitary person. Since I let work fill my life there hasn't been much room for anyone else. First magic, then law enforcement. I don't know if I regret that or not. It's just the way I am.

Every few minutes I wrestle with taking the risk of turning on my phone or not. I could at least give them some notice to get clear. But what about the people next door? They wouldn't make it.

In the distance I can hear the wail of police sirens growing closer. Damn, not here!

They may have gotten a full search warrant by now. That's not going to help if this place is wired to explode. If the Warlock sees police cars barreling through the front gate, it's all over. Done.

The sirens get louder, then pass by. They're heading somewhere else. I breathe a sigh of relief. A shallow breath.

There's another noise now. It's the distant low rumble of a helicopter. It's getting closer. The roof rattles as the helicopter passes over the top of the building.

I can hear the engine roaring through the vents. I try to visualize where it's going from the maps. The helicopter is a block or two away now. It's probably assisting the chase cars.

There's a high-pitched whine coming from that direction. Something has malfunctioned. The blades make a sloshing noise and the helicopter's engine screams louder.

The engine cuts out and all I can hear is the whoosh of the blades as the helicopter auto-gyrates to the ground. There's a metallic thud and a loud crackle, then an explosion like a transformer blowing.

Oh God.

Right near us too.

What are the chances?

The red lights on the cameras go out. The refrigerator stops humming.

The power is off.

51

TRY NOT TO PANIC. I don't understand what is going on. I sit there and wait. I focus on my shallow breaths and not moving. The cameras could come back on at any moment.

Footsteps run across the gravel outside. A metal blade is cutting into something. The middle rollup door slides up and three men dressed in bomb armor run inside. Unsure of what's happening, I remain perfectly still.

One of the men runs over, throws a bomb vest over me and fastens on a helmet.

"This way, Jessica!" he commands.

I let him pull me to my feet.

All three of them rush me out of the building and into an armored personnel carrier sitting in front of the warehouse. They slam the door shut and the driver takes off out of the junkyard, swerving around the wrecks of planes and cars.

Two of the men stare at monitors keeping a careful watch on the building. We pass through the entrance and another bomb tech shuts the gate then hops onto the running board of the carrier.

We head down to the end of the block and take a side street. In the distance I can see police cars and fire trucks. There's a cloud of black smoke in the sky.

Our driver pulls us into the open doors of a recycling plant and they slam shut after us. Finally, one of my rescuers speaks into his radio. "We got her."

I step out of the vehicle into a command center they'd set up in the last few hours. Danielle comes running up and gives me a hug.

"Thank God! Thank God!"

"The bomb?" I ask.

"We know. We checked the swabs Shannon collected and realized what we'd left you sitting on."

I point to the armored carrier. "He knows we were there now."

Danielle shakes her head. "No. He doesn't. We staged an accident."

"The helicopter?"

"The sheriff's department pilot is a former Navy SEAL pilot. He offered to do a controlled crash."

"Oh my God!" My hand flies to my mouth.

"He's fine. Bruised, but fine. We had to have an excuse to clear the area, so we staged a high-speed chase. It was live on the news along with the crash next to a chemical supply company. We've cleared everyone for a half mile. We cut the power and Ailes took over the Warlock's system."

It was all an elaborate scheme to evacuate the area without the Warlock realizing what we were doing. Did it work? There hasn't been an explosion yet, if that's any indication.

"We're going to send in techs to take out the bomb," continues Danielle. "We should have done that the first time. If we'd paid more attention to the thermal imaging we would have noticed something was out of place."

"That's my fault," says Shannon. He'd been standing over a table looking at a map. "I should have known he would try something like that."

I shake my head. "It's not your fault. We're just beginning to understand how the man thinks. If you hadn't gotten those swabs of the explosives, I'd still be sitting back there next to the bomb."

A bomb tech walks over to Shannon. "We're ready to go try to dismantle the thing."

"He's devious. Don't take anything for granted," I reply, the scent of explosive fuel still fresh in my mind.

"Trust me. We're going to take things real slow, Agent."

I take my phone out and turn it on to call Ailes.

"Thank God you're okay. We never should have let you go," he says. His voice is apologetic.

"Stop that. Someone had to go. Thankfully I have smart people to work with."

"Hopefully. We ended up making a virtual version of his entire network and overrunning the routers he was sending traffic through. The satellite was the tricky part, but Jennifer managed that. I won't get into the details."

"I'm not sure I'd understand," I admit.

"The short of it is that his software patches were a few months old. He got a little busy and forgot to update them."

"It's good to know he's just as forgetful as the rest of us. Did anyone have a chance to go over Danielle's footage?"

"We've been making a map of the floor plan. Besides Times Square, we think we can make out some outlines where he traced the observation deck on the Empire State Building."

"I guess that makes sense," I reply.

"We've been looking at 3-D models of that junkyard of his trying to figure out exactly what he's got piled out there. We found a stack of aluminum piping cut to the same size as the rails of the observation deck and some screen. He may have actually built a model of the deck and placed projection screens to simulate the walls of the lobby and the outside view."

"To fake footage?"

"Not quite good enough. More for a practice run. A really intense practice run. The same for Times Square. He probably projected images of buildings and traffic lights to make sure everything would work just right. It's insane. Have you ever seen anything like that?"

"Yeah. Remind me sometime to tell you about my rehearsals in my grandfather's basement."

"Well, the one bright ray of light in all this is that we're pretty sure some of that IP traffic from the warehouse was being routed to Texas."

"So everything is still a go?"

"It looks that way. Unless we think revealing his Michigan hideout will deter him, we're still on the hunt there."

I turn to Danielle. "How quick can we get to the airport?"

52

LOCK THE DOOR of my motel room and check my wig in the mirror. It's dirty blond and much shorter than my own hair. With a pair of librarian glasses, I was able to fool Agent Knoll in the Quantico command center. As I was the most recognizable person on the task force, he didn't want to send me to south Texas.

Agreeing to use a disguise, plus the fact that the Warlock practically told us where he was going to strike next, convinced him to let me at least come as close as our field command post six miles away. I'm in a motel that's across the road from a Texas Highway Patrol station. This seemed to be the place we'd be least likely to run into him.

I've been having second thoughts on our ability to catch him here. The Santa Lucia clue had a capital C. It was intentional.

He might want us to know where he's planning his next deception. Or this is just one giant red herring. A fake-out. We've got another team outside Boulder, Colorado, the fifth point on the pentagram, and a third team on standby at Quantico, ready to jet anywhere in the United States in five hours.

So far the group in Michigan hasn't found anything more about what he has planned next. In the warehouse they found an empty freezer inside the hidden passage and several tons of explosives, enough to have taken out the entire industrial area, but no future plans.

The bomb squad opted to dismantle the bomb but leave the warehouse looking as if we'd never been there. To the best of our knowledge, the Warlock still hasn't figured it out. Ailes turned his computers back over to him when power was restored to the area, and has been monitoring the signal traffic while a surveillance team keeps watch.

My bet is that he doesn't go back there. The staged police helicopter crash was a close call, but not so close that he pulled the trigger.

I sit down at the table and look over a map with highlighted points of interest around our Texas town. The town church has the unique honor of having been struck by lightning twice, burning down both times. A schoolhouse was wiped away in a tornado twenty years ago, killing three students and a teacher. Since then, the kids have been getting bused to a school near Brownsville.

Part of me suspects that what makes the town special isn't anything about it, other than the name and it was one of the possible locations on the pentagram. The real reason he singled it out is because it fits a larger pattern of escalation.

The first murder happened in a cemetery, hours before we cracked the code and got there. The second one took place in a more public place in Fort Lauderdale, yet nobody was watching when he dragged the plane onto the sandbar. The third murder was the most overt one of all, before thousands of people. Video of the New York City illusion is playing on the television in my room. To my frustration, it alternates with a clip of me repeating Katya's disappearance on top of the Empire State Building.

The security camera techs recorded the whole trick and made an edited tape that makes it look a lot smoother than it actually was. At Chisholm's suggestion, this was given to the media as proof that the FBI is on top of things and not deceived by the Warlock's stunts.

The problem is that, even with the edits, my impromptu vanish looks different. People who want to believe in the Warlock, and there are many of them on television, aren't convinced by the demonstration. It's the debunker's dilemma. If you don't replicate the exact effect, then they have reason to believe.

I shut the TV off when clips of me onstage with a white tiger start playing. Part of me knows I should call my father and grandfather and tell them not to talk to the media, but I'm really not sure I want that stress right now.

Earlier at the gas station, I'd picked up a tabloid that was floating the theory that the Warlock didn't actually murder any of his victims. It suggests that he simply found them and arranged for a spectacular memorial. It's full of holes and insulting to the families. But some people want him to be an antihero who really isn't hurting anyone.

It reminds me of Hitler worship. The Web is full of idiots trying to spin his evil. It's bad enough when serial killers get groupies who know they did it and glorify them regardless; it's worse when less crazy people delude themselves into justifying something they want to believe in. Entire books have been written trying to claim the concentration camps never happened, all so a handful of people who still adhere to National Socialism can point to their most famous icon as a little misguided and not a genocidal monster who has come to represent pure evil.

I stare at the map in front of me as if it will reveal its secrets and the next deception will leap forth. It's not working. Next to me is a stack of old magic books I brought to thumb through, hoping they will jar my mind.

From time to time my mind drifts to Colorado. I pull up a state map on the computer and search satellite images of the location, as if a clue will pop out at me.

Knoll and Ailes are under the impression that I might be able to see through everything and give them a heads-up to what the deception might be here. I don't know how. I just got lucky before. The only thing I believe is that this illusion is going to be bigger than the others, and he wants us as witnesses.

Magic is a funny thing. David Copperfield flew twenty feet in the air on a television special and people barely remembered it. Five years later, David Blaine floated six inches off the ground on a magic special that looked like reality television and the world went nuts. The Blaine trick looked real. Copperfield's looked like an illusion. Blaine never repeated the trick, while you can go see Copperfield float, just as he did on television, every night in Las Vegas.

I flip through the pages of a magic book and stop at a photo of a Chinese magician pulling umbrellas from a box. A few pages later a man and his wife are producing light bulbs by the dozen. Each prop is a theme.

If the Warlock's crimes are a magic act, I should be able to figure out the theme. The Chloe murder was him raising the dead, bringing someone back from death. The airplane was pulling something out of the past. The angel was him sending someone down from heaven. The best guess is that he's trying to open up different realms that embody the classical elements, water, air, wind, earth and fire, or just symbolic clues to that effect.

What other realms are there?

Chisholm's group suggests that the Warlock might try to open up the gates of hell. Our minds are so wide-open on this, we actually had a team of researchers try to track down the remaining parts of Hitler's corpse, and the graves of anyone else we would expect to find in "hell."

Hell. Hell and fire. Fire is one of the remaining elements. It sounds like it might fit. I keep asking how.

My big fear is that he might send us on so many wild-goose chases, we'll end up spread too thin. The gates of hell bring up the notion of not just fire, but also brimstone. Brimstone was an ancient word for sulfur. Of course it would turn out that Texas is one of the world's biggest suppliers. We've got teams checking sulfur-processing facilities for anything unusual there.

Our minds have been bouncing around from one possibility to the next. I'm going insane with permutations. I have to hold myself back from relaying to Knoll every idea that strikes me.

I come back to the idea of hell and fire. I used to perform an illusion called the Cremation. Two muscular assistants would seal me inside a metal coffin that was then set on fire. I was supposed to escape before I burned to death. The twist was the coffin would fall open and reveal a skeleton. After the audience reacted in horror, I'd appear in the back row of the auditorium. I never liked it conceptually. I argued with my father and grandfather about the logic of the effect. Whose skeleton was it supposed to be if I was alive? It was a logical leap nobody cared about except me.

There are at least a half dozen other illusions involving fire. They split into two themes: endurance and resurrection. Walking on hot coals, surviving in an oven, putting a hot poker on your tongue all imply an invulnerability to fire.

Resurrection illusions, like the Cremation, involve a kind of rebirth. Someone gets consumed by the flames, only to reappear unharmed. A phoenix effect of sorts. There are hundreds of versions of these ideas.

For what it's worth, I've already e-mailed Knoll and Ailes my thoughts on these specific concepts. I still don't know if they fit the Warlock's MO. He could burn down a church full of people and have them or their twins appear elsewhere and it'd still look like a trick compared with the spectacles he's already accomplished.

He's thinking so much bigger than we are and he wants us to know this. We're here in Texas at his invitation: Come watch me kill.

I look out my window at the storm clouds gathering overhead and try to imagine, if anything were possible, what would he do?

What would I do?

My phone rings. It's Knoll.

"We found the girl. And she's alive."

53

Rosa Martinez and her mother are very confused by what's going on. Knoll had Agent Johnson and a female agent named Keener go to the mother's house disguised as a couple and explain the situation to avoid arousing suspicion. They took her to pick up Rosa from her high school, presumably to help tend to her ailing grandmother. The goal was to get the two of them away from the house as quickly as possible in the event the Warlock already has them under surveillance.

In the adjoining motel room, Knoll is trying to tell them what he can. Mrs. Martinez isn't taking the news lightly that her daughter may be the next target for the serial killer she's seen all over television. They had to take her phone away to keep her from calling a friend and ruining our cover.

I stay out of the way and focus on my maps and books in the other room. Johnson and Keener have experience talking to people in this situation. The last thing I want to do is be another face in there making things awkward.

We've got six other agents in the motel and three more watching the parking lot, as well as a team using the nearby Texas Highway Patrol station facilities to coordinate with all the other law enforcement agencies. I can't think of a safer place in the world for Rosa than right here. Through the doorway I see her mother is on the verge of tears again. She keeps explaining that Rosa is a good girl and that she can't understand why anyone would want to harm her.

While Johnson talks to her by the bed, Keener is sitting with Rosa at the table and asking if she's spoken to anybody suspicious or noticed anyone watching her. Rosa is adamant she hasn't. Keener wants to know if she's been in contact with anyone online. Rosa replies that she only talks to friends she knows.

The next step will be looking through her e-mail to see if she's telling the truth or received messages from one of our suspicious proxies. Keener takes out a computer and shows pictures of men's faces from Faceplaced to the two of them to see if they recognize any of them. After twenty minutes there are no matches.

Knoll comes through the adjoining doorway and sits down at the table with me. He sees the maps, books and all my notes. "Anything?"

I shake my head. "Lots of 'ifs' but nothing stands out. He wants us to think he's capable of the impossible." I nod toward the other room. "What about there?"

"I don't know if he's made contact yet. We'll check phone records and texts. He might just have singled her out and be waiting for the right moment. Or he might not be after Rosa at all. He could be a thousand miles away and laughing at us. Maybe this is all a sick joke."

"Maybe. I still can't shake the idea that he wants us here for a reason, not just to misdirect us. At least it seems that the next evolution of this game is to play it right with us here. The angel's eyes were an invitation." I nod to the other room. "I can't think he expected us to find her."

"Yeah, I hope so," replies Knoll.

"Anything from Colorado?"

"No. The point there didn't give us a nice match like the town here did. We have our field office looking, though. And we don't have a potential victim like we do here."

"Yes, but unless he plans on leaving that point of the pentagram unfinished, there's something there. And if everything is meant to escalate, then that's going to be the biggest spectacle yet."

"I know. I know. Hopefully we can catch him here." Knoll draws a circle around the town on the map with his finger. "We've got things pretty locked down inside the zone. I don't know if he'd be able to get in or out without us seeing him. He seems to want to be close by when things happen."

"But he keeps getting further away. He probably didn't stand around and watch the reaction to the angel killing."

"He knew that would be televised," replies Knoll.

"And this? If he wants us here, he'll have no problem calling the news in if he wants it covered."

"True."

Keener walks in with Rosa. She looks scared, but calmer than her mother. She still seems in shock.

"Mind if Rosa sits with you guys? Johnson and I need to talk to Rosa's mom about some grown-up stuff."

Knoll pulls out a chair for her. "I'm going to go check out the snack machine. You want anything, Rosa?"

"A Sprite?" Her words sound frightened. She sits down and looks at the books and maps. "What's all that?"

Keener shuts the adjoining door so she can ask Rosa's mother some of the questions they don't want Rosa to hear.

"I'm just trying to figure things out." I set my pen down and smile at her.

"You look like the magician lady that works for the FBI."

I'd taken off the glasses. I put a finger to my lips. "Let's keep that a secret."

Rosa smiles. "Sure. You're very pretty. Can I use your bathroom? I haven't gone since geography."

"Of course." They'd pulled her out of school and rushed her over here. Lord knows what the past hour has been like for her.

While Rosa uses the restroom I clear the table of the books and maps. I don't know how much we want her knowing, although there isn't much point to hiding who I am from her. Without the glasses, the disguise is half as effective.

In the other room I can hear Rosa's mother explaining the family history. Where the father is and all the other awkward details we don't like to tell strangers.

I set the books aside and realize something about Rosa's behavior strikes me a little odd. She seems a little too anxious, and not just because of everything going on. She reminds me of myself when I'd tell my father a lie.

I step over to the bathroom door to ask if she's okay.

The water is running.

I can hear her whispering.

She's talking to somebody in a hushed voice.

She has a phone.

54

MY GUT IMPULSE is to knock on the door but I stop myself. If I pound on the door, that will tell whoever is on the other line that we know she's talking to them. It's probably just a boyfriend, but we can't take any chances. We're better off not alerting them, just in case . . .

I gently knock on the door to the adjoining room. Johnson cracks it open. I put my finger to my lips and point to my ear, telling him to listen. He nods and leaves the door slightly ajar.

I sit back down and pretend to read a book. A minute later Rosa emerges from the bathroom. I spot the bulge in her back pocket where she has the mobile phone. She takes the chair next to me and looks at what I'm reading.

"Heard you talking in there. Boyfriend?" I say it without looking up, as if it's the most normal thing. Just two girls making small talk.

Rosa looks over her shoulder at the door. From her angle it still looks closed. She whispers to me. "Mom doesn't know. She'd have a cat. I met him a few months ago at church camp."

Please don't let it be a counselor. I've heard enough horror stories about sex offenders using religious camps as an opportunity to prey on children whose parents think they're in a safe place.

"Is he cute?" I ask.

Rosa nods her head. "Yeah."

"Older?"

Rose looks over her shoulder again, then leans in. "Just a little."

My stomach turns. "How old?"

"He just turned eighteen. But I'm sixteen. Mom won't let me date anyone more than a year older than me."

I feel a wave of relief as I realize we're not talking about some pederastic counselor. Eighteen is well below our profile. Even an older man who could pass for that probably wouldn't fit. We'll still need to check on it, though, just to be safe.

"You ever date anyone older when you were my age?" asks Rosa.

"I didn't date much. Boys were afraid of me, I was too serious, and I was never in one place for very long." I leave out that I went on a lot of pretend dates with older gay dancers who worked in our show. We'd go to movies and clubs. It was fun role-playing for both of us. I got to pretend that I at least had a normal life for a little while.

"Yeah, but I bet they all liked you. That's why I became a cheerleader."

I have to smile. I've seen the effect a costume can have on a boy's imagination.

"What I like about Ryan is that he never asks for photos or stuff. Never any pressure, you know."

I think I know. I'm relieved to see he's not trying to exploit her. Of course, that could be because he's eighteen and doesn't want to go to jail. Or because he's waiting for one of my dancer boyfriends to come along.

"Where does Ryan live?"

"Houston," says Rosa.

Long-distance romance is always the hardest. It's also the most sincere. Without the physical attraction in the way, you tend to be at your most honest. At least that was the case for me. "Do you get to see him very often?"

Rosa makes a disappointed face. "No. Not in person since church camp. But we talk all the time." She lowers her voice. "He gave me a phone so we could talk."

An alarm bell goes off in my head.

She keeps talking, excited to confide. "He's always busy with football practice and school. But he finds the time to talk to me. Which is funny, because at church camp he kind of ignored me. Didn't really notice I was there. Then he e-mailed me afterward and said he was kind of shy. Which I can understand."

He ignored her in person. I take a slow breath. "Rosa, how did you know it was him? Silly question, I know."

Rosa frowns. "Oh, like how did I know it wasn't one of his friends pulling a prank? We talk on Skype. He's got a crappy Internet connection so it drops out a lot, which is a pain."

She's only seen him from video conferencing. We already saw how the Warlock can fake that with the added cover of a bad connection.

Thanks to Katya, we know the Warlock likes to lure his victims from afar. He kept up a fake interaction with Swanson's wife to keep her convinced her husband was still alive. We still don't know how he met Claire or Denise. They might have gone willingly with him after they met online or might have thought they were meeting up with someone they already knew and he showed up instead.

I've met friends for drinks a hundred times based on text messages. Anyone with ten dollars and access to the Internet can send a spoof text from a number you know. We're so much more vulnerable than we realize, but we're so worried about credit card thieves and eBay scammers that the idea of a serial killer using this technology against us is new. It's something I'm afraid we're seeing more of.

The Warlock is a spider at the center of a huge online web of deceit, pretending to be dozens of different personas. It's a chilling thought.

How many of our friends are people we just know from online communication? It doesn't take a freak like Damian to do this digitally.

"Rosa, what did you tell him in the bathroom? Did you mention us? It's okay to tell me. We just need to know. We need to make sure he'll be okay too."

Rosa's eyes widen. "What does he have to do with this?"

"Nothing, I'm sure. Did you mention us?"

"Yes. I know I'm not supposed to, but he's a hundred miles away and has nothing to do with this. And I was supposed to call him anyways about . . ."

"About what, Rosa?"

She shakes her head.

"Rosa. We need to know."

"I was going to go see his football game on Wednesday night. A friend of his was going to drive me."

Knoll bursts in through the side door. He's been listening with Johnson. "Rosa, we need your phone now!"

She looks scared as hell. She should be.

55

LOOK UP at the Texas sun as an FBI helicopter lands in the field next to the motel kicking up a cloud of dust. Knoll and I rush aboard and buckle up.

FBI and Texas law enforcement were able to triangulate the phone call from Rosa's phone to a moving vehicle. When it switched towers to a road passing through a thinly populated area, a spotter in an aircraft was able to make an identification of a black Suburban.

The Warlock probably wasn't expecting us to identify his victim before the crime. He sure as hell wasn't thinking we'd be able to pinpoint his location while he was still planning things.

A roadblock has been set up fifteen miles away from us. By the time we arrive, Highway Patrol and Hidalgo County sheriffs already have the vehicle surrounded. I count at least fourteen police cruisers and a Highway Patrol helicopter hovering next to ours.

Our take-down unit of eight agents dressed in armored flak jackets and black helmets is giving the driver instructions to throw his keys out the window and put his hands on the wheel. There's a moment of hesitation, then he throws something shiny on the ground. He holds his hands up and our guys pull him out of his vehicle and cuff him at gunpoint.

From where we are, he looks to be an average-sized man. An agent tosses his hat and sunglasses aside and I see thin, dark brown hair. He looks to be in his early forties.

Nothing about him stands out. Put him in a suit and he'd look like a banker. A construction hat and he'd look like a foreman. Nothing about his mannerisms suggests anything suspicious. He's acting like a man surprised by all the fuss.

Knoll is on the phone with the attorneys at the Justice Department trying to make certain we have a clear case for his apprehension. They assure us that suspicion of using electronic deception to talk to a minor is good enough cause to arrest him and search his vehicle. Rosa's claim that he was going to send a friend for her gives us a case for intent to kidnap.

What we really want is evidence that connects him to the murders and the Michigan workshop. That may take longer, but if we can prove he was talking to Rosa on the phone, then we can hold him long enough to make the tightest case we can.

After they have him secured, lying facedown on the highway with his arms cuffed behind his back, our pilot lands us behind the roadblock. Knoll and I get out to watch our forensic team search the vehicle. One of our agents videotapes everything so we can show a clear chain of custody for any evidence we find.

An electronics forensic tech examines the cell phone found in the console. He removes and plugs the SIM card into a computer in the back of an SUV. I'm looking at the face of the man on the ground, trying to figure out if I've ever seen him before. Nothing strikes me. Damian was correct; this man is as bland as you can imagine.

Actually, he seems unusually calm and isn't resisting. Often you build up an idea of a confrontation in your mind and it's nothing like what you actually find. Other times, a simple traffic stop can result in gunfire. He's just lying there in his blue jeans and polo shirt, acting as if this is all a mistake.

Knoll has a binder of all the faces that came up as probable matches before. He flips through them and stops at one photograph and shows it to me. It's him. Or a close enough match. I'm willing to bet the guy on the ground uploaded his face at one point to the face-matching site to see if he had a double.

Or someone else did. Damn the uncertainty. At least we know the man we caught is connected somehow.

Knoll is thinking the same thing I am. Why was the Warlock looking for a double in the first place? Was he just curious? We have a face match, but it's only circumstantial. We can't hold him unless we find something that ties him to Rosa. We need to prove he called her.

I walk over to the agent checking the SIM card. He's pulled up a log of phone calls and is checking them against Rosa's number. None of them match. He uses another piece of software to see if any of them called proxies.

Meanwhile, the forensic team is still searching the truck. They could be looking for days. If he ditched the phone or just the SIM, we won't have anything to arrest him on. We'll have to let him go right here.

Swapping SIM cards has become an important part of criminal activity from drug trafficking to credit card fraud. We've busted gangs that issue members pill containers with a different SIM card for each day of the week. They take one out each day, then toss it after they're done. It makes tracking them a nightmare.

One of the agents who made the arrest hands Knoll the

man's driver license. It's a Georgia license with the name Michael Haywood. If it's legit, at least we know his name. If it's not and we can prove it's a fake, we have a reason to hold him.

Knoll calls the license in to check it. I take another look at the man on the ground. I walk around to see his face. I'm still wearing the blond wig and the sunglasses. He glances up at me then away, but I can tell. He does a double-take just for a moment. He recognizes me but doesn't want me to know he does.

If I wasn't wearing the disguise he probably would have pretended to feign ignorance. It's the wig and glasses that make him doubt himself.

It's him.

Knoll hangs up his phone. "License checks out. He matches the description of Michael Haywood. No priors. No tickets. No warrants."

The forensic team remove a laptop and a police radio scanner from his vehicle. Incriminating as the scanner may be, we'll need a warrant if we want to search the laptop. Knoll walks over to the suspect for permission. The man on the ground says no in a barely audible voice.

What would I do if I knew I was being followed and I had a cell phone on me that could incriminate me? I'm sure he knows the law as well as we do. A phone would be easy to spot if he tossed it. A SIM card would be almost impossible to find. We might have to do a ground search for several miles to try to find it. Without either, the best we can hope to do is hold him for seventy-two hours, and that's kind of iffy at best. After that, we'll have to let him go if the Georgia license holds up and we can't find any proof of identity fraud.

Knoll shakes his head as he examines the license again. "It just had to be Georgia."

"Why's that?" I ask.

"They stopped using fingerprints in their driver's licenses ten years ago and purged the database."

Proving he's using a fake license would be an immediate bust. An agent is using a mobile fingerprint scanner to run his prints against known felons and other records we have on file. We've yet to find even a partial print at the other crime scenes or the warehouse, but anything that attaches him to another crime would still be helpful. The DEA will also start circulating his photograph to see if any of its informants know who he is. Anything would be something right now.

Knoll has a pained expression. We might have to let him go right here. We'd pulled him over expecting the cell phone to be a quick match. It wasn't.

I walk over to the driver's side door. A tech in rubber gloves is doing a careful sweep of the inside edges where the carpet meets the plastic paneling. She looks up at me and shakes her head. If he tossed the SIM on the floorboards or under the seat, they would have found it by now.

The highway is lined with miles of grassy fields. It's an impossible search grid. Maybe Ailes and his genies can come up with some kind of magic by triangulating the point the SIM card was yanked and compare it with his speed, but that's just wishful thinking.

A tech does a second search, pouring the suspect's coffee through a sieve to see if anything is at the bottom of the cup. Nothing. She bags the coffee cup.

The only thing left in the front seat is a water bottle. It looks empty, but she takes it out anyway and pours the contents into a plastic bucket. The bottle and cap are set aside on a table they've set next to his SUV with the rest of the evidence.

Our agents have moved the suspect out of the sun and to the back of a van so he can't watch as we search his vehicle. He's got a smug look on his face. He knows he's fooled us.

I look back in his truck and try to think of what I'd do if I wanted to have something small like a SIM card close by, but I didn't want to be caught with it.

What would a magician do?

What would I do?

I'd hide it in plain sight. Somewhere so obvious I'd make you dismiss it right away. I'd make it easy to get rid of if I had to, without you ever knowing.

I look at the objects on the table and see what he did.

56

CALL OVER to Agent Knoll and make sure the forensic tech with the camera is recording. We don't want to leave anything to chance; it's critical we preserve the chain of evidence. Finding the SIM might not convict him of the murders, but it could be enough for us to build a case. At the very least it would mean we don't have to let him go.

The Warlock probably drives a lot and has to expect to get pulled over occasionally. Some states, like Texas, have random DUI stops. Police can't search your car without probable cause, but that doesn't always mean they won't take a good look inside or flip through your phone if they have it in their custody. It wouldn't be admissible, but if they saw a few cryptic texts, they might bring in a drug dog to sniff your car. That's the way things work. I've never done it, but I know good cops who see things differently. The Warlock has to function in a world of fuzzy rules. One where police see an out-of-state license plate driving near a border town and decide to investigate. He can't afford to ditch his cell phone or SIM every time he sees flashing blue lights. He needs a procedure. He needs at least two SIM cards. One that he uses for his illicit phone calls and the one he replaces it with when he gets pulled over so police don't get suspicious when his phone flashes "NO SIM."

Magicians have all kinds of places to hide things. Even in a pair of fishnets, a sequined bikini top and shorts, I could hide a dozen objects my gynecologist would never find. It starts with using the idea of innocence to hide things.

My grandfather gave me my first magic set after he taught me the trick with the red balls. Coincidentally, it had his face on it. Made in China for a buck, it was filled with plastic props that were scaled-down versions of stage tricks. A flimsy instruction booklet explained how to perform the ersatz miracles.

The first trick I learned, because it was the easiest, involved a little round box. You would place a quarter inside of it, give it a shake, and open it to reveal the quarter had shrunk to half its size. It fooled kids and adults alike. I would perform it whenever Grandfather or Dad would put me on the spot. Somewhere there's a photo of me, wearing a T-shirt with Grandfather's face on it, and me grinning, missing a tooth. I'm proudly holding the little box up in my fingers.

The big quarter vanished when a disk underneath the lid fell on top of it, blending in with the bottom of the box. The tiny quarter, no bigger than a SIM card, was on the other side of the disk, under the lid to the box. The lid itself looked like a big bottle cap.

Like a cap to a water bottle.

I point the water bottle cap out to the tech. She picks it up, looks underneath it, then sets it back down. "Nothing."

I don't want to touch anything. I have a fear of the camera catching me picking up something we find and the footage getting played back later in court as proof that the FBI "Witch" pulled a trick. "Pick it up again. This time, tap it on the table."

She follows my instructions and gives the cap a few swift raps. She feels something click. Even with the wind blowing across the highway we hear the sound of something fall. She pulls the cap away and on the table there's a white disk that exactly matches the interior of the cap. Sitting on top of it is a tiny SIM card. Hidden in plain sight.

The Warlock can tell something is going on. He tries to twist his head around and is told to face forward by an arresting agent.

All his planning. All his elaborate schemes. Foiled by the first magic trick I ever owned. Child's play.

Knoll is beaming at me.

We got him.

I think I'll give my father a call. Possibly Grandfather. I've avoided acknowledging it, but I'm here because of them. For better or worse, what they taught me made me who I am.

57

KNOLL AND I watch the man in the interrogation room through a security camera. He sits quietly and ignores the questions. He didn't need any prompting from an attorney to do that. He's committed to not saying anything. Occasionally, he looks up at the camera as if to look back at who's watching him. He wants me to know he's looking back at me.

With his mask off, he's just another sick fuck. It's hard to connect the specter of the Warlock to the man in the wrinkled polo shirt underneath the bright fluorescent lights. That's the disturbing part. It doesn't take a demigod to kill Denise, Chloe, Claire or Swanson. All it takes is a man.

Up close he has thin brown hair that's slightly receding. He looks to be in his early forties. His face is more restrained than expressive. Light brown eyes, they see everything. You can tell he's listening carefully and thinking everything over.

He knows his best strategy is to wait things out and let his law firm, the most prestigious one in Texas, the one used by presidents and billionaires, even third-world dictators, handle things. They know the real charges we want to bring against him. They also know that a thousand things can go wrong in our attempt to prosecute him for endangering a child and intent to kidnap.

We only found the SIM linking him to Rosa. So far, his laptop has resisted our best efforts to crack its encryption. With nothing else on him or his truck, we suspect somewhere in south Texas he's got a safe house like the Michigan warehouse where we hope to find more incriminating evidence. We hope to find some clue of what he was up to. We still have no idea what his plot was going to be here.

The search warrant for his Georgia residence turned up an empty apartment. They're still trying to find any other record of a Michael Haywood.

"Haywood? Blackwood? Think there's a connection?" Knoll asks me.

"I don't know. He had to have that name before I was on the case. Just a coincidence, I guess." I hope.

We've been watching the interrogation go on for hours. Sealed away in another room, Knoll, the rest of the agents and I have been trying to parse what little we've learned for any kind of lead to more evidence.

He didn't expect to be caught, at least not this soon. Of that much I'm certain. We just don't know how much has already been put into place.

Also, nagging at the back of my mind is the larger question: Is he acting alone?

So far, everything he's done could have been accomplished by one person. It's an incredible and difficult achievement, but we've found no reason to think that anyone else was involved other than an unwitting accomplice in the case of Katya. And that's the damning thing; I don't know what's more unsettling—that one man could do this alone or that there might be others out there.

Dr. Chisholm says Haywood's behavior fits the classical loner profile to a T. Which is odd, because nothing else about him does.

We may have figured out his methods, but not his larger plan. Personally, that's the most maddening thing to me. It's one thing to have a credible theory about how he pulled off the previous murders. It's another to deal with the idea that we don't know where this was going to go from here. Ailes and his team have been doing their best to see if there are any other victims out there. Our worst fear is that a double for Rosa is locked in a basement somewhere starving to death.

There's an arrogant expression on his face whenever he's asked a question. He knows his really important secrets are still his own. We haven't said anything to the press about our suspicion of his identity. Our ability to connect him to the Warlock is so circumstantial that we're not ready to go out on that limb yet.

He looks up at the camera again. For the first time he says something more than a monosyllabic answer. "Is Agent Blackwood there? I'd really like to meet her." His voice is calm.

Our agent in the room asks him if he'll be more cooperative if he gets to speak to me. He just shakes his head. He doesn't want to say or do anything that implies he's attached to the crimes the Warlock is accused of.

"I'm not letting you anywhere near him," Knoll tells me.

"No argument here." The last thing I want to do is gratify his ego. But if I thought it would help, then of course my answer would be yes.

Our interrogator tells the man a meeting with me is not going to happen.

Haywood looks at the monitor for a long moment, knowing I'm still watching.

"A jail cell can't hold an idea," he finally says.

"Well that's almost an admission of guilt," Knoll replies to me. "The guy's playing games. The deputy told us he spent two hours on the phone yelling at his attorney before they got here."

I try to pay attention to what Knoll is saying. "What's so odd about that?"

"The line was dead. He never called anyone. He was screaming at a dial tone. He's trying to set himself up as crazy." Knoll pokes a finger at the screen.

"Wouldn't that fall under attorney-client privilege still? Even if the call didn't go through?"

Knoll shrugs. "I don't know. It's not like we're going to mention it to the judge."

"Then why do it at all?" I ask.

"Why do any of this? Nothing about him makes sense."

IT'S OBVIOUS THE QUESTIONING isn't going anywhere. I don't need to stare at him anymore. I decide to go back to the motel and finish my report, then take a car down to Santa Lucia to see if I can figure out what he was planning to do. I've looked at all the images and surveillance photos I can handle. I need to just go for myself.

Our Colorado team still hasn't found anything useful to report. That part of the mystery is still a huge blank for us.

When I arrive back at my motel room, there's an envelope under the door. I pick it up and get suspicious because it feels a little thick. But I see Damian's distinctive D written on one side and breathe a little sigh of relief. It's one of the rare times I'm glad to get something from him. I can open it without calling the bomb squad. I think.

I glance over my shoulder back into the motel parking lot, just to see if he's watching. It's empty except for our government cars. I step inside my room and lock the door behind me.

I pull a pair of rubber gloves from my jacket and use a nail file from my purse to slit the envelope open. I'll let forensics take a look after I read the letter.

Jessica,

I hope you caught the fiend. Still, I worry. Please don't go any-where without taking your prescription.

Much love!

D.

Enclosed along with the note is a flat foil pack of pills. I flip them over and look at the name on the back, Antilirium.

I type the name into my phone and it comes back as a pre-scription medication used for treating Alzheimer's symptoms. Sometimes Damian likes to make weird jokes. They seem funny to him, but he's also insane. I slip them into an evidence bag and put them in my pocket with his letter and decide to worry about the meaning later.

It takes me another two hours to finish up my notes and send them off. There's still enough daylight left to check out Santa Lucia, so I take one of our rental cars. Just to be safe, I call our local dispatcher and tell him where I'm heading.

Santa Lucia is like most other small towns in America, a collection of buildings connected by highways and back roads lined with houses to another cluster of buildings. You're never quite certain where one town begins and the other ends.

Other than a sign announcing the city limits, it's the old church that tells me I've arrived. Since it was rebuilt twice after the fires, I'm not sure if I should call it old or not. A small build-ing with a rock foundation and a white steeple, it's set back from the road in a field with knee-high yellow grass.

I pull off the road and follow the gravel driveway that leads up to the hill the church sits on. Our agents have been over it several times. The priest insists he's seen nothing suspicious. The mere mention of another fire turned the man white.

Up until a few hours ago we had a surveillance team staked out in a small shed across the highway from the church. Knoll relieved them after we found the SIM card. The church was one of a thousand possible targets. With Haywood now in custody we have to cut back on our manpower.

To the left of the church is a small graveyard overgrown with weeds. The markers look like they've been there since Texas was part of Mexico. The priest had explained that the church was only used on special occasions, for weddings and holiday services. Most of Santa Lucia's worshippers attend a mega-church outside Brownsville.

Megachurches, with their concert stages and arena seating, have become the big box store equivalent of religion. Never that religious myself, I don't know how I feel about that. If I get married, I think I'd like to do it in a church like this.

It's the golden hour right now and the shadows of the weeds give way to a warm glow. It's picture-perfect. The most peaceful place in the world. I roll down the window and listen to the breeze as it rolls through the grass.

I pull my phone from my pocket and hover my thumb over the address book. I think about calling my father.

The door to the church opens and a man in a priest collar emerges. He waves at me. I wave back and put the phone down. He walks across the gravel to talk to me.

"Beautiful day," he says.

"Yes, it is."

He turns his head to the side and coughs. "Hay fever. Gets my asthma." He takes an inhaler from his pocket. "He's real, you know."

Who's real? Jesus?
He sprays me in the face with his inhaler.
I go numb before descending.
Into darkness.

59

My body won't move. It's completely black. Part of me feels like I'm flying. I think I'm dreaming. A dream I have whenever I get stressed or feel overwhelmed. It's a dream based on a memory. A horrible memory. A memory of when I almost died.

I'm twenty and performing an illusion for a television show in Mexico. It's the kind of show with a bunch of sweaty older men in business suits and jiggly teenage girls in thongs. Everything is sensational and over the top. The week before, a stunt rider from Argentina had tried to jump three brightly colored buses in a shopping mall parking lot and slipped on his landing, sending him into a coma.

The segment I'm on is preceded by a bedside interview with the man's family as they prayed for a recovery. I'm here to promote a run of shows in Mexico City. The stunt is an escape from a wooden sarcophagus that is to be weighted down and dropped into the bottom of a lake dating from the Aztec era when Mexico City was called Tenochtitlán. You know, the usual.

As the chubby-fingered host secures me in chains and makes a few rude pats that would have gotten him banned from American television, a Mexican history professor cheerfully explains to the audience that this lake was once near a sacrificial temple and that they've found scores of bones belonging to murdered people at the bottom and I may soon be joining them.

The last thing I see before they hammer the coffin shut is the full moon. As workers pound the nails into the lid, they make a funny squeaking sound I've never heard before. From childhood in my family's workshop, I know the sounds and scents of different wood. I smell the wood and realize that while the ornate lid, carved with Aztec deities, is the same one I had constructed, the rest of the coffin is new.

The producers would later claim that they didn't do anything to the coffin. When my uncle found the original bottom half sitting at the back of a studio workshop, they changed their story to say it was damaged in transit and they had to replace it last-minute.

The chains are easy to get off. I've always been flexible and able to slip out of things without too much trouble. The difficulty is trying to keep them from falling off prematurely. But the real problem is getting out of the sarcophagus. The secret panel I'm supposed to use to get out isn't there. I kick the side with my high heels over and over, but it didn't move.

I pound the side with my fists until they bruise. There's no secret panel. I've been nailed into a real coffin.

I feel the impact as I hit the bottom of the lake. We measured it at twenty feet. If I'd done this in the ocean I'd keep sinking until the coffin imploded. That's small satisfaction, knowing I can just as easily die in two feet of water. The coffin is supposed to be airtight, but it's not. Water is filling up the interior . . .

———

I'M JARRED FROM THE DREAM as I feel a bump. My head hits something like carpet over metal. I'm in a trunk. I know that it's been a common safety feature for years to put a release on the inside of a trunk in case someone gets accidentally trapped inside. I have no idea how an adult could get accidentally trapped that way, maybe a child. But here I am.

My arms are behind me. I twist my body over and reach my fingers out to where I think the back of the car is. I feel the thick plastic handle and pull on it. It yanks free. Someone has severed it from the mechanism.

I bring my knees up and start kicking toward the top of the trunk. I know the driver will be able to hear me. I don't care. I'd rather pop it open in a busy highway than wait for him to park somewhere isolated and try to sneak away from the vehicle.

After three kicks I feel the car stop. This isn't a good sign. It means we're probably someplace secluded. I swivel around so I can kick him in the face if he opens the trunk. A minute goes by of me waiting. I wish I'd brought my hands in front of my body by sliding the cuffs around. I'm too afraid to do it now in case I'm caught in a vulnerable spot.

I wait for the sound of the key in the lock. It never happens. Instead, I hear the click of the trunk being opened remotely. The lid pops up a few inches. It's dark out. I see a sliver of moon through tall trees.

Then the trunk flies open and a figure standing behind the trunk, near the back door, shoves a canister in my face and sprays me again. I see stars and clouds, then nothing.

60

My family knows I have at least an hour's worth of air if the coffin stays airtight. On television they say only ten minutes. The plan is to raise me up after twenty. But I'm not going to make it five if I don't do something. I'm going to drown.

I race through my options. Hidden under my costume I have a small knife. A gift from my uncle. Using it to carve through the wooden lid would take years. Instead, I feel for a weak spot in the sides using my fingers.

I touch a spray of water coming through a small gap between the planks to the side of me. I shove the knife blade through to force a bigger opening. Water squirts into the coffin and my fingers slip as I work the blade between the crack.

The coffin is filling up faster. I've made things worse.

I keep sliding the blade back and forth anyway. The edge catches on something. It doesn't feel like a nail or another board and only gives slightly as I push into it.

I imagine the outside of the coffin. This must be the canvas strap holding the weights that keep the coffin from floating back up to the surface. I force the knife into the material. I only manage to bend it backward. I switch to a sawing motion, but nothing gives.

Water is up to my chest. I only have a few minutes left.

I'm desperate. I pull the knife out and move it a few inches farther down. I repeatedly jab at the strap from the inside, hoping to puncture and weaken it.

I want to cry. I want to scream. I do neither. My world is the strap. That's all that matters.

The blade snaps through something and I feel a sharp vibration like a string being plucked. I saw at it again. I can hear the sound of something sliding free. I've cut the strap!

But I'm not moving.

I take a deep breath.

My grandfather once told me about doing a similar escape from a packing case in the Hudson River. It got stuck in the mud and a vacuum formed, keeping him from pulling the box free after he exited through the secret panel.

I throw my weight against the side of the coffin to rock it back and forth. It's hard with all the water inside. It sloshes around in the darkness.

I'm afraid I'm already too heavy. I'm exhausted and just want to wait it out. I feel the water coming in through a gap in the lid and wonder if I can use a stocking to plug the crack. Maybe it could give me another few minutes of air.

I reach down to rip it off my leg and bump my back into the side of the coffin. I feel everything tip to the side. The coffin keeps turning.

I'm floating up! It's a gradual ascent, but definitely in the right direction. An eternity later I hear shouting. Men pull the coffin from the water and drag it to the shore. Crowbars pry open the top. I see my grandfather and uncle looking down at me. Their faces are white.

"I'm okay," I tell them.

Grandfather doesn't miss a beat. He turns to the camera, still several yards away, and shouts, "She's gone!" He runs to the edge of the water and pretends to look for me.

When the bright light on the camera is pointed at him in the lake, frantically looking for me, my uncle uses the lid of the coffin to conceal me as I hide in the bushes. The television crew never sees me leave.

My uncle drives me back to the hotel while my dad and grandfather make a big show of the fact that I've vanished.

He gives me a sad look as he lets me out of the car. We both know they love me, but that's the kind of people they are. Never ones to let a potential tragedy go to waste as publicity. I thank him for the knife and book a flight out of Mexico that night.

It is the last time I speak to my family face-to-face.

Now I realize that may have been my last chance.

61

My FAMILY ISN'T WAITING on the other side to spring me free. There is no secret escape hatch. I'm in a trunk of a car. Every few hours my captor stops the car and sprays me with a canister of a chemical that sends me into a lucid dream state. I retrace memories of childhood and occasionally feel like I'm flying. The FBI chemist explained that the chemical the Warlock used was similar to a drug that witches in the Middle Ages used to use to create the sensation that they were levitating.

I experience that feeling when I go in and out of the sleep. My head is numb; my mind is a television set turned to an empty channel. It's hard to focus on anything for very long. I remember the coffin and my uncle's knife. I try to find it on my body, but it's not there.

I try to cling to the facts.

I need to focus.

My gun, my badge, everything has been taken from me. Even my shoes. I don't feel like I've been touched. But I'm so disconnected with my body, I don't know if I could tell right now.

The driver is taking me somewhere. I don't know where that is yet. My last memory is of trees. Tall trees. Taller than what I saw in south Texas.

When we get wherever we're headed, I'm going to die. He's going to kill me. I know this because he said the Warlock is real. He believes this man is a higher being.

Damian had warned me that the Warlock might have accomplices. He went out of his way to make it look like he was acting alone. Many psychopaths like to use the word "we" to imply they represent more than one person. To pretend they're not just one lone nut job baying at the moon in the middle of the night.

This man, my captor, is probably acting under the Warlock's orders and not just some disturbed rogue who decided to honor his idol. I know this because he uses the spray we think the Warlock was using.

If I'm awake, that means he's going to spray me again. I decide to pull my hands around my body before he does that. I want to feel around the trunk again. If I can find a tire iron or some kind of weapon and hold my breath, I might be able to fight back.

It's harder than I anticipate to slide the cuffs to the front of my body. My arms feel like they're made from rubber. I have trouble knowing where they are in the darkness. The effort takes an eternity. I finally bring the cuffs to my face and stick my tongue out to tell what they are. With the right tool I can pick just about anything.

I taste glue and plastic. He's put plastic cuffs on me, then wrapped them over and over again with duct tape. It's the kind of binding you put on someone when you know you're never going to set them free.

There is no doubt he's going to kill me.

I could try to slide them off against the inside edge of the trunk. But I'm afraid he'll spray me again and it won't matter.

He'll just add more tape. I feel around the floor of the trunk for anything to use as a weapon.

My hands touch soft fabric. It's my jacket. I can use it to cover my mouth when he sprays me. That might help just a little. I'm still vulnerable here. As I slide the jacket across my chest I hear something crackle inside a pocket. It sounds like a pack of gum.

I stick my hands inside and feel the bag with the letter and the blister pack of pills that Damian gave me. That seems like an eternity ago. I would have preferred my uncle's knife. I push them back into my pocket, then remember what the note said and what the pills are for.

They're an Alzheimer's medication.

I try to think through the fog back to the presentation by our chemist and the molecule on the screen.

My chemistry is rough, but I think Damian's pills are some kind of inhibitor. An antidote of sorts?

I bounce as the car stops. I pull them free of the packaging and swallow all of them. It's hard. My mouth is dry and I haven't had any water. They don't want to go down my throat. The trunk is going to open any second.

He's going to spray me.

The pills are starting to choke me. I have to do something.

I have to survive.

I bite the inside corner of my lip. It's easier than I thought, given how numb I am. Blood rushes past my tongue. The dry pills become moist. I swallow and try not to think about what I've done so I don't throw up.

I feel the pills go down my throat, finally. I don't know what effect they're going to have. All I can do is wait.

I move my tied hands behind my back. I don't want him knowing I can do that.

The trunk opens. I see a figure standing several yards away. He's holding a video camera with a light aimed at me. At first I think he's talking to me, then I realize he's talking to the camera.

62

THE LIGHT FROM the camera makes it hard to see his face. I think he is the priest from the church, or at least the man pretending to be the priest. He steps closer to the car and keeps the camera light pointing toward me.

"As I promised you, Lord. There she is. Unharmed . . ."

He notices the blood flowing down my lip.

"Goddamn it!" He sets the video camera on the ground and walks toward me. He pulls a gun from his waistband and points it at my head. "I took the gag off so you wouldn't choke back there. Now look what you've done!"

"Let me go." I try to make my voice calm and reasoned.

He ignores me and brings the gun to my face. He uses his sleeve to wipe the blood free. If my hands were in front of my body and able to move more quickly, I could maybe knock it out of his hands. Then what? All I see are trees. I have no idea where I would run to.

He steps back and picks up the camera and starts over again. "As I promised you, Lord. There she is . . ."

So this video is supposed to be seen by the Warlock?

I scream as loud as I can. "He raped me!"

"I did not! She's lying! She's a lying whore!"

He lowers the camera and gives me an angry look, then storms over to the trunk with the gun in his hand. "I swear to God, bitch, I'll hit you in the head with this if you say another thing."

I need to keep him talking. "Let me go. I know it's not your fault."

He shakes his head. "He told me you'd say anything to get me to let you go free. Even try to tempt me."

"He's a fake and a liar." I have to do something to disrupt his train of thought. He's like a cult member repeating a line over and over again.

"You wouldn't understand him. Your world is so small," he says.

"I see through his tricks. He's just a cheap magician."

"Everything is a trick to you. You're just a magic whore from a family of whores."

"You're not a murderer. This isn't you."

"You're right. I'm not. I'm a temple priest about to perform a transformation." He steps back with the camera and aims it at me again. "You were right, Lord. She'll say anything. She'll accuse me of anything."

I can't let him finish this video the way he wants. "This man violated me. He said I was his to play with."

The man can't decide if he should stop the camera or not. "Go on. Tell your lies."

"He said he had doubts about you. He said that he was afraid of you and only doing this to protect himself. He asked me if I could help him."

He drops the camera and runs toward me. He punches me on the jaw. The blood I've been swallowing flies all over my blouse. The subject of sex made him very uncomfortable. This is his weakness. This is how I humiliate him. I rip my blouse open on the edge of the trunk, revealing a black bra. "Video this, asshole. How's he going to feel when he finds out you violated his sacrifice?"

He looks genuinely confused. He wants to hit me again, but he knows it will only make things worse. I watch a vessel bulge in his forehead, then fade away. He smiles. "It's a test. He knows you'll try this. It's not working."

He picks up the camera again and aims it at me. "Everything you said is true, Lord." He spins around and aims it at a mountain in the horizon. "There she waits, my Lord."

I don't recognize the mountain, but its shape is unmistakable. Half of it is caved in. I've been asleep for more hours than I can count.

Have I been out for days? All I know is that I've been brought to one of a dozen volcanoes in the United States. I'm too numb to tell if it's cold out. This could even be an active one in Alaska or Oregon.

The Warlock's follower pulls the canister from his pocket and sprays me again. It's a long spray. He does it until it's empty. I'm pulled backward into a black lake.

63

I FEEL LIKE I'M flying again. This time the sensation is milder. I realize I'm being carried. My head is filled with champagne bubbles. Damian's pills are fighting the drug. I'm not sure who is winning. I can't sense much other than a shoulder in the pit of my stomach and the up-and-down motion of walking.

He sets me on the gravel and steps over me. I can barely move, so I keep still. I don't want him knowing that I'm conscious. I can see the car a hundred yards away. It looks like we're at the end of a long road. Part of me thinks only a minute or so has passed since he sprayed me. I can't imagine him carrying me up the side of the mountain.

A pneumatic hinge makes a gasping sound. The man picks me up again, slides me into a seat and fastens a seat belt around me. It takes him a moment to position me since my arms are still bound behind me. I lie slack and maintain the deception. Fighting him is impossible and pointless.

He shuts the door. I can see trees through the window. It feels like we're in a small car. One of those European ones you see winding through back alleys in Italy. I don't understand why he changed cars or put me in the front seat.

I hear him climb in the other side and shut his door. His fingers place something on the dashboard and strap it in place. Out of the corner of my eye I can see the video camera's red light.

Recording what?

He flips several switches and the dashboard begins to glow. I hear the sound of an engine starting up and feel the front of the car shake a little. Only it's not a car.

We're in an airplane.

He revs the engine and we lurch forward. Trees move past the window as we turn toward the start of the runway. I tilt my body to the side and bring myself slightly forward, still pretending to be unconscious.

The Warlock's helper addresses the video camera. "I wish you were here right now. It doesn't feel right. But I know that I can't understand all the parts of your mystery. I'm just thankful you've given me this honor."

The plane starts to taxi down the runway.

He's going to take me into the air.

He's going to fly me over the volcano.

He's going to push me out in some sick ritual.

I still can't move enough to do anything. I try to push my hands under my body as the airplane bounces down the runway. The seat belt keeps me pinned.

The tip of the plane lifts off and we're airborne. He turns the stick to the right and we do a wide arc to avoid the treetops at the edge of the runway. We go in a circle and I'm able to look at the narrow strip of concrete below us.

It's an old forestry runway. The trees have grown to the edges. Probably long abandoned, the only access is from the air and an abandoned logging road. It's the kind of place you'd only know about if you flew over it. The strip looks so small. I can only imagine a seasoned pilot being able to pull off a landing there.

The plane climbs higher. He points the nose toward the volcano. I look out at the wing and realize we don't have any running lights on.

He speaks to the camera. "I remember the first time I took you flying. I never met anyone who learned as fast as you. I should have known. I realize now that you were just testing me."

It sounds like a love letter. I want to challenge him with this, but I don't want to give up my advantage. If you can call it that. I can still barely move my fingers. I try to do some of my stationary yoga flexes to get the blood flowing through my muscles. If I can get my hands around my body fast enough, I might be able to get his gun and make him bring us back down to the landing strip.

I have to wait for the right moment. I need him to think he's safe. That'll be when he undoes my seat belt. He'll have to do that if he wants to push me out. Only this time it won't be onto an old runway to break bones like the Warlock probably did to Claire. He wants me thrown into the caldera of the volcano.

I doubt there's a lake filled with lava inside there. Probably just a bunch of steaming vents and ash cones. The effect will be the same. The impact will trigger some seismological gadget and somebody will be sent out to inspect the disturbance.

Either way, they'll find my smoldering corpse in the middle of a fiery volcano. Retribution. It'll show the reach of his power. With no witnesses and him locked away in jail, it'll be another mystery to build on his legend. How did the Witch end up in the volcano?

It won't be a big illusion like the other three, but will prove to the world that even behind bars he can make strange and horrible things happen.

I wonder how many other people there are like the man who has captured me. It's a scary thought.

"We're almost there. I'd like to climb and cut the power and glide, really soar on the wind, but I think I'll have to save that for later. Or at least until I lighten the load."

The volcano looms. We're on a path to go over the collapsed edge. I hear his fingers flip a few switches and then the sound of his seat belt unbuckling. He leans over to my seat. I can feel his breath on my neck. His hand slips across my waist and touches the seat belt. It pauses for a moment. A finger caresses my abdomen. He lets go of the seat belt and grabs the door handle instead.

I've only got seconds. I watch his wrist turn the handle. He pushes it open and the air rushes into the cockpit. One hand grabs my bound hands while the other unfastens my seat belt. He has me tightly. I can't slide my hands free. I can't get loose. I'm being lifted off the seat.

I can see the caldera below the wing.

Wind rushes past my hair.

The plane is tilting me out of my seat.

I feel my balance slipping.

My FINGERS TOUCH his waist. He's trying to shove me out of the plane. I grab the leather of his belt and hold on. He pushes me forward and feels me clinging to him.

"You bitch!"

He lets go of my hands and punches me in the back of the head. I see stars. My fingertips touch metal. Instinct takes over. I grab his gun behind my back, slip off the safety and squeeze the trigger, hoping to hit flesh. I keep firing it until all the rounds have been spent.

The turbulent air rushing through the open door is punctured by the loud explosions.

He lets out a groan. Blood trickles over my fingers. He slackens his grip on me and falls back into his seat. He pulls the gun from my fingers, shoves it to my head and pulls the trigger. It's empty.

I twist my body away from the open door and use my hands to grab the seat belt. He's staring down at his leg. The bullets have gone through his side and part of his thigh. There's a lot of blood, but I don't think I hit an artery.

I speak in a calm voice. "Land this plane now and you'll live."

He's still looking at his body in a state of shock, trying to assess what to do. The plane is spiraling downward. I must have hit the control panel too. The lights are flickering. His pilot instincts take over and he puts his hands on the stick and fights to bring the plane back under control.

The interior light strobes on and off, then goes dark. The engine dies. The only illumination comes from the red light of the camera and the sun rising over the horizon. For a fleeting moment, I think I see something glowing in the caldera.

The pilot turns the stick to the left and tries to bring us into a shallow descent.

His face is twisted with rage. "You bitch! You bitch! You've gotten us killed! Now is not my time! He said now is not my time!"

He tries to shove me out the open door again with his right hand, but he's too weak and he knows he has to bring us in for a landing. As soon as he puts both hands on the control I slide my hands around to the front of my body. I'm vulnerable for just a moment, but I don't want to give him another chance to push me out.

The plane passes between two tall trees. He tries to keep the nose up, but we're still falling. I slip my seat belt back around me.

He speaks through gritted teeth as he concentrates on bringing us down. "You're still going to die."

"Not if you bleed to death first."

"Goddamn you! There's no place to land!"

He tilts the plane to the side and banks us between another cluster of trees. Ahead of us is a tiny road that only goes a few hundred feet before twisting behind a ridge. He shoves the stick forward and brings us onto the narrow ribbon. The plane shudders horrendously. I'm thrown against the restraints. If I hadn't put them on, I'd have been tossed out the window.

The plane skids down the road and twists to the side. We spin around and slide off the edge and fall backward down the other side of the ridge the road is on. A tree trunk clips the wing outside my door and rips it free. The plane keeps skidding and pinwheels again.

The left wing hits a tree and is broken off. The wing flips over the top of the plane. The tail section hits a log and crumples as we come to a jarring stop. My back feels like I just fell off a building and my head is rattled.

The pilot looks like he passed out. Damian's drugs and my adrenaline have kicked in. I unbuckle my belt and leap out the open door and start running up the side of the ridge. It's a hard climb up the dirt and gravel. I keep falling and have to use my bound hands to stop myself from slamming my head into rocks.

The plane has made a deep furrow in the dirt. I try to climb it and reach the road. I steal a glance back and see the man stumbling from the airplane. He's got one hand over his side and another on this gun. He staggers and aims it toward me.

The gun clicks on an empty chamber. I turn away and keep climbing. Behind me I hear the sound of metal on metal. I ignore it until I realize it was the sound of an empty magazine being tossed at the plane. I hear the clicking of another one being slammed into place.

I see the edge of the road above me. I take two more strides and pull myself up to the asphalt and roll over. On flat ground, I hope I can outrun him in his injured condition. If I'm lucky he'll bleed out.

I sprint down the road and away from the mountain. I hope to find help, but I know a road like this can seesaw back and forth for forty miles down the side of the mountain before reaching a town.

There's a gunshot behind me.

I run.

65

MAKE IT ANOTHER hundred yards before my legs feel like they're melting through the road. All the drugs in my body and my exhaustion are starting to take their toll. I try to keep jogging. It's hard with my hands still bound. The corners of my vision fade while my body resists the urge to black out.

I hear another gunshot and something whizzes past my ear. The sound echoes through the ravine we're in. I look back. He's only a hundred feet behind me. He has the gun pointed straight at me. He's still holding his wound, but it doesn't seem to have slowed him down.

He shouts to me, "You're not going to make it!"

"I already did! You failed him! You failed him big! And now you're going to bleed to death out here," I shout.

He falls to his knees and keeps the gun aimed at me. "At least I can take you out first."

The gun is pointed at my chest. His hand wavers slightly, but he uses his other to steady his grip. He's got a clean shot.

There's a loud crack that echoes through the trees. His shoulder jerks back. Blood sprays from his arm and the gun drops to the ground. He falls on his face and screams.

I run over to the gun and pick it up with my bound hands

before he can get back up. I point it at his head. He rolls over and looks at me. There's a bullet hole in his shoulder.

"Goddamn bitch!" He tries to move but he can't get to his knees.

I look around the trees to see where the bullet came from. There's no one around. It sounded like a rifle shot.

In the distance I hear rotors. A moment later a spotlight pokes over the trees in front of me and a helicopter flies over the side of the mountain as dawn begins to break in the distance. The chopper hovers overhead sending a wash of air around us. Dust and dirt are kicked into a cloud. I keep the gun trained on the pilot.

My body wants to collapse, but I remain rock steady. I don't even know if I have the energy to pull the trigger. I just stand there and keep it pointed on his head.

He writhes on the ground and tries to shield his eyes from the spotlight with his good hand. Under his breath he mutters curses. Some of them sound like they're in another language.

The helicopter banks to the side and I see an FBI agent in tactical assault gear leaning out the side with an assault rifle. He leaps off and lands in the grass. He's followed by another agent. They run over to me, keeping their guns trained on the pilot.

One of them shouts to me over the sound of the helicopter engine. "Agent Blackwood, is there anybody else in the area?"

I look at the pilot's shoulder wound and back at the forest. "Nobody hostile."

"Are you okay? Do you need medical help?"

I don't know. I'm more worried about losing our one witness. "I'm not urgent. This man may be bleeding out. We need him alive."

The helicopter lands on the road and two more in tactical

gear climb out. They zip cuff the man on the ground and apply first aid to his wound. They tell me a medical chopper is ten minutes away.

I'm about to fall down, but I insist they take the pilot first. He might be our only connection to the Warlock.

The chopper takes him, and I fly to the hospital in a second helicopter. The last thing I remember before passing out is sitting between two other FBI agents as the helicopter climbs into the sky.

I catch a glimpse of the caldera. Someone gently takes the gun from my hand and places a blanket over my shoulders, then holds on to me as we fly.

I dream of nothing.

66

I WAKE UP IN a hospital bed in Portland, Oregon. Ailes is sitting in a chair reading a book. When my eyes open he gives me a smile.

"There you are, Blackwood," he says. "Feeling a little more coherent?"

"I hope so. How long have I been here?"

There's a row of empty paper coffee cups on the sill behind him. "Two days. They had to clean all that stuff out of your system," he replies. "Your family is here."

"My family?" The word sounds unusual to me.

"Your father and your uncle. They're staying at a hotel. I'm not sure how things are with you and them, but I thought it best for them to be close by."

I'm not ready to deal with my father just yet. Maybe when I have a little more strength. But I'm glad he came. Maybe ten years a little too late. But he came.

"What about the pilot?" I ask.

"He didn't make it."

"Damn." If we could have gotten him to talk, who knows what he could tell us. "What about Haywood?"

"Still sitting there. Not saying anything. If the pilot had

survived, we might have been able to play them off of each other." Ailes's eyes dart away for a moment as he hesitates.

I'm still cleaning the cobwebs from my head. "What?"

"If there's one accomplice . . ."

I get it. "You think there might be more."

"A cult. We still don't really know what he was going to do in Colorado or Texas."

"If he's in custody he's going to need help to pull it off," I reply.

"Our mystery shooter who took out the pilot may have been doing Haywood a favor after all."

I shake my head. I know it was Damian. I can't come out and say that to Ailes—although I'm sure he knows. Damian tracked me down somehow and took out the pilot before he could kill me. Once again, his protecting me puts his actions under suspicion.

I sit up in my bed. There's a bouquet of orchids on my night-stand. Orchids . . . a favorite I've only told a few people. I reach for the card.

"It'll take some unconventional thinking to get them," says Ailes.

I open the card.

Jessica,
Try not to miss me too much, darling. I have to go away for a while. Our devious little friend has started something we'd all be better off if he hadn't.

I can't always be there for you. So please keep safe. Lucky for everyone, we don't all play by the same rules . . .

Love,
D.

I hand the card to Ailes. He reads it and gives it back to me. "What does he mean?"

"He's going to try to find them before we do. Before they have a chance to get to me," I reply.

"And do what?"

"Kill them. Kill them all."

"One man?" asks Ailes.

"How many guards are here?"

"Two on the door. Another two watching the lobby. I've been here for a few hours. I dozed off for a bit. Why?"

"Did you see anyone place the flowers here?"

Ailes stares at the bouquet. His mouth opens to say something, but he's speechless. He runs to the hallway to talk to the policemen guarding the door. Damian was in my room proving my point. Ailes runs to the hallway to talk to the police officers guarding the door.

I lie back and stare at the ceiling.

Damian's kiss is still warm on my cheek. I'm bothered by how much it comforts me.

If I don't stop him he'll get them. I don't doubt that for a moment. I can sit here and let that happen. Everyone will tell me I've done everything I could. I've gone above and beyond the call of duty. The Warlock is in jail. Maybe we haven't proved it's him, but I know.

Meanwhile, my obsessive sociopath is out there trying to protect me. He wants revenge, not justice.

Maybe it would be better if I let him do that. But I made an oath to uphold the law. I can't let Damian fight my battles. I don't need a protector.

I pull the IV from my arm. The floor is cold. It's better than feeling numb.

I put on my clothes and go into the hallway. Ailes is dressing down a local police officer. "Jessica?" he says as he sees me standing, still a little unsteady.

"We have to stop them. We have to stop them all. It ends."

"I know that. There's nothing more we can do right now." He gently grabs my arm.

"Yes there is." I feel my knees beginning to buckle.

"We don't know how many are out there. They're fanatics. They think this man is God."

My fingers dig into his forearm, more for balance than emphasis. "Then we kill their god."

He relaxes his own grip. "I don't suppose putting you in restraints will work . . ."

I fight back the urge to just lie down and let things wash over me. Things are clearer to me now. I see an end to this game. "Not a chance."

67

THE MAN WE BELIEVE is the Warlock is sitting in a small room watching the television on the other side of a wire grid. The only sign of movement is his eyes flickering across the images on the news. His bound wrists rest on the metal table where they're handcuffed.

A guard unlocks the door and lets me inside. Haywood, whatever his name, sees my reflection in the television. His spine snaps straight for a moment before he relaxes into his normal posture.

It's the little reactions like this that tell me who he is. As a cop and a make-believe mind reader, you look for how people react when they don't think they're being observed. This shows you their true nature. I unsettle Haywood behind his mask.

We still don't know his real identity, but in consulting with the DEA, we suspect he may have been someone on their radar for a while under another name. In the last ten years several new synthetic drugs appeared on the market, they suspect designed by the same person. Coming up with new drugs can be extremely lucrative. The designer never has to meet face-to-face with his clients. He never has to produce them in large quantities either. He gives them a formula and a process in exchange for a percentage of the profits. If they screw him over on the money, he takes the next new thing somewhere else.

As I walk around the table to the chair opposite of him, his gaze follows me. There's the faintest of smiles at his lips. I sit down and stare back at him.

"This is a pleasure," he says as he uses the remote to lower the volume.

"Is it?" We'd kept my disappearance out of the news. This is the first time he knows that I'm alive.

"Very much so," he insists. "I was afraid . . ." There's a hesitation in his voice. "I was afraid you weren't worthy."

"Worthy of what?"

He gives me a slim reptilian grin. I can tell he's trying to compose himself. He wants everyone to think things are going the way he intended. He's still processing the realization that I'm alive, and that his attempt on my life through his accomplice was botched.

"Have you been traveling much?" he asks.

I ignore the question and ask my own. "Why?"

"Exactly." He says it as a statement.

"I have to call the parents and loved ones of the people you killed. They're all going to ask me why. What should I tell them? That nobody paid attention to you when you were little? Girls wouldn't talk to you? That you have such low self-esteem that you decided that the only way to feel anything was make people think you were special? Any words I should pass on to them when I tell them I met with the person that murdered Chloe, Denise, Claire and Jeff?"

His eyes drift to the floor and the expression vanishes. "Yes. I feel for them. I don't expect them to see the shape of things. But I took no pleasure in their deaths. They are very much loved."

"They may not quite understand what you mean by love."

"Love is sacrifice. Isn't it, Jessica? It's dealing with inconsistencies and hypocrisies. It's seeing the good among all the bad. It's why somewhere deep down you're capable of love, even though you've been surrounded by, shall we say, some very complicated men?"

"I don't think you know the meaning of love."

"Maybe not. Maybe not. But I'll leave you with this question. What was I feeling in my heart when I watched you sitting there in the darkness all alone in my warehouse in Michigan? Why did my finger never waver over the button that could have cratered you in an instant, wiping away every sad thought from your face?"

I don't know what to say. We never told him we found the Michigan warehouse. All this time he knew? He saw me sitting there and never set off the explosion? It has to be a trick. Why else wouldn't he?

"Did I strike a nerve?" he asks. "Tell you what, if you can answer me one question honestly, I'll do the same."

I give him a cold stare.

"It looked like you were staring at something in the dark back in that warehouse, Jessica. For the life of me I couldn't remember what was there. Then I realized it must have been something that wasn't there. A person. Who were you looking at? In the darkness, who do you see?"

My mouth opens but I don't have an answer.

"Their lives served a greater purpose. Where others had doubt, they now have certainty. We live in an age of miracles."

"All you did was construct elaborate lies."

"Isn't that the root of all faith? The belief in something that isn't true—at least something you have no reason to believe is true? And what do you know? Maybe I am a god."

I raise an eyebrow at the holding cell. "So you're here by choice?"

"Jesus could have escaped his Roman prison cell if it was necessary."

I roll my eyes. The television is playing behind me at a low volume. He shifts his gaze from me to the screen for a moment.

"It doesn't matter if you believe me. It only takes a few." The last words come out slowly. He's distracted.

"There's a gift shop next to his cell in Jerusalem," I tell him. "Do you think he planned on that? Think things got a little off-message after he died?"

Haywood is pretending to not watch the television set. "His disciples . . . they spread the word . . . they . . ." His words trail off as he tries to focus on the television. His fingers twitch as he thinks about turning the volume up.

I stare straight back at him and don't acknowledge the television. Behind me the pilot, the man who tried to kill me on the Warlock's order, is talking to a camera. Diagrams of the Empire State Building and medical reports flash on the screen. He's exposing the charade.

" . . . I began to suspect it was all a lie . . . but I was too afraid . . ." says the pilot.

I give Haywood a thin smile of my own. "When Jesus died, Peter didn't go running around calling him a fraud. Did he? That's the real problem in being a god; you don't get to control the message."

Haywood's facial muscles slacken for an instant, then grow tense. His wrists pull at the handcuffs fastened to the table.

Behind me the pilot continues the exposé, calling Haywood a charlatan; the whole thing a lie. Haywood is furious. His most trusted confidant is revealing everything. His Peter has become a Judas.

We don't know what the pilot really knew. It doesn't matter. Like any other magician, Haywood knows his weakest link is the people he trusts with his secrets. Right now he's watching his most devout disciple call him a fake.

It's a trick, of course. Eventually he'll realize it was his own trick. It's Gerald on the tape using his computer program to mimic the pilot. We pulled enough audio and video from the camera on the plane to make it work.

The whole thing was done on the sly without official approval. Ailes ran it by Chisholm over drinks in a Georgetown bar. Both understand the game is deeper than just arresting people. This is psy-ops. Going after cults is sticky business. The only effective way is to destroy them from within.

We don't know who else he has out there. But I'm sure when they see this they'll have some soul-searching to do. If they're smart, they'll come to us before Damian finds them.

I stand. Haywood stares up at me and tries to say something. He wants to sound confident. Words fail him.

"You don't know the whole plan!" he shouts as I head toward the door.

"I don't care. Nobody cares. All you are is a liar now. A liar and a murderer." I let the door slam behind me, leaving him alone in the cell. Without an audience.

68

To: Alan Parkworth, Assistant Director, FBI Cyber Division
From: Dr. Trey Goode, Director, NSA Intra-Agency Cryptographic Working Group

Alan,

As per your request we ran all the linked files from the "Warlock" defacement of the FBI home page through the GlyphR system. Sorry it took so long to get to it. I think you guys need to take a look at the raw data for the .PNG image of the defaced FBI logo. The image is 120K but actual image data it only about 20k. There appears to be another file encoded in there.

Assuming best-of-breed encryption, it'd take our system a long time to get through this. Back-of-the-envelope calculations suggest your crypto machine using the Kunaki-Stein Elliptical might be able to do it in approximately six years, six months, six days . . . Yeah, I know how ominous that sounds.

We tasked our cypher for thirty hours on the first sequence as a test. We found one possible word: Eternicon.

Does this mean anything to you guys?

I wish we had the resources to commit on this. But since it looks like you guys caught the guy, it might be a waste of time.

Sincerely,
Trey

ACKNOWLEDGMENTS

Special thanks to my father, a federal agent, whose cases and incredible experiences inspired me and whose unwavering support encouraged me. Thanks to my brother, an FBI agent, for providing me with helpful information and forgiveness for the dramatic license I took. Justin Robert Young for his essential help at every stage of this book. My literary agents, Erica Spellman Silverman and Robert Gottlieb. My editor, Hannah Wood, for her dedication to this book. James Randi, a great mentor who taught me how we're deceived, and more importantly, why we need to believe. Ken Montgomery, Mary Jaras, Gerry Ohrstrom, Matt Ridley, Dr. Paul Zak, Joke & Biagio, Brian Brushwood, the Weird Things podcast listeners, Diamond Club <> and the Mayniacs.

ABOUT THE AUTHOR

ANDREW MAYNE is the star of A&E's magic reality show *Don't Trust Andrew Mayne*, and has worked for David Copperfield, Penn & Teller, and David Blaine. With the support of Johnny Carson, Mayne founded a program that uses magic to teach critical thinking skills in public schools for the James Randi Educational Foundation, and his "Wizard School" segments aired nationwide on public television. He lives in Los Angeles.

WWW.ANDREWMAYNE.COM